Hope Clark's books have been honored as winners of the:

EPIC Award (three-time winner)

Silver Falchion Award (three-time winner)

Imadjinn Award (three-time winner)

Daphne du Maurier Award (finalist)

Route 1 Reads East Coast winner for the state of South Carolina

"C. Hope Clark delivers addictive, character-driven suspense. Every. Single. Time."
—Debra Dixon, award-winning novelist and bestselling author of *GMC: Goal, Motivation, & Conflict*

"Those who haven't read any of C. Hope Clark's books are short-changing themselves. You can't begin one of her books and then put it down. Two-time Killer Nashville Silver Falchion Award winner.
—Clay Stafford, *Killer Nashville Noir*, Founder of Killer Nashville

"Author C. Hope Clark brings to life the uniqueness that is Edisto, peppering the island with endearing and strong-minded characters that linger in your mind long after the last page."
—Karen White, *NY Times* Bestselling Author

"Hope Clark has created another fascinating heroine in former Boston PD detective Callie Morgan. A fast-paced mystery set against the backdrop of a tiny South Carolina island where murder never happens—or so the locals would like to believe."
—Kathryn R. Wall, author, *The Bay Tanner Mysteries*, St. Martin's Press

The Novels of C. Hope Clark

The Carolina Slade Mysteries

Lowcountry Bribe
Tidewater Murder
Palmetto Poison
Newberry Sin
Salkehatchie Secret
Lake Murray Money

The Edisto Island Mysteries

Murder on Edisto
Edisto Jinx
Echoes of Edisto
Edisto Stranger
Dying on Edisto
Edisto Tidings
Reunion on Edisto
Edisto Heat
Badge of Edisto
Edisto Bullet
Edge of Edisto
Edisto Storm
Hidden on Edisto

The Craven County Mysteries

Murdered in Craven
Burned in Craven
Craven County Line

Hidden on Edisto

Book 13 of The Edisto Island Mysteries

by

C. Hope Clark

Edisto Bridge Books

EDISTO||||
BRIDGE

Edisto Bridge Books
140A Amicks Ferry Road, PMB 4 Chapin, SC 29036

Print ISBN: 978-1-968423-24-7

Visit Hope at chopeclark.com

Cover design: Debra Dixon
Interior design: Hank Smith
Photo/Art credits:
Beach Scene (manipulated) © Les Cunliffe | Dreamstime.com

Dedication

Dedicated to Lawdawg

Chapter 1

SIX PROTESTERS, most in jeans and tee shirts, the autumn sun bouncing off their shades, picketed in a semi-circle outside the small building on Jungle Road. They didn't appear to be experienced at picketing, though. The moment a voice rose loud and animated, the others hushed them to a respectable level. Honestly, there was more laughing and cutting up than dissension in Edisto's first ever protest.

Backside resting against her patrol car, Police Chief Callie Jean Morgan watched from across the street, holding a chuckle, wondering if the lightheartedness stemmed from relief at Edisto Beach returning to normal after Hurricane Nikki. Clean-up had gone on for over six weeks, most repairs about done. Maybe some of that factored into the jovial behavior. Some might marvel at the efficiency, but on the coast, recovery was honed to a fine science.

Recovery included Callie's broken nose acquired during the storm. Though not as tender anymore, she found herself still protecting it. Her romantic, live-in significant other Mark DuPree assured her nobody else noticed, but at home he kissed it gently from a habit of nursing the injury.

Officer Annie Greer walked up with two cups in her hand, coffee that would ordinarily be steaming anyplace north of South Carolina, but the day shined bright with little breeze and a not-too-warm, not-too-cold sixty degrees. "We got enough lock-up room for all these dastardly evil-doers?"

Callie appreciated her officer's humor. Edisto had no jail.

This level of public display would never have crossed anyone's mind until five years or so ago when post-COVID tourists relocated from the north to better weather, lower taxes, and year-round outdoor activities. A southern winter felt like capri weather to them. The altered tourism gave the economy a shot-in-the-arm during a time of year that used to mean no traffic, unemployment, and seasonal hours. Year-round natives weren't too crazy about the shift. Those with businesses, however, kept quiet, banking the extra income with relish. Each year more rentals filled up and filled up faster than the year before.

Change in the air for Edisto, for sure.

A sign toter who could be a hippier version of Callie's mother Beverly followed the line with her message, *We're already Edis-slo*. She'd pumped her sign up and down the first half hour or so but now strolled with the others.

We're calm enough, read another sign in a mellow green, a red cross mark through a marijuana leaf. Its owner strolled as well, as if practicing what she preached.

Take that crap back across the big bridge. That protester had a swagger, swaying the sign back and forth, his khaki pants frayed and dragging across flip flops. His head shined bald on top, long gray hair hanging on the sides to his collar. He was tanned from a lifetime in the sun, a boonie hat dangling down his back.

Annie passed the second coffee to Callie and took a relaxed stance alongside her boss against the cruiser. "You sure Amos didn't partake a little before taking up a sign? He's got the moves."

On cue, the thin, middle-aged, scruffy-bearded man let the stick of his sign rest on the sand, then he did a slow-motion dipsy dance around it, before taking it back up again.

Callie took a sip of her coffee, black because who had the time to sweeten coffee anymore? "That's his normal speed," she said. "Been that way since he was born. Wouldn't be surprised if he had a stash, though. Wouldn't be surprised if half these sign toters had imbibed before, but a CBD store on their turf doesn't sit well with them for some reason. And freedom of speech is a real thing." Callie motioned with her cup at him. "He's not even against the place. He's just keeping things light-hearted for the sake of the owner."

Annie motioned with her cup toward a lady not far from Amos' age. "That one's a trip."

The middle-aged woman walked with purpose, in a more upscale outfit of slacks and a straw hat with a scarf attached. She made comments to folks not marching to her satisfaction. "Do more, people. Step it up. We need a chant! *We have no need for the weed!*" She popped Amos lightly with her sign. "You don't belong here. Scat."

Amos cackled, dipped out of her reach, and recommenced his dance.

Officer Annie gave a humorous wince. "They haven't exactly stopped traffic, have they? Nobody's really watching but us."

"Malorie makes more noise elsewhere, trust me." Callie took another sip then poured the rest on the ground. Being almost eleven, it was likely left over from the morning rush at the coffee shop down the street. "Malorie raised holy hell with council over this place. She never misses a meeting or a chance to play devil's advocate on every issue on the agenda. Any more like her, expect more protesting like this."

Poor Malorie considered herself old guard, disgruntled with the Northern blood moving in. Forget the fact that she'd had to squeeze herself into the culture two decades ago. Her heart was in the right place, but she'd never be completely accepted by the legacy. Layers of society made up this beach.

A wafting coolness blew up the road, and Annie wrapped both hands around her cup like it was about to snow. Callie caught sight of the owner peeking from behind blinds, judging the temperature of the crowd.

Sixty-ish with reddish gray, naturally curly hair, chopped short enough to be off her collar and bouncy, Kitty wore tie-dye and denim to fit into the community, but her welcome measured lukewarm at best. Edisto liked to think of itself as family-oriented, different than all the other beaches. Safe and simple. Hopefully this half-hearted discontent melted away by day's end. Hopefully not everyone was as uneducated about CBD as Malorie.

This particular business entity had planned its grand opening to coordinate with incoming Thanksgiving visitors, and, subsequently, the Christmas crowd three weeks later. What had once been a one-bedroom beach rental had morphed into a short-lived real estate office then received permission from town council to go retail commercial . . . as a CBD store.

To some, that meant weed, regardless of the strength or definition.

Cars trickled by the two officers, Callie recognizing every third as a regular. An infamous powder blue 90's Mercedes convertible approached, the driver stopping behind the patrol car.

"Uh oh," Annie said.

Callie waited to see how the driver exited before passing judgment. The door wouldn't be slammed because this car was much beloved, but *uh oh* was right. Callie read the dust storms kicked up by the bejeweled sandals on size ten, pedicured feet. Hurricane Sophie approached landfall.

Annie leaned in. "Where's Miss Sophie stand in all this?"

"Doesn't take cop training to tell that, Annie." Callie pushed off the patrol car. "Hey, Soph. How'd yoga class go this morning?"

Sophie Bianchi was an island icon, the yoga maven who supposedly held spiritual talents connecting her to the other side. A handful feared her powers. Most admired her. Men and women alike would date her given half the chance.

She was still dressed in leggings from teaching yoga, a soft rainbow kaleidoscope of color today. Her turquoise tank and gold, loosely woven shawl matched the sandals. The frosted pixie shag bobbed with each step. Her trademark coral nail polish was fresh, applied each and every morning.

One might suspect such an oracle-like person to smoke a joint here and there to better connect with spirits, but nobody could say for sure. Callie, however, lived next door to the woman, fully aware of the stash under Sophie's upstairs bathroom sink.

Sophie's opinion about this store, appropriately named Edisto Calm, ran chilly. She never thought the license would pass, so she hadn't gotten involved, not wanting pot to be a topic of conversation with her yoga students. She preferred her Zen inherent, and her reputation more on the natural side.

But now the venue was about to open which appeared to rattle her more than it should.

"What the heck are you doing?" Sophie asked, hip cocked.

"Watching a lawful gathering to ensure it stays peaceful," Callie said with the monotone she saved for keeping a situation composed. Maybe she threw in a taste of sarcasm since this was Sophie, and the event had been so unassuming.

"Don't talk to me like I'm an idiot."

Callie reworded her explanation. "These people are protesting tomorrow's opening. They are making their opinion known. To their credit, they are being orderly. A couple already left. I'll be leaving in a second." She let that sink in. "Want to do lunch at McConkey's? It's finally open after the storm damage."

But Sophie wasn't up for being placated. "Where's the owner?"

"Where do you think? Inside, getting ready for tomorrow. Wisely, she's not having a thing to do with these people." Callie had spoken with Kitty Ingram that morning in a phone call relaying the first couple of picketers had shown. Not that Callie hadn't known about the mini march since they'd applied for a permit, but when two protesters turned to eight, she'd cruised over. While they didn't have the temperament for trouble, she didn't want them to attract someone who might.

"I need to speak to that Kitty person," Sophie said, blowing hard through her nose, glaring at the building like the person inside might sense the heat of her ire. "I'm sure I represent the majority on this beach, and she needs to hear from me."

Annie's eyes widened, seeing the potential for altercation after all.

"And tell her what?" Callie said. "You're too late. It's approved and it's opening."

"But she isn't welcome." Sophie took a step to cross the road.

Callie laid a light hand on her friend's forearm. You don't want your name in the newspaper, Soph. And the owner is quite aware that some take issue with her business."

Annie waited to be told what to do. Assist with Sophie, leave and not listen, tend to the picketers . . .

"I've got this," Callie told her officer. "No need for you to stick around anymore." She could handle Sophie, and Annie didn't need to hear what blackmail Callie might have to use to shut up her friend.

Catching the message, Annie tipped her head. "Nice seeing you, Miss Sophie."

Callie winked at Annie to just leave.

She did, and Callie shifted in front of Sophie's line of vision to interrupt her mental loop of frustration, accented by a draft pushing a lock of hair in front of her eye that she slapped back.

"Soph," Callie said. "CBD and pot are miles apart and you know it. Cannabidiol is not psychoactive. It has medicinal properties, something you ought to appreciate." Callie had the sentences ready from having had to explain the differences so many times these last few days. At least a dozen times today. She had already discussed the science to Sophie, but she could stand to hear it again. "And THC stands for tetrahydrocannabinol, the main psychoactive chemical in marijuana, not CBD. Apples and oranges."

"Don't preach to me," Sophie said. She'd been unnaturally disturbed by the whole idea since town council's approval. "CBD and marijuana are bought for similar reasons, meaning this in-your-face shop alters Edisto's image. It'll hurt the aura." When Callie didn't react, she added, "It'll damage the beach's reputation."

Callie had little say in what businesses came and went, though she was obligated to speak up if one might disrupt the community. But she saw the store as harmless. It almost married into the Brigadoon feel of how Edisto was its own universe, separate from the rest of the world, a means for visitors to find their chill.

Besides, a lot of businesses on the beach failed to last much more than three years anyway. Ella & Ollie's had recently closed its upscale establishment, as had the Old Post Office restaurant. Only last week a pizza joint gave its notice. Entrepreneurs in this neck of the woods had to ride the waves in terms of income, and the troughs could last a month or two, enough to sabotage anyone's balance sheet.

A picketer called, "Hey, Sophie! Come join us."

Sophie spun, turning her back to them. "I can't be seen getting involved."

"Then why are you here?" Callie said. "Leave."

"I hate this. I'm torn."

"Just ignore the place. Besides, you don't want to alienate your own enterprise. Some of your people may also be customers here."

"Maybe you're right—"

Marie, the Edisto Beach Police Department's office administrator, came over the mic. "Break-in at 1100 Myrtle. Called in by a neighbor."

Annie came across first. "On it."

Callie would join her in a moment, just as soon as Sophie left, which she appeared to be on the cusp of doing.

"Sophie!" Malorie, the most active of the low-speed picketers, cupped hands around her mouth, attempting to be heard. "Get your tight little yoga ass over here and take up a sign!"

Callie spoke under her breath. "Don't take the bait. Just go."

Sophie glared. "Malorie. I should have known. Maybe I ought to get involved."

Callie sighed loud enough for her friend to hear. "Soph. . ."

"Would that be so wrong for me to step in?"

"I am not getting into this with you, Soph. You're smart enough to know better than to get sucked into Malorie's mayhem and damage your own aura."

Initially, Callie had expected Sophie to prance front and center in the noise making about Edisto Calm . . . until Sophie had explained her reasoning.

Turned out that one very important person supplied the pot needs of Edisto Beach. Sophie wasn't daring enough to divulge the source, but Callie understood the person to be a long-term Edistonian. Like a legacy type of person not so much in bloodline as to the enterprise. Sophie was protecting someone.

Her friend spoke like she'd read Callie's mind. "Doesn't take long for CBD to turn into THC out the back door."

"Now you sound like Malorie. You know better than that. Just let this play out. It's not like you have a choice." Callie's mic went off again, this time Annie.

"Chief, you better get over here."

"What's up? Anyone hurt?"

Annie cleared her throat. "Um, no."

"Okay, I'm about to leave." She clicked off.

Kitty peered out a window again. Malorie saw her. "Get out here and hear our concerns!" she hollered. "Coward!"

Malorie turned toward Callie's side of the street, settling on Sophie. "Get over here, crazy yoga lady. Maybe she'll listen to one of her own kind! You idiot marijuana people give Edisto a bad image."

Aw, damn.

"You people!" Sophie yelled. "What the heck does that mean? And since when do I give Edisto a bad image, you old shriveled up piece of driftwood." She bolted across the street.

A golf cart veered to miss her. It made a hard stop into the passenger door of the police cruiser.

Amos whooped and high stepped, laughing.

The front door of Edisto Calm snapped open, and Kitty rushed onto the porch. "If you get hurt it's not my liability. You hear that, Chief? Are you seeing all of this?"

Callie made sure the golf cart driver was okay and shooed him off, the damage no more than scratches.

Grinning from ear to ear, Amos backed off, relishing being the spectator.

Sophie nudged herself into Malorie's face, hands fisted on each hip.

"Sophie," Callie cried, looking both ways for more golf carts. "Back away." She raced toward the picket line, only to suddenly smell the all-too-familiar smoke.

Amos had lit up a joint. "Kick some ass, Chief."

"Seriously?" she hissed. "Put that damn thing away."

"Let me light you up one and you won't be so uptight either."

"You're on someone else's property. I'd back the owner's complaint if she came after you."

Amos blew out another puff. "She won't care. Trust me."

Gasps and shouts of picketers snatched her attention away from the joint. Malorie lay on the sand, Sophie leaning over her. The others had backed up a few yards, finding refuge under a palmetto tree.

The fluffy Malorie rolled to her knees, trying to stand, attempting to scream louder than Sophie who stooped within inches of the woman, fussing straight into the picketer's ear.

"Sophie. Back away!" Callie ordered, rushing over.

"Shoot your gun in the air, Chief!" shouted Amos before he gave a whooping holler.

Callie reached the yoga maven, snaring her arm before she could put Malorie back on her tush. Her mic went off again. With one hand on Sophie, she answered with the other. "Chief Morgan."

Annie. "I didn't make myself clear. Someone broke into the house on Myrtle. He's still here."

Callie's blood chilled a little. "Wait for me. Stay safely back and let me get there. Do not engage."

"No," Annie said. "It's okay. Someone took care of him."

Callie escorted Sophie to the other side of the patrol car, keeping a firm grip. "What does *took care of him* mean, Annie?"

"I mean he's cuffed up on the back porch. A cut on his lip, and he claims his arm's broken."

"Is the owner there?"

"No. House is being rented. Owner lives in Florida."

"Then who . . .?"

"No idea, but there's a note tucked in his back pocket that says *You're welcome.*"

Chapter 2

CALLIE KEYED HER mic. "Hold tight, Annie. I'll be right there."

Then she backed Sophie against the vehicle. "I have half a mind to cuff you, throw you in the back of my cruiser, and make you ride with me the rest of the day."

"You heard her," Sophie said, then spun around to scream across the roof of the car, "Malorie, you're a bitch!"

"And you're a witch," Malorie screamed, leaning to one side in a bit of a stagger, possibly hurting from the fall. Callie hoped not.

Sophie's yoga kept her fit and lean, but Malorie was more the typical sixty-something who'd retired to do little more on Edisto than meet ladies for five o'clock drinks and ride on a boat someone else captained.

"Bitch is worse," Sophie returned.

"Witch is wickeder!"

Recognizing the rising heat, Amos strolled over to escort Malorie to the seat beside him on the Edisto Calm porch. He offered her his joint, and after a stunned second, she refused.

Callie appreciated Amos's assistance. Honestly, Malorie ought to take a hit. Would do the up-tight woman some good.

She turned to Sophie. "You better hope she doesn't file charges. But I don't have time for this crap. Get in your car, and I'll follow you home."

"What if I wasn't going home?"

"Well, you are now."

"What if I don't want to go home?"

"Then you ride with me."

Sophie thought about that, some huffs and puffs still coming out of her. "How will you know?"

"Hush. You're being childish. You and Malorie are both against Edisto Calm being here. Leave it at that." Callie shook her head. "I seriously don't have time for this," she said under her breath. She escorted Sophie to her car, ordered her in, and motioned for her to drive ahead. Then she got into her own vehicle and followed.

Sophie's beach house, *Hatha Heaven*, happened to be next door to

Callie's, *Chelsea Morning*, and both weren't three-quarters of a mile down Jungle Road from Edisto Calm. Nothing on Edisto was far from anything else.

Sophie parked in her drive. Callie spoke out her passenger window. "Go inside. Do not return to that store. Do not contact Malorie. Understand? I'm telling my people to check on you."

"There's only you and Annie today, so don't go all 5-0 on me like you have all these *people*. Besides, I have to go to work," she said. "I'm going to be late."

Wonderful. Sophie was hostess at El Marko's, the Mexican restaurant in the strip mall not a block up from Edisto Calm. "Better yet. I'll have Mark watch you." Conveniently, Callie's beau was owner of the eatery.

She had to go! Annie had a situation that didn't make sense, and Callie wasn't feeling good about that. "Your street-fighting can only damage your own image. I'm going. You behave."

Callie left, fingers crossed that her friend's promise was trustworthy.

Frankly, she would be happy if bitchy-witchy arguments were all she had to contend with on the beach. Break-ins happened, a common risk with empty rentals in a tourist area whose population changed from ten thousand by summer to seven hundred by winter. That was a lot of empty properties with few people to watch them. With Thanksgiving around the corner, however, the number was more like four thousand, but that still left enough tempting opportunity.

Catching someone usually took a neighbor identifying the violator, like in this case. The standard culprit was often someone from the bigger island, but even holiday tourists got tempted. Edisto wasn't a party place, so teenagers got bored. But Callie halfway expected to know this burglar even if Annie didn't.

She sped up. The beach community was five to six miles in circumference from Scotts Creek up Palmetto, around to Dock Site and back to Jungle then to Scotts Creek again, so getting anywhere took no time, even at thirty miles per hour. At cop speed, Callie reached the Myrtle Street address in a couple of quick minutes.

Annie's cruiser sat parked in the shell and gravel drive of one of the better homes on the Sound side of town. Four thousand square feet give or take.

No one waited on the front porch, so Callie trotted to the back side. Every house had a front and back view. Along Myrtle, the back of several houses like this one meant overseeing Hole 5 of the Wyndham golf course, far enough away not to be recognized by anyone playing that hole.

No looky-loos gathered in the front, always a good thing, but when Callie came out on the other side, a small group of four stood at the base of the stairs.

"Any of you the renter here? Or the owner?"

They all shook their heads, which meant they were a collection of nosy neighbors. "Okay, then who's the person who called this in?" she asked, not knowing two of the people. One she might have seen before, but the elder man she recognized. He lived next door. "Mr. Weston? Was it you?"

An eight-foot-tall wax myrtle blocked her vision of above. "Annie? You up there?"

She heard the officer but couldn't see much of her other than some movement through the leaves. "Yeah, Chief."

Weston came forward, wanting to talk. "Give me a sec, Annie," Callie said and turned to the man. "Go ahead. What did you see?"

"I was fixing lunch . . . my kitchen is on the corner, and the window is on this side," he said, using hand gestures to point back to his place. "I was halfway through frying an egg sandwich when I saw him yank open the back door." He gave an exaggerated nod. "So I called you people."

"You get a good look at him?"

"He moved like he was young. He wore a mask, so can't tell you whether he was black or white."

Or yellow or brown, but this was rural South Carolina so the odds were that Weston was right one way or the other.

"See anyone else?" she asked.

"No. Were there more?"

Her brow went up. "You tell me. I just got here."

He shook his head but didn't seem so sure about it.

"You stayed inside?" she asked.

He nodded. "Never left the house until your lady officer showed. I'm not into interrupting criminals and risking my life. Don't get paid enough for that."

Honestly, Callie didn't either, but she did it anyway, supported by the insurance from a deceased husband, a murdered father, and the beach house given to her mortgage free from her parents. This neighbor Weston didn't work anyway. He'd retired from being some chief somebody at an engineering firm for a major government contractor.

She pulled a pad out of her pocket. "Recognize anything about him?"

"What do you mean?"

She peered up at him like she had reading glasses on her nose, not difficult for her to do since she ran six inches shorter than most people. "I mean, anything about this man ring a bell?"

"No, Chief. I have no earthly idea who he is."

"Not perhaps one of the people renting the house?"

To that he scoffed. "I don't keep up with who rents what and when. Just saw him break in."

Damn it. She hated to see strangers invading this beach. She best get up the stairs and see what the heck this situation was. Hopefully Annie had double checked on whether the guy was just some renter who'd lost his keys. Annie had been cryptic in her description of the burglar, though.

Callie took the stairs two at a time. Upon reaching the landing, she slowly opened the gate that kept someone's dog or toddler from breaking free and tumbling down. She scanned the scene then glanced back down at the part of Weston she could see through the bush. Not much of a view from down there. She returned her attention to the state of this affair.

Annie stood guard over a man in his early thirties. Awkwardly, he bent over the porch railing, arms outstretched, his wrists cuffed around a flagpole. Old Glory flapped ten feet overhead. He'd wedged each foot between bannisters to avoid toppling over.

She mouthed *what-the-hell* at her officer. Annie delivered the man's wallet with one hand and a slip of paper with the other.

"Hurry up, lady. My legs are cramping!"

Magnus Sims. Age thirty. His driver's license photo gave him more of a sense of middle eastern ethnicity than the real man's appearance, but his heritage appeared a hodge podge. He could've been born in Adams Run up the highway as much as overseas.

License said Ravenel, South Carolina, not far up the road, and she thought she recalled the general vicinity of the address. A local, more or less. He'd either recognized the opportunity of vandalizing rentals or was friends with someone else who had. Empty rentals rarely held valuables, so even when broken into, little was taken. Just because a house looked affluent didn't mean the rental owner dared to display items that could easily walk off each week as one tenant replaced another.

Which meant the hungrier burglar would invade an occupied rental. Tenants left valuables all over the place from jewelry to wads of bills, thinking they were safe. Problem was, burglars ran the chance of running into people, which led to being seen, and of course, stiffer criminal charges.

Still, the two-million-dollar question remained. Who had subdued him?

"Sir, is your name Magnus Sims?" she asked, adding for him to also confirm the address on the driver's license.

"Yes and yes. Can you just get me down?" the man asked. "Your officer here is enjoying herself watching me teetering on the brink of a serious demise. I've been here for almost an hour."

Decent vocabulary for someone too dense to burgle properly.

Callie took particular note of his arms being outstretched and shackled. Normal angles. Nothing out of the norm. "Did you tell her your arm was broken?"

"I might've exaggerated about that," he said.

Callie took his picture from several angles then told Annie to key him loose. Both put hands on him. Annie released the cuff on one arm, using it as leverage to control him, while Callie maneuvered the other arm behind his back. She held the man's waistband minus a belt and eased him to his feet. He immediately sank to the floor, rubbing his legs with the free arm. Annie gave him a few moments then stood him back up and repositioned the cuffs. She moved the man such that he looked straight at her boss.

"Magnus," Callie began. "What were you attempting to do?"

"I thought this was the house I was supposed to rent, and when my key wouldn't fit the front door, I came around back . . . to try . . ."

Callie shook her head and looked at Annie.

"I called Wainwright Realty already," the officer said. "I have the name of the tenant. It's not Magnus Sims."

"Strike One. Want to try again?"

"It's under my girlfriend's name."

"Who is . . .?"

He twisted a look over his shoulder at Annie, who stood there grinning, her look telling him he would get it wrong.

Callie gave him the long hard pity look she gave those caught in their first lie. "Let's try something easier," she said. "Who cuffed you to the flagpole?"

That question amped him up. "Never saw him. Honest to God."

With a smirk at Annie, who returned a comical shrug, Callie tried again. "You broke into the house, and someone sneaked up behind you, dragged you outside, bent you over and restrained you to a flagpole. Yet you caught not one glimpse of him?"

Instinctively he tried to raise an arm to talk. The cuffs drew him up short. "I swear. He slid my balaclava around so I couldn't see." He nodded to the black cover in a bunch on the porch plank floor. "The cuffs were on before I knew it. I figured the owner came home."

"Annie?" she asked, wondering the same.

"I took his cover off, but no, nobody was home," said the young officer, her short blonde bob blowing strands into her eyes. "With this guy restrained, I searched the house. Then I called Wainwright Realty to see if they knew this guy, and if the place was rented. It is rented but they were out. Wainwright doesn't know this guy, and they are sending someone to repair the door as we speak. They don't want the renters upset."

"Good deal. Anything missing?" Callie asked.

Annie shook her head. "Appears he didn't have the chance, but I looked for anything amiss. Everything appears in order. I'll ask the renters later, but I found nothing in his possession."

Callie looked the man over. "Well, we got you for breaking and entering, but nothing burgled. Did you know the house was rented?"

"I waited for them to leave. I am not into hurting people. That means you can let me go, right?" Magnus's dark eyes weren't angry or intimidating, instead pleading. "I don't have any kind of warrants or record or anything. Go ahead and check." Getting caught with his hand in the cookie jar seemed less concerning than being totally unsure what had just happened to him.

Callie looked to Annie. "You check his name?"

"I did," the officer replied. "He's correct. Nobody's looking for him."

Callie paused for a few breaths, leaning toward cutting him loose. He was sloppy. He wasn't used to doing this. How he addressed her next couple of questions would help her make that decision. That and she had no lock-up on the beach. Anyone arrested had to be taken to Walterboro forty-five miles northeast of them, which meant one less officer for the better part of a day.

"Everything okay up there, Chief?" hollered Weston from below.

"We're good," she said. "Y'all can go on home now." Then she changed her mind. "No, hold on. I have another question or two for you. Give me a sec."

Some silence. "Okay."

She returned to those last few questions for Magnus. "Did you hear or smell anything about this person who stopped you?"

Magnus paused, the thought of using senses other than sight catching him unawares. "He was stealthy as hell, so no, I didn't hear him."

Callie wondered how stealthy hell was but didn't interrupt. "Smell?"

Magnus sniffed like he had to be reminded of what Callie meant, like whoever it was had left their scent hovering in the air like two-dollar cologne. He shook his head. "No. I'm remembering nothing."

"Did he speak once he caught you?" she asked.

"No."

"What sound did his feet make going down the steps? As in sneakers versus boots. A big person or a lightweight one?"

"No sound at all," he said. "He didn't even breathe! I'm telling you, the damn guy was a ghost!"

"What makes you think it was a guy?" she asked.

That Magnus could identify with. "Because he was fast and strong. At least my height. I never knew what hit me. Twisted my hood around, and in an insane flash he restrained me. He led me outside and hooked me to that flagpole in seconds."

"Without a word?"

"Without a word. He seemed almost like a ninja person, or some special forces dude. Tells me one thing, though."

The special forces remark caught her attention, but she let the man finish his thought. "What's that?"

"I don't want to meet him again."

Callie read the piece of paper found in Magnus's back pocket, a ripped piece of a notepad. *You're welcome.* No point worrying about handling the message. If this person was so good at nailing a burglar without leaving a trace, he wouldn't leave prints. "Did he wear gloves?" she asked.

Magnus's eyes widened. "Yes, he did. I felt the leather when he cuffed me."

That made up her mind. "Uncuff him, Annie."

"But Chief . . ."

Callie held up a finger . . . and leaned up to stare Magnus in the eye. "Are you leaving my beach now?"

"Yes, ma'am."

"You fear my guy now?"

From behind him, Annie gave a puzzled expression.

"Yes, ma'am," Magnus said, then leaned down. "Who the hell is he?"

Callie backed away and motioned for Annie to free him. "Why would I feel the need to tell you?"

Magnus rubbed his freed wrists. "Guess I wouldn't tell me either." He continued feeling his wrists, waiting, and when she didn't immediately reply, he asked, "Am I free to go?"

"If you walk with me to the street." She took his sleeve, and he accompanied her down the stairs.

Weston turned his back, slapping the guy closest to him to do the same thing, like they didn't want to be seen.

Callie continued with Magnus under the house, mounted on pilings like all the other residences, and took him to her vehicle. "Now you can go," she said. "Where are you parked?"

"A block over."

"Let me give you a ride," she said.

He laughed. "You trying to get me in your car and slip me off to jail?"

She chuckled back, trying not to mock him. "No, you're free. I have your name and driver's license, so I can ID your vehicle unless you stole someone else's."

"God, no. That's just stupid."

Like this B&E wasn't.

"I think I need the walk," he said.

She flipped a hand. "Then take off."

Damned if the guy didn't launch into a trot and head toward Fort Street, where she'd park a car if she needed to be clandestine about it.

Annie came up beside her. "I'm confused, Chief."

"So am I," Callie said under her breath. "Wait here and keep a watch until the Wainwright people get the door repaired."

She returned to the back of the house where Weston and company waited. "Mr. Weston," she said. "Did you see anyone other than this guy from your kitchen? If you saw this guy break in, I'm wondering if you saw the second?"

His frozen expression told her, but she needed to hear him say it. "There wasn't anyone else."

She studied him harder, but he seemed pretty solid about his answer.

He leaned in. "Was there someone else?"

"Yes, and they stopped this man from doing any damage or taking anything."

Weston had to think. "Guess I missed the second one going in when I went to get my phone."

"Possibly. But thanks for being the good citizen and calling it in. It got us here fast enough to prevent any accident or harm." She reached out to shake his hand, but when she drew back he wasn't inclined to let go.

"What is it, Mr. Weston?"

"So the other guy got away?" he asked.

"Yes, the other person left before we got here," she said. "But all's good now. Again, thank you."

The owner would be contacted properly and told a burglar had been scared off. The door would be repaired within the hour by the realty company managing the property. The tenants would be spared a scare.

All was good.

Kind of.

The average citizen might question her judgment on this, but logistics favored what she'd done. People thought law enforcement black and white, when it rarely was. If she charged the man, he'd get off likely with no more than a slap on the hand, a fine, and probation at the most. The courts had more serious problems than this.

She returned to where Annie stood by her car, talking to the repairman who'd just pulled up in a dated two-door Ranger. Waiting until he had his tools and headed to the back, she looked to Annie for an update. "He ran down Fort Street, like you thought, Chief. So I'm to wait until this Wainwright guy is done?"

"Yes." But it was time for a training moment. "Has it crossed your mind as to who our vigilante might be?"

"I have no idea," the young officer said. "We have no description."

Callie rubbed her chin. "How would he be aware of a crime even taking place?"

Annie did a screwed-up thing with her mouth, a mild shrug following. "Okay, and maybe this is a long shot, but what if he's Magnus's buddy getting the jump on him, you know, like a joke? And Magnus lied about some stranger sneaking up behind him. If this is his buddy, and Magnus is embarrassed from all this, then neither will be back."

Hmm. "How did they pick which house?"

"Old fashioned casing the streets," Annie answered.

Or knowing someone familiar with the area, like the repairman currently fixing the busted lock.

However, Callie confirmed that Annie's answer could work as well, giving her credit for trying. As Annie got into her car, however, Callie decided to take another walk around the Myrtle Street house. She didn't expect anything, but it wouldn't hurt to search.

She wasn't as naïve as Officer Annie, but she believed Magnus and his claim of not knowing the man who interrupted his task. The stranger's skill set, however, sounded unique. Made her envision some crazy ex-military seeking to make himself relevant or be a hero since he had no more wars to fight.

Or the whole stealth description could be no more than Magnus painting his own worth.

The house Magnus broke into would be guarded well enough now between Weston's wariness and the tenant's raised awareness. She hoped Annie was right, too, that the foiled burglar would not be back.

But the term vigilante kept sticking in Callie's head.

Chapter 3

SHORTLY, ANNIE radioed Callie that the Myrtle Street house was secure. Janet Wainwright, the island's real estate magnate, called Callie for a brief conversation about the plusses and minuses of charging the guy who'd broken in and stolen nothing. With the man's name in hand, however, Wainwright conceded to Callie's decision. No doubt the retired Marine might happen to drop in on the address in Ravenel. That would be Callie's guess. And Wainwright would make the tenant's mild inconvenience worth their while financially for a future stay.

Peace restored.

Callie cruised Palmetto Boulevard for the umpteenth time of the day, one eye on anything that moved, to include watching for Magnus and the stranger who had tied him up, like she'd recognize such a gent. With both on her mind, she scanned between houses into back yards on one side, and to the beach on the other.

Author George Orwell was attributed to saying people were better than you think they are. Callie'd read *1984* and *Animal Farm* like every other kid in high school, and while she'd never seen the quote, she got the gist of what he meant from how he carved his characters. She'd attempted to hang decisions in her law enforcement life on those words going all the way back to her career in Boston. First, because the guilty 'til proven innocent style of policing was practiced by far too many. Secondly, in growing up she was pretty sure she'd seen the best of her mother, and there were no altruistic expectations for that woman, so she vowed to see it in everybody else.

Not the most righteous of logic but it was how she looked at herself in the mirror at night. Think the best of people. It was hard in practice, but she tried. Cops, tainted from experiencing the negative of humanity, didn't normally think that way.

Not arresting Magnus counted in that direction. Her decision had been a combination of having no jail handy and the fact he'd been caught before he'd really done damage. He had no record. The scare might've steered him off her beach. The arrest would've only made him bitter, with some inclination of getting even. She fell on the side of thinking better of him.

Mr. Orwell would probably agree.

You think too hard, Mark often told her when her mental faculties got knotted up amidst the philosophy of enforcing the law. The losses in her life numbered more than any five people, maybe ten. She couldn't accept they were there one day and gone the next without a strong reason for why. She had no answers, though. That left unsolved mysteries for her to shoulder. She functioned best by a rule book and defined lines to travel within, but they didn't always work.

She'd missed lunch, and hadn't wanted a late one with the mood she was in. Not a mood, exactly, but more of a spider-sense. With Mark being such a positive individual, she strove not to bring her moods home to him to solve. Nor to the restaurant. But when it came to cases, he was all ears, and his pre-retirement, law enforcement experience came in handy.

Over the next three hours, she wrote three traffic tickets and assisted with jumping off a golf cart battery. Someone tipped their shopping cart over in the parking lot of Food Lion, and she moved a domestic spat from the middle of Dock Site Road to their rental thirty feet away on the marsh. She found a small poodle dog, drove a few blocks with it in her lap hanging out her window until someone recognized it as theirs.

But the whole afternoon she couldn't get the vigilante from Myrtle Street out of her head.

Being close to five in the afternoon, her stomach started talking to her. Mark ran El Marko's from eleven AM to the same PM. Sometimes earlier, sometimes later. He had a small staff who came in to prep in the morning. He closed at night.

The sleeves she'd rolled up by day had come down with the drop in temperature, and she almost donned her jacket from the seat beside her. But with the door to El Marko's only a quick trot from the parking lot, she chose to just scurry into the warmth.

She liked this time of year. The in between of summer and winter. Holidays made her feel emotionally complicated. She loved the windy, sighing emptiness of October to mid-November. People behaved better that time of year. At least with the police.

Callie entered the restaurant. With dinner time not in full swing, Sophie sat in a corner on her phone. When she spotted Callie, she leaped up like she'd been caught at shirking her duties as the so-called hostess.

Callie waved her off and headed to her regular table at the back, near the kitchen, a table smaller than others so it would fit in the cramped space. Since nobody else wanted that spot, Callie always had a waiting VIP seat.

No menu needed either. Mark would just surprise her. Since the wait staff knew her, by the time she took her place, an appetizer was on its way out the door . . . in the hands of her lover.

"How was your day?" she asked.

He also set a Bleinheim's ginger ale before her. His dark Cajun hair fell two inches over his Hawaiian shirt collar. Nobody'd ever questioned how that style shirt belonged in a Mexican restaurant, but he wore them daily, with a whole wardrobe of floral color in his closet. "Slow and steady with lulls," he said. "How was yours? Busy? Noticed you missed lunch."

"Slow and steady with lulls," she repeated, taking a swig of her alcohol replacement. Mark kept a stash of the spicy hot sodas for her benefit alone. When she'd gone on the wagon, a dear friend had introduced them to her. The heavy-handed bite of the ginger was to remind her that alcohol was no longer her thing.

"The protesters broke up not long after you left," he said. Edisto Calm sat within sight of the restaurant. "I think they liked you watching them."

"They had nobody else to watch them." She snickered from behind the ginger ale bottle, taking another sip. "Besides, I had to get your employee out of there." She nodded toward Sophie, back on her phone near the door. "She about got into a brawl with Malorie McLauren in front of everyone."

"Over what?" he asked.

She popped one of the mini quesadillas in her mouth and gave it a few chews before answering. "Not totally sure, since my understanding is they both don't want Edisto Calm to exist. Malorie doesn't want the place there, period, just because of how it might represent something not family friendly. Sophie, however, seems to believe it'll compete with the real thing."

He peered over at his employee, like he saw her in a new light.

Callie read his mind. "She's not about to go in public high, but she does partake. She seems to think the owner will be selling gummies out the front door and weed out the back."

A burrito smothered in jalapenos arrived, steaming. The waitress held it before Mark for inspection and go-ahead before setting down the plate. Callie loved that.

The little things mattered with him, and she loved that about him, too. "If that place starts selling the real McCoy," he said, "word will spread. Surely the owner knows better."

"I don't know," she said, touching the burrito and deeming it too hot to eat. "The old Piggly Wiggly had someone in produce who supplied the general population."

He grimaced, looking at her like she ought to know better.

"Before my time." Callie subtly motioned with her fork. "I told Sophie the owner wouldn't dare, but she doesn't see it that way. She's protecting her supplier, I think." She took a bite, finding it still warm, having to suck in a breath to take the temperature down. Then she went for her ginger ale.

"Give it a second," Mark said.

She swallowed, feeling for any raw spots on the roof of her mouth. "Wait till you hear about the break-in."

Mark turned more serious. As retired SLED, the state's law enforcement division, he had the background to understand Callie's job. She could mention things about her day and him have a reasonable handle on what to worry about and what not to. Edisto's behavior usually wasn't worth the fret.

Both read Edisto as a less than dangerous place to oversee and enjoyed the laid-back environment . . . except when real crime showed up and nobody took it seriously. Between Callie's background from Boston and Mark's from SLED, they watched the beach with a keener eye than the other officers, most who'd never seen a body and would likely never draw a gun.

The officers numbered eight now. Thomas Gage was her most seasoned, and he'd seen more than his fair share of bad guys with a sprinkling of corpses, even at thirty years old. He thought the world of Callie, and she cherished him, secretly praying he never left.

Officer Annie Greer had witnessed a handful of events to teach her a few lessons. She'd arrived on Edisto almost a year ago and stayed, partly due to Thomas.

The others, however, consisted of guys closer to retirement, putting in time. They relied upon Callie to tell them what to take seriously with these tourists, the rental owners, the natives, and the employees. There was a fine line between what was arrest worthy and what wasn't worth damaging the community's economy over. These older uniforms tended to overlook most incidents anyway.

Callie relayed the break-in on Myrtle, wanting Mark's two cents on what may have happened and how she handled it. She described the conversation with Magnus, and the style in which they found Magnus trussed up and waiting. No proof of the guy who Magnus didn't have a chance to see. Also, Callie had no budget nor the tools for forensics, and with no real crime other than a door Wainwright had already fixed, there wasn't much to stick to the man.

"I'd have let him go, too," he said. "Not that I'd tell you how to run your town."

"Nice save," she said, finally taking a big bite of the just-right temp burrito.

"One of your officers wouldn't do this would they?" Mark asked.

She frowned. "What, break into a house?"

"No," he said, then she got it.

"You mean the other guy. Sneak up, snare Magnus, tie him up and leave him for someone else to clean up after?" She grimaced at how weird that sounded. "Sorry, not seeing that. Why not claim the collar?"

"Just playing devil's advocate here. Maybe a beach visitor who's a cop by day? Or retired cop who had a shrewd enough eye to catch this guy in the act but didn't want to get involved?"

"Why not call me?" she asked.

"Again, the not-wanting-to-get-involved part."

The theory felt rather far-reaching to her, but having a vigilante on the beach felt just as far-fetched. "These houses have little to steal, though, Mark. Natives would likely understand that. This guy Magnus isn't immediately local. First, where did he get the idea without knowing someone? And what are the odds someone just spotted him and had the guts to stop him?"

"Think he was followed?"

"I do," she said.

"Maybe his own buddy did this? Told him about these houses being easy marks during the off season, then when Magnus followed through, the buddy set him up, trussed him up, and took off. Sounds like a joke young single guys would play."

That suggestion sounded the most feasible. She hoped that was the case, too, because that theory carried lower odds of being repeated.

"Your tenant isn't bucking your letting him go?" he asked.

"I let Janet take care of that. She assures me all is well in that department."

"Good. Then eat," he said. "Your dinner's getting cold."

Mark sat silent, sometimes watching her, sometimes staring off like he had something on his mind.

"What're you thinking about?" she asked once she'd downed the burrito. People were coming in for the supper hour, and Mark would have to return to work in a minute. This was how they carried on a lot of their conversations, right here at this tiny table against the wall, between, during, and after meals. The beach was small. Commuting wasn't the issue like in Charleston, where getting to and from work consumed one to two hours of the day. Still, they struggled to find alone time. With him being a proprietor and her a cop, they waved in passing, sent chatty texts during breaks, then caught up over food, in this spot. Everyone in town knew it, usually leaving them alone. But it was also where all the other officers could readily find her, too.

"Just mulling over that break-in," he said, after a pause. "Any chance you've attracted an admirer?"

She hadn't thought about that, but she could see how he would. "You mean a groupie?"

"Groupie, borderline stalker, some enthusiast about the law."

"A wannabe?"

His lips were mashed, and he shook his head. "This person sounds too knowledgeable for a wannabe." He pushed his chair back. "This is a bit outside the box, don't you think?"

"Yes, I'll be careful," she said, reading him. He had to return to work, but he would ponder this the whole evening, ready to discuss it again once he arrived home near midnight, when she laid in bed, in and out of sleep, waiting.

It was sometimes difficult for him to watch her police, doing things he used to do, wishing he could be there beside her. Getting shot in the leg had earned him early retirement, but he had the skills, and when he wanted to hear about her work, she talked.

As for the break-in, Callie figured she had nothing to worry about until she did. No harm done. A real badass would've hurt Magnus, not left him for her. Mark would chew on this, though, wanting to iron out all the wrinkles in every tangent of an idea.

In other words, he wanted her safe.

She appreciated that, and, after he gave her a quick peck, watched him walk away, loving her in his mind.

Her meal done, a kiss still felt on her lips, she stood and searched out Sophie, to ensure she hadn't slipped back outside to challenge Malorie again. Her neighbor and buddy needed a leash at times. "Hey, Soph. I haven't missed anymore street fighting, have I?"

"Never laid a hand on her," she said. Seated at the front of the restaurant in leggings, a multi-colored tunic top hanging over her thighs, Sophie looked every bit the fit yoga lady she was known for being. A scorpion pose wasn't beyond her reach, an incredibly difficult manipulation. If Sophie took on Malorie, she'd win, but Edisto didn't need a kiss-ass yoga maven fist-fighter amongst its natives. Or its entrepreneurs, for that matter, which Sophie was with her yoga business. The Chamber would kick her out so fast.

"Well, don't think about the store for a while," Callie said. "Let Edisto Calm run its course. It'll evolve into a benefit for the community or fold. I'll keep it legal. Heck, you'll probably keep it legal with your hawk-eyed nosiness, but, Sophie, Miss Kitty Ingram has a right to open a shop just like you and anyone else."

Sophie chewed on that thought. "Gives the beach a bad image," she said, falling back on the same words as that morning with no other reasoning to give. "I'm visiting when they open. I'll be one of the first to cross that threshold. Just seeing me will instill the fear of—"

"Fear of what? What're you thinking, girlfriend?"

Sophie wasn't believed to be much of a bother by the islanders but was considered a strong part of its fabric. She could bad-mouth the new store and make a difference in its business, though.

Callie couldn't stop her from going in the store and casting one of her arched eyebrows in an *I-see-you* look. To most people she was comical, cute, and unique. To those who believed in the spiritual world, she was a conduit to its essence, which some attributed to her having the potential of curses. Her own son Zeus called her a witch.

However, to Kitty Ingram, someone new to the beach, Sophie might easily be perceived as a threat, and Callie didn't need the animosity. Business owners might take sides.

Callie went for a little reverse psychology. "Draw too much attention and you send business her way. Ever think of that?"

Apparently, Sophie hadn't, because she quieted.

"Let's let the beach decide," Callie said, in a hope to wrap this up.

Sophie emitted a hard breath and rose to seat a couple who'd walked in. Time for Callie to move on, too. Hopefully she had changed Sophie's mind.

Outside, she smelled a nip in the air, the sky already emptying itself of light. She could go home or make another round of the beach's thoroughfares. This in-between period wasn't comfortable. Technically off work, she had nothing to do until Mark came home between eleven and midnight.

If she went home, she'd be alone for five hours, with little to do other than read a book. She wasn't much for television, hating the fact it took three remotes to find something decent to watch.

Alone time didn't set well with her. Solitary made her think too hard, and if she didn't have much to think hard about, she fell back on thinking about a drink, or the son she missed at school, or the mayor mother who drove her mad with her own deceptions and schemes.

She missed her dead father, the two officers she'd lost two years ago . . . and her murdered husband. Spiraling, some called it, and it didn't look good on an alcoholic.

Sometimes she visited her biological mother who lived a couple doors down. She and Sarah had bonded well since Callie learned of her true lineage only two years ago, but she tried to limit those visits to twice a week so as not to become a burden. Sarah assured Callie her door was always open, but every adult had a life of their own.

That emptiness often made her wander back to the restaurant to have Mark nearby and to avoid temptation. Sometimes she'd ask her old boss Stan to pass the time with her . . . or simply find him there. He'd about recovered from his broken leg, using a cane these days. She'd bought him a hand-carved design to make him look suave.

Half the time, however, she traveled the peaceful night streets giving Edisto way more service than it paid her for in terms of salary.

She guessed it was driving the streets tonight.

From behind the wheel, she eased into what little traffic there was because of the early evening and it being dinner time. A car passed about every couple hundred feet. The sun set lovely today, in a creamsicle orange, and driving along Palmetto Boulevard, she smiled and settled into the routine.

But she still thought harder with nothing to interrupt said thoughts other than the occasional wave of a resident.

What she hadn't mentioned to Mark was a certain ex-Army Ranger they'd both met during the hurricane not quite seven weeks ago. He avoided arrest because he'd morphed from an abductor of young women to somewhat of a vigilante hero, and nobody had felt the need to pursue him. Magnus's mention of *stealth* popped him into her mind.

He'd parted from his Ranger partners, no longer in agreement with their criminal activities. They'd had a sweet racket, hurting no one and making money doing so. In one brief moment, in a loud exchange with those partners, under the whump-whump of a medical chopper, this guy mentioned staying on at Edisto. He had the survival skills to live in the jungle. He had no home. He had no family. He'd saved a couple of lives during that hurricane time, which caused a loose, quasi-respect to build between him and her. Mark was there. He got it, too, but he didn't totally trust the man.

It was funny how they didn't talk about the Ranger anymore. They didn't mention how he'd broken the law then changed his mind and come to the rescue and saved lives.

It was one of those gray areas where the law might be a little too tight, where a uniform might take the latitude of looking the other way. She'd let him loose like Magnus, like there was some good left in him.

Not having seen him since the hurricane days, she assumed he left. Now she wasn't so sure.

She also wasn't so sure what to think about that.

Still, a far-reaching idea.

Chapter 4

Bruce

AFTER THE HURRICANE, Bruce Bardot lived a week in the woods, most of the time under an old man's lean-to-shed off Laurel Hill Road. By night he slept beneath tarps and such, the eighty-year-old man oblivious, only coming out of his ram-shackle home once or twice a day to either check his chicken coop for eggs or feed the birds, this time of year the eggs being few. Both the shed and the coop had been strategically built so that the owner could take a dozen steps one way, then a dozen in the other, then come back inside, the effort taxing his aged bones to their max.

The location was far enough from the beach in one direction and civilization in the other to allow Bruce to catch his breath and think.

He'd been with his two Ranger buddies for several years but never settled. They traveled to several places a year, pulling an abduction scam. But kidnapping young women for ransom, even if they returned the girls unharmed to wealthy parents who could afford to pay, while lucrative, was wrong. And dangerous. It took coming up against that police chief on an evacuated beach during a hurricane, an insane twist of fate, to show him how far he'd strayed. To pry him from his comrades. Necessary pain.

For now, and however long it took, he'd remain off the grid, something he was quite capable of doing. He'd about decided to stay in the Edisto vicinity a few months, maybe befriending this old man, but it took studying the lay of the land and the traffic patterns before making that choice.

He liked what he saw about Edisto Island though. There were enough jungle and remote places to keep him hidden for a long while, versus farms, national forests and parks where people were liable to find you sooner or later. This felt more secluded, less noticeable.

His phone having long lost its charge, and Bruce not exactly wanting people to know his whereabouts anyway, he remained obscure. He didn't need old buddies to locate him, or the local uniforms to ping him.

No doubt he was still in the Edisto Beach police chief's mind. She'd been the main one he'd assisted. She was sharp.

Instead, he walked. He covered miles, with fifteen miles a day well within his abilities. He stayed in shape since his tours as a Ranger. The better shape he was in, the less he needed civilization and its rules, its laws, and its judgment. He'd learned there was one set of laws in war, loose ones, necessary ones, and another set at home, the second set leaving a lot to be desired. In his walking around the island, he'd learned Edisto was bigger than he thought, too. A good thing.

The walks let him think. If his old partners continued doing what they had done with Bruce, karma would soon snare them, coming like a sniper from the hills, undetected and lethal. He hoped not. He hoped that his departure altered their plans as well. With him being their loose end, and them being his, he had no choice but to never see them again.

He wasn't rattled. Nothing rattled him, really, which some found odd, including an ex-wife who claimed he'd been born with a brain missing its emotional center.

They called him a good medic, though. A phenomenal one, frankly, per the doctors he'd worked with. He'd toyed with medical school, but the PTSD in his record wouldn't let him set foot in a university door. During the hurricane, he'd helped save a couple of people on the beach, a meager attempt to make amends, then he'd parted ways . . . from the world.

Didn't take traipsing around more than five miles, however, for him to see that Edisto Island was as close to isolation as he could immediately get. He didn't do cities. He didn't do crowds. He couldn't even do a damn apartment, for God's sake. He had to see his perimeter. He preferred control over what could possibly come at him.

All he knew was what felt most normal. What felt safe. He rather enjoyed being the one who kept things safe, thus the need to see three-sixty around his surroundings, or as close as he could get to it.

That's why the worn-out, lean-to shed was cozy for the likes of him.

And walking gave him peace.

Even with the overgrown greenery of the Edisto jungle, he could see more than most people did on a city street. He sensed beings. He spotted movement to the level of minutiae. He sensed what was dangerous and what wasn't. Walking kept him tuned.

He liked it here. Plenty of wildlife to live off of, and enough scattered roadside markets to fill in the gaps. He could live like this for a while.

The fifth day into his new Edisto existence, he deviated west on Raccoon Island Road, to gain a fresh set of bearings. Each day consisted of mentally mapping. He'd have every paved, dirt, gravel, and silt path etched in his brain in a matter of two weeks, give or take a day from what he surmised. He'd studied the beach and island enough prior to the hurricane to have a sense of the whole. Rain or shine didn't matter. He'd been trained to ignore weather and adjust. He went out, period.

That fifth day, however, he heard the woman moaning long before he saw her.

Taking a detour through the woods, keen to her locale, he routed himself around such that he could reach her from where she wouldn't suspect; she or anyone else who might've heard her moan.

A path lined with vegetation from what had to be an unseen house showed habitual wear to her mailbox. Something had made her totter and slip off the three-foot route. One sneakered foot had mired up into some creature's dug-up hole, filled with recent rain and hidden by fall leaves knocked down by the same.

From the worn-out whimper, she'd been there a while.

He panned the forest. No building, no cars on the road. All good.

He ran fingers through his hair, damp from the irregular drips of old rain off the trees, then he straightened himself. "Hey," he said, lowkey. "Don't be afraid."

"Oh!" She jumped anyway, with the delayed reaction of someone bumping seventy.

"Need help?" he asked, approaching slow enough not to scare, fast enough not to look like a creep.

"No," she said, awkward on her back, the ground around her slick from failed attempts to right herself. "I chose this moment to set myself up for some hot hunk of he-man muscle to find me and whisk me off to a cave to ravage me. You up for the job?"

He grinned, daring to stoop beside her after that entertaining retort. "This scheme work for you in the past?"

"Every time," she said, forcing a grin against some part of her that hurt, per the wince. "Problem is they all leave. Can't stand the mosquitoes and the humidity so they leave for some other wench. Their loss."

Carefully pushing away the mud, enough to relieve the suction and see that the ankle wasn't twisted in an unnatural angle, he managed to sit her up and extract her leg from the muck, the shoe left down in the hole.

"Ain't broken," she said, wiggling toes with way more vigor that he thought she would.

"Clearly not," he said, sitting on his haunches. "Want to try to stand?"

But she pointed to the hole. "Not until you retrieve my shoe. Just bought these six months ago. Didn't cost much, but they've still got a heap of mileage left on them."

He retrieved the shoe and headed in the direction of where she pointed to home, her leaning on him and limping until he just swooped her up and carried her the last thirty yards.

She giggled. The giggle turned into a cackle, and he had to laugh a bit himself.

The house popped up out of nowhere, on the swamp, close enough such that the aroma of its mud hung thick in the air. By the time he settled her on a kitchen chair, she asked where he was from, and if he had a place to stay.

"Making do," was all he'd said. "Staying in a place just big enough to stash my duffle. Nothing like this castle."

She smiled at her newly acquired knight. "Would my spare room beat that?"

The ancient, white clapboard marsh house might be old, but it beat the shed. She seemed safe enough. "You here alone?" he asked.

She grinned wider. "Why? Worried someone will catch us together?"

She wasn't intimidated in the least, and he couldn't contain another chuckle. "Absolutely."

"Nah," she said. "I'm alone. Nephew drops in once in a blue moon, but only when he needs something. Not because he gives a damn."

He studied her, reading her, deeming her a lonely soul he wouldn't mind sharing conversation with. Maybe just long enough to see her healed. A regular bed would be nice.

"A night maybe," he agreed. "Two, depending on your ankle."

She gave a lewd, sideways grin at him, pushing gray strands out of her eyes, a bit muddy from her ordeal. "If we're going to be roommates, we need each other's names, don't you think?"

"Why, is this that cave you mentioned?"

"Depends. Is this love at first sight or just some fly-by-night, old-fashioned porking?"

He busted out laughing this time, something he hadn't done in . . . as long as he could remember. Maybe back before the tours overseas, before the uniforms and guns, heat and sweat and blood. PTSD of his caliber didn't feel settled enough to laugh. That said a lot about her.

"Bruce," he said, rolling her sock down and off her injured foot. There was some swelling, but nothing serious. Finding a big stew pot, he filled it with warm water and returned to her, setting the foot in it to gently wash off the dirt.

"Ooh, honey. You just bought yourself longer than two days. Name's Serenity." Her body melted a bit. "Since I could be your mother, it's Miss Sere to you. And I'm not about to steal your virginity, so rest easy."

Laughing and feigning disappointment, he continued washing the foot. When finished, he emptied and refilled the pot and did the other. Soon her feet were dry with new socks and mule slippers he found under her bed.

"I'll take your offer to stay, Miss Sere." The name was pronounced Siri, like on the phone. It suited her.

That night they shared leftover collards and a small piece of ham, and he'd found enough flour to make them a plate of biscuits. After retrieving his duffle bag from the lean-to, he returned to stay in her guest room. The sheets were musty from lack of use, but the mattress beat the dirt floor of the other place.

He'd help her out until she could walk, he told himself. Told her the same thing. Six weeks later, however, he remained, agreeing to stay only if he could earn his keep.

He also rather appreciated the reclusive locale of the place, with the house's rear having a fantastic one-hundred-eighty-degree view over that pluff mud swamp, the front consisting of woods accessed by that worn path and a private rutted drive.

She loved him to pieces. In a genuine, grandmama way she sopped him up like gravy.

Serenity Rush Whaley claimed lineage back to plantation days, but Bruce knew nothing about such things. Living in the moment was all he could handle. Who spawned him didn't matter, which was part of why he'd been so perfect for the military and the repeated tours.

One evening, she sat on her back porch swing that he'd re-anchored to new supports in the ceiling. The house was heated by wood, and he enjoyed chopping the pieces as much as she enjoyed watching him chop it. Being November, she'd need more of it soon.

"How's your foot, Miss Sere?" he asked. The foot had long healed. It was their joke. She pretended to limp at times, telling him she needed to be swept off her feet again.

"Don't know if I'll ever be right," she said, then cackled. "You might need to stay on a few more days."

"I'll try," he said, chuckling back to himself.

He drew up short at the sound of a knock coming from around front.

"You hear that?" He reached her side, listening hard again. Woodpeckers could reverberate through these woods, but this was human.

The knock came harder. "Aunt Sere?" called the visitor.

Bruce looked to her for explanation.

"My nephew Larue," she said, standing, none too happy at the interruption.

"I would rather he not know me," Bruce said.

She paused but didn't question. "Hide inside."

He knew where to hide. He slid into the kitchen pantry barely six feet inside the back entrance, the door cracked enough to hear.

She shuffled to the front door. "Y'all didn't tell me you were coming. Didn't even hear you drive up. I might've made dinner for you, Larue. What'cha need, honey?"

"Why do I always need something, Aunt Sere?" said the boy Bruce assumed was Larue, the voice sounding like someone in his early twenties. Bruce wished he'd hidden closer, so he could get a look . . . get a read.

Sere didn't mince words. "I asked because you don't show up without a need. It's not dinner, so what is it?"

He acted like he hadn't received a backhanded insult. "This is Magnus, Aunt Sere. He's my buddy from Ravenel. You got any money?"

Bruce tensed. A dozen thoughts coursed through his mind, the main one being what he might have to do to these two guys to stop them from robbing his landlord, his friend. Worse, where he'd have to go once he made himself known, which would be any place but this island. That would leave her exposed.

He stood still and listened harder.

"What day of the month is this?" she asked, acting like she had to ponder the question. Bruce had come to know her as much quicker than that.

"The twentieth," said by who had to be Magnus. A little older sounding. Thirty maybe.

Miss Sere slapped something that sounded like her leg. She chuckled like she always did. "Come on, baby, you know that's way too far from the first when I get my Social Security. That check is spent within a day or two of when I get it. You ask me this every time you visit, and the story's always the same."

"Don't you keep money here?" Magnus asked. "Everybody saves money."

"Apparently not you, or you wouldn't be asking for mine. Besides," she said. "I pretty much have all I need."

"Told you," Larue said.

Sere rolled on, unphased. "What y'all got there?"

Bruce again wished he'd hidden someplace better to keep an eye on her.

Magnus spoke up. "Look, Auntie, this is just some things we need to store in your house. That's the main reason we came around. Not for your money."

Liar.

"Will it go bad?" she asked. "I'm sure I can find room in the refrigerator."

"No," he said, shaking the contents. They had a little rattle to them. "Just some gifts I want to hide. With Christmas coming up, I can't hide them at home. My little sister knows every hiding place in the house. What'd'ya say?"

Bruce perked at the request. What better place to hide stolen property or illegal contraband than some old woman's run-down house in the middle of a swamp?

"Why sure, baby. Got a coat closet right inside the living room there. Or put it behind the couch. I never get visitors, so it'll be safe wherever you decide."

Bruce heard steps move, and he could approximate about to where since he'd become quite familiar with the place. A couple of thumps told him the items weren't massive.

"Hey, while I got you boys, can you do me a favor? I need kindling and wood chopped out back. I did a little bit, but an old woman can only do so much. Come on through."

The boys said nothing. They also didn't move.

Magnus spoke first. "Let's go, man."

"Wait a minute, man. Can he store more junk here, Aunt Sere?" Larue might have phrased it as a question, but he didn't sound like he was giving her much of a choice.

"Sure, baby. How's your mother?" Sere asked.

"She kicked me out."

"Oh, baby. Like you have no place to stay? I have a room, but I'd need you to fix a few things in it to make it worth staying in. You might need you to buy some sheets. I do have an old blanket, but you'll have to shake the bugs out of it. Now, if you live here, on the first of the month I'd need you to take me into town to run my errands. I didn't hear your car. You still have it, right?"

"Gotta go, Aunt Sere. I got a place." Then in afterthought, and Bruce couldn't tell how sincere, Larue asked, "You doing okay?"

Bruce could hear the pretend grin in her words. "Hurt my ankle. Might need you to take me to the doctor this week. What do you say about Thursday?"

"Glad you're better. Gotta go, Aunt Sere. Later."

Larue didn't make it past the threshold before Bruce slid out of the pantry, out the kitchen door, and around the house.

Larue remained on the doorstep as Bruce came around. The back of Magnus's canvas jacket had just disappeared through the trees. Bruce noted the just-shy-of-six-foot height, black hair to his collar, and a balaclava rolled up over his head as a cap. As he thought, early to mid-thirties. Not a power builder but fit enough. No pot belly.

Not someone Serenity needed to confront.

From behind the trees, Bruce noted Larue coming from the house to his left. Magnus had already disappeared to his right. Instead of waiting for Larue, Bruce covertly traveled tree to shrub, coming out close enough to Raccoon Island Road but not out in the open. He hid in wait for Larue to reach the car Magnus leaned on, oblivious to being watched.

"Breaking into these rentals is a lot of trouble for not much reward," Magnus said, pushing off the vehicle to go around to the passenger side as Larue opened the driver's side of the fifteen-year-old Toyota Scion, the paint dulled to a cross between blue and gray.

"That junk we just stashed isn't worth a hundred dollars," Larue said. "We need to break into the occupied ones."

"Or break into the owner's closets if you're going in the rentals. I told you to go straight for those. They're usually in the hallway, or off the master."

"This is chump change shit. And what do you think an owner is going to stash in a closet that anyone can break into? Extra toilet paper? Shampoo? Their favorite coffee? Get real, man. We're hitting the rented ones. You got a grip on those, or do we just watch and go from there?"

Larue shut his door, the window down. "Doesn't take a genius to spot them, man."

"Tomorrow, then. We go for another address. One that's rented."

"Just a second. First, we watch where the cops are. They rarely patrol more than two at a time. All it takes is one ticket, one golf cart wreck, someone running off from the restaurants not paying, and you've got both cops occupied. That's how we decide where to hit."

Bruce was impressed. Apparently so was Magnus. "Dude, I hear you."

"Myrtle Street, though," Larue said. "Or that end. Away from the commercial places. Those houses are bigger than what you've been toying with, and the restaurants and shops are on the opposite end of the beach."

"Why aren't you hitting up these houses on your own?" Magnus asked.

"Got caught one time. They know me now. But listen, that CBD store is opening this week, so they'll be watching that. I saw the signs going up. We can drive by and double check, but I'd bet money on the cops being there. Leaves over half the beach open for us. What time? I can be your lookout."

"I'll do this alone."

"No, you won't. I gave you the lay of the land."

Magnus thought about that. "Noonish, then. Even if the cops aren't involved with the CBD store, they'll probably be at lunch. Speaking of the store, why aren't we breaking into it? There's way more reward there."

"Baby steps, brother. Baby steps. With it being new, it'll be busy. Put it on the list for later. Let's go before Aunt Sere notices we ain't left. You're putting me up tonight, right?"

They drove off, Magnus's answer lost in the wind.

Bruce hadn't been eight feet away.

When he returned to the house, Sere was going through every closet hunting him, calling his name.

He made noise coming in the front, stomping his feet like he had dirt on them so as not to scare her. "Wanted to make sure they were gone," he said, when she appeared from a bedroom, eyes questioning.

"I was worried about you," she said, coming up to him, each hand stroking his arms. "You're safe now. I got rid of them."

Safe. Like he was the one staring down two deadbeats trying to mooch off an old, retired lady. Like he couldn't take on both men, kill them with minimal effort and dispose of them in this swamp like they never existed. All he needed was a reason, and they'd almost given him one. "They ever threaten you?"

"Nah," she said. "Larue's shiftless but not a threat. Him and whoever he brings always leave when I talk about them doing any sign of work." She spoke like they were no more than the mailman asking her to sign for a package. "Come on. Let's finish that wood. I'll make you some tea."

As she disappeared into the kitchen, he stopped at the living room coat closet to find a lone burlap bag, a cord knotted around the top. It took some messing to release the knot, but he did. Nothing but a few collectibles used to decorate the rentals. The hundred-dollar value Magnus gave the stash was overestimated.

"Think I'll go for one of my long walks tomorrow," he said. "Do you mind? I need to get my miles in since it's supposed to be a nice day."

The next morning he rose early to do Miss Sere's chores, then took off on his walk. By ten thirty he arrived on the beach. By eleven he wandered Myrtle Street.

By noon, he'd cuffed Magnus to a flagpole.

Chapter 5

THE NOVEMBER crowd took to the beach and the shops with the weather clear, warm, and welcoming, and the next morning a decent number of them packed in at the grand opening of Edisto Calm.

This time Callie sat across the street and down, watching, hopefully not deterring business from Kitty Ingram's new place. Officer Thomas Gage served as the other officer on duty for the day shift, and he patrolled the beach solo, tending to travel more along the eastern end of town, nearer to the CBD store and other commercial enterprises. Occasionally he slid down to the western end to make his presence known, but odds were that anything that happened today would be on the eastern end or on the beach itself. More rentals on the east end. More residents on the west.

Edisto Calm had opened at ten, with people lined up a dozen deep to enter and explore.

Callie watched both sides of traffic, occasionally checking her phone. A whistle through teeth jerked her attention back to where it should be, on the crowd. A big wave from the whistler took her briefly aback then threw her into laughter in noting the old, retired Boston Police Department Captain preparing to enter such an establishment for what was a ninety percent chance of making a purchase for personal use.

Stan Waltham, her prior boss, who'd followed her to Edisto a couple years ago to retire, mingled with the crowd, his tall, hunky stature not difficult to miss, especially with the cane. While he wasn't a long-term resident, he was indeed a full-time resident, and therefore well known. His garb tended to be the large-print Hawaiian floral shirts, which his build could carry off, while Mark's Hawaiian prints sported more taste. And as she'd hoped, Stan's custom carved cane brought compliments instead of pity. It had become his style.

She would stride over there and razz Stan if she wasn't in uniform. There remained a sense of misplaced immorality about hemp products to just enough ignorant people for them to question a uniform being on site.

The door opened. Kitty strode out, dressing the part in her chic hippie charm. A tie-dyed ruffled top swayed over creamy slacks and sandals. She carried what appeared to be a natural tan tone with some freckles. She might be from Atlanta, but at first glance she fit the island environment like she was born and raised there. She could tell you every manner to use CBD products in every which way possible.

"Welcome one and all to the grand opening of Edisto Calm. We carry premium CBD products made from American grown hemp. Everything is third-party tested, and we offer a thirty-day money-back guarantee. Today, we offer a fifteen percent discount on everything."

A forty-something lady, a tourist from the brand-new sarong to the lack of tan, raised her hand. "Do you carry suntan lotion?"

A college-aged boy sniggered at the inquiry, but Kitty let him, answering instead, "Not exactly suntan lotion, but it is proven that skin treated with CBD cream winds up less red from UV ray exposure. Since it naturally carries an SPF of 6, it provides some protection while moistening the skin and allowing safe absorption of the all-important Vitamin D we need."

Oohs rose from the gathering.

Kitty held up a finger. "Also, if you get burned, CBD cream lessens inflammation and eases pain."

Aahs this time.

Another lady, who might've even been with the first one, asked, "Any pet products?"

"Yes, ma'am. Listen," and she eased the door back with one hand. "We've got what you need for rising in the morning to going to sleep at night. From mind improvement to body soothing. From humans to pups. You might even find something to assist in your effort to lose weight. Come on in. And thanks for y'all coming so bright and early!" The proprietor slipped back inside, and Stan scooted through, swept in with the others.

The woman exuded a sweetness that drew one in, and she'd used that personality to sway the town council from the get-go. Earlier, Kitty had even spoken with the six picketers who'd arrived around nine and gently asked them to picket off her property. Then she'd handed each a muffin. Malorie had jerked her hand back like the hemp that could be in the snack might seep into her skin and morph her into something alien. The others, however, accepted the peace offering. Callie had started to walk over, but when they disbursed after finishing off the muffins, she saw no need.

Kudos to Kitty.

Amos, bless him, had offered to stick around and appease Malorie. His crowing told anyone paying attention that he didn't give a damn whether anyone was for or against him or the store. He just entertained.

Amos liked anyone and everyone.

Malorie tired of having no allies and left.

In what appeared to be the same frayed khakis and flip flops from the day before, Amos had gotten in line with the others. A couple of people gave him space, and Callie wondered if body aroma accompanied those old pants. However, he soon traveled inside like Stan. Callie could envision Stan asking Amos the pros and cons of what to buy.

It didn't take long before a couple of the earlier protesters exited, darting off to their cars like nobody could see the logo on the bags they carried, making Callie wonder just a little as to what product had convinced them to cross the line to the enemy's side.

With his own bag in hand, Amos returned outside to the porch, designed to feel cozy and laid-back in tune with the store. He settled himself into a lanky, lazy curve of a sit on a bench and promptly commenced to light up.

Callie about stepped in front of an El Marko golf cart used to deliver Mark's Mexican fare around the beach. She waved it by then trotted across Jungle Road. "Amos, no."

About that time, Stan came out, his nose up in recognition of what he'd been assured wasn't supposed to come from a CBD store.

And scurrying in from the parking lot was Sophie, fresh out of yoga class with her finger pointing one way and her fussing backing it up. "I told you she'd be dealing out of there."

Callie trotted faster. "Sophie. Come here." She intercepted her friend at the edge of the property and redirected that energy back to facing the parking lot. Sophie pissed and moaned the entire time.

"I told you, I told you, I told you," she said.

Callie toyed with escorting her to the patrol car, to hide all this energy from Kitty's potential customers.

"Sophie, take it down," she said, stopping between cars in the parking lot, about forty yards away. "Let her have her day."

"But you can smell it from here!"

True that. The aroma had reached them from Amos's blunt.

"That's Amos, not Kitty, and you ought to realize that. I was headed over there to discreetly ask him to leave," Callie assured her. "You stay here, hush, and wait, please. Don't hurt the business."

"What if I wanted to go in? I really do want to see what the attraction is. I told you yesterday I was going to. You can't stop me, and I'm sure you don't want to make a scene out here. Not on Miss Kitty's *big day*." She ended her point with air quotes.

"Not until I deal with Amos, and not unless I go with you."

"That's not fair—"

Callie put an arm around her friend, who returned a what-is-this look. "It is precisely fair. You've broadcasted two days in a row that you're looking for trouble." She squeezed the toned shoulders, repeated for Sophie to stay put, then pivoted and marched to Amos. He'd gathered a couple of fans from the looks of things. He would light up for everyone standing there given half a chance.

"No loitering, Amos," she said, the others taking a step back at her advance. "And no smoking." She hoped he put that thing out quickly, and that the others didn't expect her to arrest the man.

But he accommodated her, one man nearby giving a light groan of disappointment.

Kitty poked her head out the door. "What the heck is this?"

In an animated manner, Amos pulled out a little mint tin out of his pocket, opened it up and mashed out the fire, then slid the remnant inside and tucked it away.

Kitty reached inside the door and flipped a switch. A fan came on overhead. In a second thought, she reached over him to the hanging cord and yanked the fan's speed to high. She didn't go right back in though. Instead, she leaned in Amos's personal space. "Don't push me. I can get a restraining order if you don't behave."

Amos looked at Callie, brows bobbing in jest.

She gave him a half grin. "She can, you know."

"Trust me, she won't," he said. "Besides, everyone does it, Chief." He waggled his brows again, exaggeratedly bushy compared to his lack of hair up top.

"Yea, Chief," said the disappointed man watching how this was going to play out.

She turned to him. "Do I know you, sir?"

His humor faded a bit. "No, ma'am."

"Do I need to get to know you?" she pushed. He wasn't a local, for sure.

Nervous, he replied, "No, ma'am," again, and turned toward the parking lot. She didn't think he'd been in the store yet, but no problem. He could return later. Two others dispersed on his heels, each already having made a purchase.

Kitty returned inside, but not before she handed a quick thank you to Callie and a wink at Amos.

Amos grinned up from his laid-back repose. "Party pooper."

"Amos," Callie said, then took a deep, belly-button-reaching breath. Half for her own purpose and half to tell him she wasn't tolerating this behavior on her beach.

His chuckle was a contagious one, and he gave her a dose, and as expected it disarmed her a tad. "Charm isn't going to cut it, Amos. You cannot do this, and you know it. It's too much trouble taking you in for something so trivial."

"If it's so trivial, then overlook it."

She glanced around, not needing ears. "I do enough of that as it is. As long as it's illegal in this state, you cannot just broadcast your habit. Especially not in front of a commercial enterprise. You'll give her business the wrong image. She could press charges, you know."

He shook his head in a few short jerks. "Nah. She likes me too much."

Wonderful. The local pothead and the CBD store owner. A match made in heaven. Callie'd heard rumors. Guess they were true.

Callie's lips mashed in a smile. She turned to see if Sophie had followed directions and waited or if she'd crossed the street, only to find her four feet behind her.

"Boo," she said, giving Callie a small jolt.

Amos gave a growling snigger.

"I'm going in, *Miss Police Chief*," Sophie said, still hesitating a second in case Callie objected.

"Be my guest." Callie stepped aside. She turned to check on Amos. He'd stood and hung over the railing. She took a final sniff, grateful that the fan had dispelled the scent.

Guess it was safe enough to leave these two. She scanned the area in her habit of staying aware of surroundings . . . and then she froze. A man in his thirties traipsed down Jungle Road. He'd passed where she was parked and headed west, toward the center of the town. Instinct told her to look again. A feeling told her he was familiar.

Not familiar in a resident kind of way. He dressed like a soul without a nine to five for a long time, such that his loose style was inherent and there for good.

She watched him for a good five minutes.

Surely not.

Callie was afraid to look away in case he vanished, which might make her question whether he'd been there in the first place. She watched until he reached the slight curve in the road.

"Callie," Sophie said with an irritation that told her that the yoga lady had called her name already. "Are you deaf?"

Callie finally took her eyes off the man she could no longer see. "No. What is it?"

Again, surely not.

"Can I ask you a stupid question?" Sophie asked.

"Sure. You ask them better than anyone," Callie said, returning attention to her.

Sophie scowled. "Am I allowed to talk to Miss Kitty?"

"Wait," Amos said. "If I date Miss Kitty that makes me Marshal Dillon, doesn't it?" He again bobbled his brow, apparently a trademark habit. The man was full of himself.

Sophie popped him across his bald head. "Shut up, Amos." Then to Callie, "You can't do anything to me unless I hurt her or trash her place, right?"

"That's not all you can do to get in trouble, but go on in. Get it out of your system."

Callie stepped aside as six more people approached, and then she returned across the street. She cranked up and left, eager to scan the area.

Unless he veered off, that walker still might be taking Jungle Road.

She could radio Thomas and ask him to look out for him if he detoured.

It wouldn't hurt.

Surely that wasn't him.

She peered back at Edisto Calm. A few more people went in as two came out, bags in hand. The place was doing great.

Callie had told Kitty to call if an issue came up, and if her patrol car wasn't outside, it wouldn't be far away. Almost eleven, and the day had gone swimmingly. This business might not be so detrimental to Edisto. Might even settle it down more. She could live with that.

"Thomas?" she radioed. "Where are you at the moment?"

"Finishing up a ticket at the corner of Palmetto and Portia Street."

She thought a second.

"Come back," he said. "Something up?"

"No, just checking," she replied. "I'm making a circle of the beach then headed to lunch. The new store seems to be fine."

They signed off, and Callie pulled away. She headed west on Jungle Road.

She passed her place, then Sophie's, then her mother's house on the other side. She got within five houses of Lybrand with no sign of this man.

He had been the spitting image of Bruce Bardot. She'd figured he left the island. She'd hoped he had even more.

She didn't want to think about what to do with him if their paths crossed. He was the bad guy you saw as more good than bad. The antagonist in the story that the audience learned to love and root for to win, regardless of what he'd done wrong before.

She didn't want him on her beach, though. Good or bad, she'd prefer doing without the dilemma. Seemed she couldn't find him now anyway.

Chapter 6

CALLIE TRAVELED the major roads on the beach then made her way back to El Marko's for lunch, with still no sight of the walker. Mark had met Bruce before. She had nobody else to talk with about him but Mark. She'd convinced herself that she'd never see Bruce again. Nothing lost, nothing gained.

Yet here he was . . . possibly.

She entered the restaurant and navigated to her token table in the back. Sophie wasn't there. Of course she wasn't. She was scouting out the CBD store. Inside, outside, interviewing people who'd been in there. Her day would be occupied with her obsession about Kitty Ingram, and odds were she'd call in sick to Mark. Good thing it was the time of year when people could seat themselves and the wait staff was still able to keep up.

Callie sat, her ginger ale making its unrequested appearance as usual, and after the first taste, she let her fingers slowly spin the bottle on its coaster, thinking.

Bruce . . . the man who'd saved Stan's life when they were stranded during Hurricane Nikki. She'd snagged his medical talent to salvage Stan's broken leg. Stan would never be able to identify him, though. He'd been too far out of it.

What if Bruce was identified when he was attempting to be on the straight and narrow? And why did that bother her?

He'd been one of three ex-Rangers who hadn't adjusted well after their military service and had taken to earning their income snaring wealthy young women, collecting ransom, then gently returning them to their families. The kicker was that they were handled well, never allowed to see their captors, kept healthy, and returned unscathed. Bruce's medical skills and an IV bag of glucose kept them sedated and well-nourished in between. The event that wound up on Edisto had gone awry. Callie had returned the girl to her parents, who couldn't say anything about her ordeal, and Callie was the only person who knew enough to suspect Bruce as part of that team.

Callie had discovered the girl lost near the police station, noting the slightest of unconscious recognition by the girl when she touched Bruce's medical bag and caught a whiff of him. A lone glimpse.

If Callie had attempted to arrest the man, there was no evidence. The girl couldn't identify him. The family killed any news coverage not wanting to expose their daughter to public scrutiny. Heck, the girl saw Bruce as one of her heroes.

If Callie hadn't seen Bruce part ways with his partners and heard his anger in telling them he could no longer do what they did, she still wouldn't have put two and two together.

She had liked the man.

"Wow, you're deep in thought," Mark said, sitting before her, the plate in his hand exuding aromas that beckoned her back to the present.

She scanned the room, estimating how much free time he had and if it was enough for a discussion.

"Yeah," she said. "We've got to talk."

"Sounds ominous," he said, half in jest.

She hesitated, not having even confirmed the glimpse of Bruce as legit.

Her mic called her. She turned down the volume, rose and scooted outside, so as not to disturb Mark's lunch guests. "Callie here."

"Break in on Myrtle." Marie, her office administrator, coordinator, all things the police department was, except badge toter.

Thomas came on. "I'm nearby. Headed over. Eat your lunch, Chief. I'll call if I need you."

She returned inside, the table empty except for her food. She was surprised it wasn't already in a to-go box. Her personal chef had become accustomed to her being called out amidst a meal. Sitting, she dove into the burrito, her guard up that she could be pulled away.

Mark returned. "Are we still talking about your problem or is it on hold?"

"The latter," she said. "No, wait."

He sat.

"I think I saw Bruce Bardot."

It didn't take him long to make the connection. "It's been weeks."

They were two of the three who understood what finding Bruce Bardot meant, with Stan having been briefed once he'd come to his senses after the hospital stay and was fast on his way to healing. Thomas and Town Councilwoman Donna Baird had met the man but labelled him nothing more than a beach visitor whose vacation had the poor timing of meeting a storm.

Callie felt an uncomfortable need to watch the room, to see who could hear . . . like it mattered. "I can't say for sure it's him, but I feel it is."

"Boss?" came a voice from the cracked open kitchen door. "We just got a call in order. A big one. Kinda need your help."

Mark turned around from the interruption.

"Go on," she said. "We'll talk later."

He moved in, not only for their goodbye kiss, but to ask, "Any missing persons on your radar?"

"No," she said, giving him a second peck. "We'll talk later."

He left her there alone, with about four bites left on her plate. She finished her meal, swilled the drink, and left.

On the way, she called for an update from Thomas.

"Might want to get over here," he said. "The renter is upset, and this is a story you want to hear directly from them."

"Address?"

He gave the location, again on Myrtle, five houses down from the one yesterday. "We're out back on the porch," he added.

Touching the gas a bit, she arrived in no time, finding Thomas's cruiser in the drive, behind one other vehicle. She got out and headed toward the conversation in the rear.

Up the stairs, Thomas sat on a wicker chair, across from a man and a woman, ages estimated to be in their fifties. The man couldn't take his eyes off his wife, and the wife seemed unable to stop talking.

Thomas made introductions to Mr. and Mrs. Jordan.

Then to the couple, he asked, "Mind if I show her inside? You two just sit here and nurse those drinks while you catch your breath."

They didn't sit back, but they nodded that they'd be fine despite the stiffness in their posture. Smiling in assurance, Thomas left. His gaze darted to a spot to the right, which made Callie notice what looked like smears of blood. He led the way inside.

A coffee table lay on its side, the chess board and its playing pieces scattered across the floor. A broken lamp. Nothing else was destroyed, but dark red spots showed on the throw rug and across the back of a tufted unholstered chair which wasn't facing where it normally would if Callie had decorated this room.

"Fight?" she asked.

"Yeah."

She peered through the glass at the tenants consoling each other.

They didn't look like they ranked too high on the aggression scale. "How about just walking me through this so I don't have to guess and get it wrong."

"The couple was gone," he said. "Out to eat. They came home to someone in the house. Seems they liked coming in the back door instead of the front due to the logistics of the stairs to the car, so they entered and practically bumped into the people robbing the house."

"People?" Callie asked. "How many?"

"Two," he said. "But the uncanny thing is that they were fighting each other."

She squinted at him. "You mean the two burglars?"

"Yeah."

A small laugh escaped her, though none of this was funny. "Okay. The blood on the porch . . . and over here on the rug and furniture. Whose is it?"

His eyes widened at the realization he hadn't covered the important part first. "Oh, the renters are fine, Chief. Not a scratch on them."

"Then this is from the thieves."

He held up a finger. "From one of the thieves. They said one seemed to be stopping the other."

"Any chance they can make an ID?"

Thomas moved toward the built-in bookcase on the wall. At the base of it was a black balaclava on the floor. "No, but I'm betting there's blood on that."

Thomas continued. "Mr. and Mrs. Jordan said one man was bigger than the other. The one doing the ass-whooping kept his knitted mask on. Mr. Jordan said the lesser one left pretty bloodied up. And get this . . ."

Callie studied the room, trying to place all the characters and see their movements. "I can't wait. What?"

"The winning burglar apologized to the Jordans."

"Say what?"

"They said the bigger burglar literally threw the lesser burglar out onto the back porch where he fell flat, then got up and ran off."

"Thus, the blood on the planks out there."

"Right," Thomas said. "Then he turned to the couple and said, *'Apologies for his intrusion.'*"

Callie would kill for cameras. Rentals didn't often have cams, because tenants didn't appreciate being recorded. "Any chance of a camera on the back door at least?"

"The Jordans pointed out a cam on the back right corner, but they don't have access We'll have to talk to Wainwright Realty."

Better than usual. "I'll take care of that," she said. "Anything stolen?"

"That's the thing," Thomas said. "They say nothing is missing."

She had questions, and she wanted no misunderstanding or misinterpretation. "Let me talk to them." Without waiting for a response, she exited, taking the seat where Thomas had been.

She told the couple she had questions. The Jordans seemed eager to comply.

"Describe the fight," she said.

Mr. Jordan jumped at the chance, Mrs. Jordan literally sitting back to let him take the reins. "One was dominant," he said. "He seemed to dislike the other one. The second one didn't get more than two swings in before he was whipped. The big one had moves. He was fast and slick, and the smaller guy never laid a hand on him."

"Any idea why they were fighting?" Callie asked.

"There were no words. At least not from the big one. The smaller one cursed because he was totally outmatched, but that was it. The bigger one kicked, and I mean kicked, the smaller one out the door. Once he got up, he took off like a scalded dog. That's when the bigger one, the winner, told us '*Apologies for his intrusion.*'"

Callie held up her palm, to stop them at that point. "Not *our* intrusion or *the* intrusion, but *his* intrusion?"

"Without a doubt," piped up Mrs. Jordan. "It was downright mannerly. Like the lesser one hadn't done his job right or wasn't supposed to be there at all. Like the other showed up to police the bad one."

Ordinarily, Callie would label such an odd-sounding replay of the conversation as misheard, especially amidst the scary shock of experience. But just the day before, she'd had a vigilante stop another break-in and leave a note saying, *You're welcome.*

Could this be the same guy? Or guys?

"Did you get a look at the one who got beaten up?" she asked.

The couple looked at each other. "Maybe," the wife said first. "Possibly," said the husband.

Callie retrieved her phone, scrolled into photos, and stopped at the driver's license of Magnus Sims. "Is this by chance one of them?"

Mrs. Jordan nodded vigorously. "That's the one who got beaten up."

"Did you see the other? Remember anything particularly memorable about him?" Callie was happy to have at least one of the culprits identified, but she was more interested in the more righteous sounding one. The one that might do something along the lines of leaving a note that said *You're welcome.*

Both of them shook their heads. "He kept his hood on," the wife said.

But the mister hesitated. "He moved like he was choreographed. Like he sparred in a gym or took Oriental fighting classes. I don't know the difference between Jujitsu and Taekwondo, but he could read the other guy's moves before the other guy could tell himself what he was doing. No challenge whatsoever."

Callie's pulse picked up. "Think they were partners who just . . . I don't know . . . fell out over what to steal?"

"Oh, no," said the wife.

Her husband peered at her, like how would she know anything about a fight.

"Didn't you hear him, honey?" she said to her spouse. "The little guy said to the big guy, 'Who the hell are you?'"

"I'm not sure I heard that."

"Well, I did. And the man that got beaten up took off with the other on his tail." She redirected to Callie. "I ran to the front to see out the window. The first kept running up the street."

"What about the second?" Callie asked. "The big guy."

"He veered between houses. He was way faster, so I'm not sure what he was doing. He could've caught the first at that speed, though, if he'd wanted to."

Maybe he did, just not on the street in front of eyewitnesses.

Callie continued with the questions, the descriptions, repetition of same to see if their stories contradicted themselves. In the end, she believed one guy broke in, the other followed him in, and the latter kicked the former's ass.

The first was identified by the wife.

The second, however, Callie felt she just might know. There were no coincidences.

Vigilante service at its finest – part two.

Just how many parts were there going to be?

Chapter 7

Bruce

MISS SERE WELCOMED Bruce back in the early evening with chicken soup and biscuits. She understood how to use salt and onion, plus flour to thicken the soup and hide the limited amount of chicken, to make it seem way more than it was. The mild dip in temperature made the steaming bowl a welcome meal.

He almost felt bad for leaving her alone as much as he had of late. He had, however, stopped off at the lone Edisto grocery store and replenished some basics, to include a frozen pork shoulder, which made her eyes widen in delight.

"Two days in a row," she said, rushing to put the small bag of groceries away before setting bowls on the little kitchen table. "You made me miss you, kid. You're not gonna sneak away from me, are you?"

Miss Sere always served in the kitchen, never using her formal dining room. She felt she did not have the proper china and such to occupy it, so the twelve-by-twelve area tended to collect furniture and knick-knacks that were too old and worn to bring much if sold. . . so she hoarded. Bruce wasn't sure why she had told Larue to hide items in the closet when stashing that sack. Anywhere in that dining room would've hidden it more.

Therefore, with knees almost touching, they ate in the kitchen.

"I would give proper notice when I leave, Sere." Their monikers for each other had gone informal. Hers merely Sere. His simply Son or Kid.

"Don't you worry," he said. "But if you ever tire of me being here, all you have to do is say so." He'd lived alone before. He'd lived alone amidst people. He'd lived alone in his mind for years, accepting himself as the best company of all.

However, he'd come to enjoy this rough-edged, soft-hearted old lady. She wasn't quite as robust as he'd first thought, but she got by. She didn't ask too many questions of him, and, likewise, he didn't of her. She held history and secrets, opinions and memories like he did, not willing to share what wasn't necessary. Sharing was overrated. Trust was just what it needed to be.

They were two people who had no place else to be needed, each roughly sending comfort in each other's direction.

His visit had evolved into weeks now, approaching two months. He might've left earlier if not for Larue showing up with his buddy. Though he could hurl some hefty weight, Bruce didn't trust either one as far as he could throw them.

Larue mooched off Miss Sere. Bruce's gut told him as much, and he listened to his gut over anyone and any other impression in the world. The first of the month, when she got her Social Security check, had come and gone without the boy coming around . . . this time . . . but another first of the month would come around in a week or so. Bruce wondered just what exactly he could do about that. He hadn't even made his presence known to the nephew, but if he did allow his quiet, intimidating presence out of the closet, Larue would most assuredly keep his distance, at least as long as Bruce lived there. Once Bruce was gone, however, no telling what Larue would do to make up for income he'd missed.

He munched on his third biscuit. "How much does Larue take out of your monthly check?"

She'd taught him to eat them hot, with two pats of butter, or rather margarine since it was way cheaper, absorbed into the flaky layers, then warm syrup poured over it. He could eat as many as six after a workout or long hard walk like today, and if the meal was light, even more. If he wanted leftovers for a late-night snack, he'd stop at three.

"I limit him to a hundred," she said.

"How much do you get?"

"About a thousand."

Jesus, that was nothing for someone to live on. Someone normal, he self-corrected. He could live off of less.

"Since he didn't ask for any last month," she said, "I'm sensing he picked up work or found other means." She studied her bowl of soup, something telling him a hundred dollars fell on the low side. He could see Larue coming back and catching up on missed payments, too, like he was owed.

His opinion about Larue had solidified today, though. He was behind the break-ins. Magnus had emitted a creepy vibe from the outset but today proved that Larue came from much the same mold.

He clenched his right hand, a bit sore around the knuckles. Damn good thing he wore gloves when on a mission.

Yesterday, the first burglary, he'd hidden in the woods between the house and the golf course and watched things play out. Seeing the chief let Magnus loose had disappointed him, but since Magnus hadn't stolen anything, and with this beach functioning on such a small police force, he shouldn't be surprised. With the young officer watching Magnus leave the premises, Bruce had taken a wide detour to see which vehicle he might escape to. Like at Sere's place that day, Bruce had scurried close enough to hear the two guys weren't yet deterred from their plans, consisting of more than the one-off burglary.

After being let off the hook yesterday by the police chief, something he ought to be damn appreciative of, Magnus had hit the same street today, at the same time of day, only five houses down from yesterday's escapade. Yesterday Larue waited for Magnus, and Bruce had listened to them continue to scheme. Today . . . Bruce found the same old tired sedan one block over and two down, with Larue waiting behind the wheel.

They could've hurt that couple today.

During his long walk back to Sere's, in analyzing that day's crime alongside yesterday's, Bruce came to some conclusions. The two were hitting houses on the opposite end of where the police were. That would be the western end, the same end he and his buddies had rented during the hurricane . . . for similar reasons. There was more action on the other end of town to keep a cop's attention.

They'd also hit midday, when the cops would be at lunch and the renters most likely on the beach or eating out or shopping. Two cops on duty, most likely, and as he'd learned in walking the beach today, feeling out the busyness of traffic and tourists, there was a grand opening of a store. A CBD store. From the crowd, a taste of controversy would keep the authorities closer to that part of town.

In all his estimations and guesses, he'd hit the jackpot in thinking Magnus, and most likely Larue, would hit near where they had before, about the same time. He'd reached Myrtle Street around eleven and camped out, eyes open for that beat-up, dated Toyota sedan. He'd seen it, jogged to it, and followed Magnus. Larue had waited in the car. Bruce chuckled at the younger being the wiser.

"A second helping?" Sere asked.

She needed those leftovers. He still had some cash in his stash, and most of what he'd spent had been for her groceries. He worked off the rent, but he could tell she would have paid out of pocket just for his company . . . and the security.

"No, ma'am. Those biscuits filled me up." Biscuit flour was cheaper than chicken.

She stood to clear the table, and he finished off half a biscuit, to fill that last empty spot he had. After popping in the late bite, he flexed his knuckles.

"What did you do to your hand?" she asked.

He looked at it, as if its ache surprised him. "Don't know. Chopping wood?" Indeed, he'd done his fair share of that.

Bruce couldn't tell Sere it came from putting the fear of God into Magnus Sims for breaking into another house. He couldn't tell her that his knuckles, though gloved, had split Magnus's lip, his brow over the right eye, and his jawline. More blood than Bruce wanted, and in hindsight, he wished he'd just trussed Magnus up again, but the couple made enough racket coming up on the back porch to make Magnus turn around about the time Bruce came up from behind.

If he hadn't taken Magnus down, no telling what he might've done to that couple. Instead, he whomped up on him, pushing him with each punch past the couple through the back door. The final wallop had put him face down on the porch. From there he'd let Magnus jump up and take off, with him on his heels. He had reason to get away as much as Magnus did, and having Bruce on his tail only made Magnus put more distance faster from the couple.

Larue had once again acted as the getaway driver.

If he had his way, Bruce would disappear them both.

Sere might not have birthed her nephew, but whatever happened to Magnus would affect Larue, and Bruce wasn't too sure how much that boy mattered to this woman. It sounded like he and his mother were the last family she had. Even if Larue took her money and the sister-in-law hadn't come by once, much less called, when that was all you had to call your kin, you tended to cling to it.

There was something to be said about not being the last person left.

Question was what to do about those two guys now. He had hoped they'd discarded these empty dreams of theft and riches. Today was proof they hadn't.

Sere started washing dishes. "Want me to do those?" he asked.

"Wish you would," she said, turning off the water and drying her hands on a threadbare dishtowel. "I'm feeling a tad puny today."

He got up and went to her, moving her such that he could study her complexion and look in her eyes. The more he'd come to know her, the more he saw her hiding symptoms. "Are you supposed to be on any medication?" he asked. Most sixty-somethings were on one thing or another. Pills for blood pressure, diabetes, cholesterol, and a dozen other common ailments filled seniors' medicine cabinets. He hadn't seen the first med in the house short of aspirin and a pink stomach soother.

Sere limped more some days than others, too. She breathed heavier at times when she hadn't exerted the effort to warrant it. A few times he watched her take longer to sit on her porch swing, like the bending made her think twice, then once she was seated, she took a long while to rise, even choosing to nap in place rather than find her way to the bed.

She reached in her pocket, and he heard the pills rattle in the bottle she pulled out to show him. Metformin, for diabetes, to lower blood sugar. There were six in the bottle. A relatively cheap medication. It had three refills. An easy drug to get most any doctor or PA to prescribe.

"That it?" he asked, doubting that this was all this lady should be taking. She moved okay, but she tired easier than she ought to, and she could stand to lose about thirty pounds or more.

"They said I ought to be on some kind of heart pill, but I don't want it," she said.

His frown made her turn back to the dishes. "Can't let these dirty plates sit all night."

But he stopped her, escorted her to her recliner, and turned on a sit-com she liked.

While he had daylight, he did outside chores. An hour before dusk, he returned to the sink.

There were only a handful of items to wash with just the two of them, but he still dallied, watching out the window to the marsh. It was that hour before dusk, when colors faded to shades of gray, but not dark enough to not see wandering wildlife hugging the shore. A raccoon moved along the water's edge. If Bruce stood still long enough, he would see that family of deer again. The buck was a ten-point that only made an appearance when it was fully dark, and Bruce only knew that most of the time from his tracks found in the morning. He often walked the line with his coffee, watching the animal population come to life with the dawn.

He pondered putting a buck in Sere's freezer but worried she didn't have the room. A doe, maybe. He had no license to hunt, so he'd dress it himself. Few would question the gunshot since it was deer season.

He turned the water off, folding the damp dishtowel and draping it over the sink's edge. He'd been arguing with himself for the last week about how much to get into this woman's life. A lot depended on how long he stayed, because to come to her aid for much more than putting a chicken in the freezer carried with it a bit of an obligation to see things through. Whatever those *things* were.

He also hated to leave when he could've done something. It would be wrong to be Sere's knight then yank the assistance away. She was lonelier than she admitted.

But how long was long enough?

"Sere?" he called, walking into the living room. When they didn't sit out back and listen to the night life, they sat inside, him usually on the sofa, her in the recliner that had to be over twenty years old, a split on each padded arm, and another behind the head. She'd taken to putting a dishtowel over the head spot, in an attempt to hide the oily, worn area from decades of hair mashing the same circle and leaving residue. At least it was leather. It never would've lasted this long other-wise.

She'd fallen asleep, her head tilted left. He eased it back upright. Otherwise, she'd awaken with a crick in her neck.

Bruce had wanted to discuss Larue. How close was she to him, and how much was he in her business? Her financial business. She'd already bragged about owning the house, but she had no children of her own. Larue would have to be a total moron to not wish to be her heir. Unless it went to his mother. He'd ask about that, too.

Why should he care, though?

Because he had nowhere else to be, and no one else to defend.

If he'd learned anything in his thirty-seven lonely years on planet Earth, it was that you had to live for something. You had to have direction, not just existence. He'd failed outside of the military, entering it because otherwise he would have gone to jail. He knew it. His foster parents told him so.

The eight kids in his foster home learned defense and self-preservation through experience. It didn't take a genius to recognize the foster kids were only a reason for the two adults to grab a check for beer money. He'd been lucky enough being placed with his brother, so he didn't complain. Turned out his brother's luck hadn't lasted that long.

A year into their residency, a sixteen-year-old who notched his closet door frame to keep track of the broken bones and scars he inflicted, chose the brother that particular day.

Cajoling, bumps, shoves. What felt like hours hadn't been twenty minutes before the abhorrent asswipe went too far in the yard . . . that grassless, silty dustbowl of a yard where the kids were forced to spend most of their time while the adults, if you could call them that, had sex and polished off twelve packs inside.

The coroner ruled it an accident. Kids playing, a trip over a bare tree root, a head hitting the corner of the concrete steps. Who was going to contest the finding?

From that point on, Bruce swore to a set of his own notches, with a vow to incur on the killer the same number of scars and broken bones he'd inflicted on others. Unlike the culprit, he did so quietly, discreetly, with a stealth that made even the guilty kid wonder who did the deed.

Bruce got good at causing pain and making the recipients stay quiet about it.

At seventeen he left; on the condition the foster parents give approval for him to enter the Army. He'd done enough research to know that in the military they pointed you in a direction of purpose, approved your purpose, ordered your purpose. Outside of that environment, however, purpose wasn't so simple. He wanted someone to tell him what to do. Two days longer at that foster home and he would've killed that kid.

Bruce pushed aside the memories and relaxed on the sofa. He oversaw his fate now. No buddies, no boss, no military, just himself.

He flipped past the news stations he abhorred and found another sit-com. Thirty minutes of senseless humor was about all the television he could stand.

Still, what was his purpose being here? He'd been without purpose for over two months now. How would he leave having made Miss Sere's life better? Was he supposed to? What if she woke up in the middle of the night and found him gone? A good thing or a bad thing?

Sere inhaled, accenting a snore with it, and exhaled, settling herself deeper, as if she was in this chair for the long haul.

How many nights had she done this when she was alone?

She looked older than her years, her gray hair aged and dull, her complexion dry and untended. Her eyes needed better glasses. The ones on the table to her side were limited, drugstore magnifiers at best.

He had no long-range plan on Edisto Island. He had no long-range plan for life. The only purpose he could pin-point at the moment was Miss Sere and seeing to it that no one took advantage of her. The only way to do that was to commit.

But to what, how, and for how long?

For now, it was late and he committed to the sofa, closed his eyes, and muted the sitcom laugh track so she would sleep better, at least not wake up in the dark without being able to see he was still there.

A fisted triple knock sounded on the door. Bruce sat up, quickly checked on Sere who continued sleeping, and toyed with answering the door himself.

Chapter 8

CALLIE PUT out a BOLO on Magnus Sims. She started to, then changed her mind, in doing so on Bruce Bardot. Nobody had seen his face. Not even Magnus in his close-up encounter with him today. She was fairly sure Bruce wouldn't let many people see it period.

She laughed to herself. She wasn't even sure it was Bruce. A BOLO would be foolish.

Once again Wainwright Realty was forced to repair a rental's busted lock, but this time, the broker asked that Callie stop by at her convenience, meaning ASAP to the notorious real estate broker. The office being across the street and down a block from El Marko's, it was an easy request. Callie pulled in the parking lot, noting how the gold and red lantana bushes that accented the Wainwright flower beds in the remarkable colors of the broker's blessed Marine Corps had about lost their hue this late in the fall. The first frost would knock them dead.

Janet came out of her office with back rigid and straight, just as Callie walked in the door. White cropped hair shined against that perpetual tan, the angles of her cheeks sharp and underlining that she firmly meant whatever she said. Janet Wainwright always meant business.

Surprisingly, the receptionist was still the one from the summer, a rarity. Janet's reception staff normally came and went like the weather, making this one quite remarkable. Her long-term tenure also meant that with her dominating Marine-driven boss in the room, she knew better than to speak.

"Janet," Callie said, with a nod.

"Chief," Janet answered, not nodding. Anything to be the bigger alpha in the room. "In my office, please."

A semi-order, but Callie had learned to speak Marine with the lanky sixty-plus year-old woman who had spent half her career as a drill-sergeant on Parris Island. This was a woman you wanted on your side . . . as a friend, as a peer, as the agent representing the sale of your real estate. She downright owned wherever she planted her flag.

Most of the time she meant well.

"I'm tired of repairing broken doors," Janet said, before Callie had a chance to take a chair in front of the wide, mahogany desk. "Caught the perp yet?"

"We have a name, Janet. It's only a matter of time."

"Heard you let him go at the first house."

Callie expected this. "Yes, I did. Didn't see him as much of a danger, and he hadn't had a chance to steal anything."

"Thanks to someone else, not you, I hear. And that someone saved him for you to arrest, yet you didn't. Wonder what he thinks about that?" This beach was too small for any tidbit of information to remain secret for long, and Janet would use it to her advantage.

"Yes," Callie said. "We have no idea who this vigilante is, though. That's why—"

"Twice, Chief. And some other person stopped him both times. Same man?"

How the hell had she learned that so quickly . . . oh yeah, the door repair guy.

"Yes, Janet, someone stopped him both times, but we don't know who that person is."

The retired Marine hadn't moved from her stance of sitting rigid in her chair, elbows on her desk blotter, stare riveted on Callie like she was a target. "What are your plans?"

"First, I want to ask you about cams on the houses. The second house, the event from today. That address had a rear cam and another on the front. Got any footage I can see?"

"They don't work," she answered. "They're a deterrent only."

Wonderful. She could ask Janet to change that and make them active, but that meant going to the owners and begging permission, then deciding who would monitor those cams, and letting renters know that their comings and goings would be scrutinized. Thus, the reason the cams didn't work.

"Are any of your rental cams live?" Callie asked. Might as well find out now.

"A couple," Janet said. "Financial needs outweigh the security. Renters don't like—"

Callie stopped her with a raised open palm. "No, I get it." She scooted closer to the edge of her seat. "So, when I cannot catch burglars, I can now assume any cams are for show and not to bother you."

"Correct," Janet said, totally unflappable about Callie giving her a side-handed insult. "So, again, what are your plans in dealing with this crime spree?"

"Two houses is not a spree," Callie said.

But Janet wasn't accepting that. "To the public, to my renters, to the average person out there who talks to any of the renters, and probably your officers when they stop for a beer someplace, this isn't some idiot too dumb to burgle correctly. It's a spree. And I'm sure town council would agree."

Come again? Was this woman threatening to take Callie to the council? "Not sure I read you properly, Janet. Normally your warnings are plainer than that." She tried to sit back, like she hadn't been affected. "Or did I read you wrong?"

"You read me correctly. Find this man. This spree will reflect on me."

Callie chose her words carefully. "Working on it, Janet. Headed out to the man's house now. Will let you know when we have him. Hopefully your renters will press charges when we do."

"I'll see that they do," Janet replied.

The broker would give them some amount of financial reward to make it worth their while. She'd also discount their next visit. Wainwright Realty held onto clients with vise-grip business acumen.

Callie left unrattled. This was the Marine's *modus operandi*, to intimidate people into doing what she wished. Her livelihood was dependent on a low crime rate, though. Edisto Beach held a history of limited legal violations short of the occasional theft of a fishing rod or items left on a beach towel. Sometimes people walked out on a tab, and golf carts made people stupid, in her opinion, but the atmosphere remained low-key, relaxing, and safe. It was her job to keep it that way.

A few drownings, heart attacks, but no rapes as long as she'd been there. There had been deaths. More than the average person was aware, and she diligently tried to keep it silent. She could only think of one case where someone had been in the wrong place at the wrong time and randomly died. The rest, and she counted them off in her head . . . more than she realized . . . were personal. The person was targeted. She couldn't stop people coming to Edisto Beach who had a past of upsetting someone.

There she went, letting her mind spin off in a loop that made no sense and accomplished nothing. Things had been great this year. They still were. Her crime of the day was an amateur thief, for God's sake. The worst problem she'd had since the beginning of the year had been the hurricane, and nobody died.

Seems her past had her afraid of what might happen, like she was overdue for a hit.

The blood on the furniture and floor of the latest property had taken her aback, but not for more than a split second. She was glad Thomas had been her officer on duty for this. He'd been present for the worst of the situations on Edisto Beach, and they had a bond of sorts. He didn't talk as loosely, and he respected her on a higher level.

Having lived and worked on Edisto as long as she had, she'd come to expect something new around every corner. She understood too much about bad people and the quickness in which something could go wrong. This burglary today had somehow tapped something she'd rather enjoyed being dormant. Only for a couple months, but still, the peace had been nice.

She felt the urge to go seek out Mark, then changed her mind. She couldn't run to him with every twinge of discomfort. He understood her, without a doubt. His own law enforcement demons, his own loss of people through violence had affected him as well. Their late-night talks would freak out a lot of people.

He was the third love of her life. All three had been law enforcement. She doubted anyone else would understand how she was put together, honestly.

She rode the beach roads for the next hour, keener that usual in studying faces, like either of the two men from this morning would be walking the streets, but after Janet's tongue-lashing, she felt the deeper need to serve and protect.

She looked up Magnus's tag to find a small 2009 GMC truck in his name. Red. Two-door. She wouldn't expect it to be much of a truck and if this guy was robbing houses for a living, he wasn't too good at it if this was what he drove. Still, she scouted for it, wondering if he was in cahoots with someone else.

Then, with everything seemingly okay on the beach, with the CBD store uneventful in its first day of business, she put Thomas on notice while she headed to Ravenel. The small, rural town was in Charleston County and outside her jurisdiction, but she wanted to make sure Magnus lived where his license said he did. And if he did, she'd bring him in after a call to the Charleston Sheriff's Department.

They crossed lines like this all the time, mostly her crossing into theirs more than the other way around, but few uniforms wanted to travel much in rural areas. At least not for some lowlife of this caliber who'd broken into two houses and stolen nothing. She'd get concurrence after the fact if she learned of anything, and they'd be glad to give it. It was thirty miles give or take, but she covered the ground like it was twenty.

Ravenel had been no more than a crossroad for years, but it professed two thousand residents now, with a proposed hundred-house development in the works. People lived anywhere they could to be close to Charleston yet live cheaply. They wanted to be near beaches but far enough to say they were leaving Urbania. They wanted things both ways, and sometimes it made for tourists who expected a lot out of Edisto Beach, forgetting they came there to get away from it all.

Everything grew too close along the South Carolina coast. Some days it broke her heart.

Her internal compass led her correctly to a small street off Old Jacksonboro Road, with the address of the dated, white vinyl siding house not difficult to find. The place was long overdue for a strong power washing from the mildew creeping on the south side. No sign of the 2009 red pickup. Any vehicle, for that matter. Still, she got out and knocked on the door. No answer.

She went next door, about two hundred feet away, taking note of the older man watching her from across the street, from his own vinyl siding house, yellow. Some company must have given a group discount around here for re-siding old homes.

Next door to Magnus's address, a pup yapped at the doorbell, and a girl who couldn't be more than eighteen answered the door, hair loosely gathered atop her head, a one-year-old on her hip, the floor behind her littered with toys, shoes, and dog things. "Yes, ma'am?" she asked, noting the uniform with respect.

"Hate to bother you," Callie said, introducing herself, pausing a second for the girl to introduce herself as simply Aimee. "But I'm looking for a Mr. Magnus Sims?"

"He lives next door," the girl said, hitching the baby higher on her hip.

Callie smiled. "Yes, I gathered that, but he isn't home. Do you have any idea where he might be during the day? Or when he comes home at night?"

That's when Callie got the side-eyed look of wariness. "What's he done?"

"He might've witnessed a crime," Callie said.

The girl *humphed*, again hitching up the child who had to weigh a quarter of what she did. "More like committed a crime," the girl said. "He's my baby-daddy and ain't worth a rat's ass. Ain't done a damn thing to support this child, and here I am living with my parents. Living within a spit of him, yet he don't see his child more'n once a month, and that's if he happens to see us outside."

"Child support?" Callie asked, not sure she wanted to go into that side of the man's background.

"Nary a dime. Says I have to prove it's his first, and he won't do a blood test."

Callie had pulled up information to see if ol' Magnus had a record, but all that showed was half a dozen paid tickets. None outstanding. "He ever stole from anyone?" she asked, taking the opportunity to tap this girl's anger and see if she'd spill Magnus's secrets.

"Besides my virginity?" the girl spouted, tilting her head at the baby. "First time. Lucky me. Should've played the lottery that day and used some of that luck to afford this kid."

"No, ma'am. Has he been involved in anything illegal?"

The girl mashed her lips. "Besides knocking up a minor? Sorry, wish I could tell you something. He don't tell me anything. I talk to him about as much as the old man across the road."

Callie looked over her shoulder at the other house. The front door was cracked open, and while she couldn't see the gentleman, she suspected he kept an eye on the cop car and the cop knocking on doors, expecting to be next.

"Is Magnus working a job?" she asked.

"No idea."

"Then how does he afford that house?" Not that it was much of a house, but it had to have cost something. Or at least the real owner charged rent.

"It's his momma's house. He lives with her. Our mothers are second cousins."

Wonderful.

This was getting nowhere. She handed the momma-child her business card. "Please, Aimee, if you think he has gotten into trouble, or he brags about doing something he shouldn't, call me. He's involved in something. Just trying to decide to what degree."

"Would he know it was me?" she asked.

"Wouldn't come from my mouth," Callie replied.

Apparently, that was good enough. "Well, gotta go feed this fella. Good luck," she added, and somehow Callie thought she meant it. She crossed fingers she'd call, but Callie wouldn't hold her breath.

With a spin on her heel, she headed across the street, knowing full well the old guy expected her. "Sir?" she called before she got to the steps. "Mind having a word with me?"

Nothing.

"It's about Magnus Sims, your neighbor?"

The door eased back. "A distant great-great-nephew, if you must know, but what about him?"

Another relative. The gene pool out here might be a little tainted. Callie guessed him to be ninety if he was a day. Seriously old. A strong wind could lift him up and drop him into the next county. "He witnessed a crime on Edisto Beach. Need to speak to him but can't seem to catch up to him."

"Stealing?" he asked. He'd once been a big man, and even with his bent-over posture, he measured six inches taller than Callie. "Boy loves to rob people. Robbed me once. Wasn't worth a hundred bucks what he took, so I let him have it. Figured that loss was worth him being in here and seeing there was nothing else to take."

There was some logic to that. "Does he operate alone?" she asked.

"Don't know, don't care," he said. "He brags, though."

Okay, she'd ask . . . "about what?"

"How he's gonna find him a place to stay on Edisto Island. Been hoarding what he steals somewhere over there. Hopes to move one day and get out from under us." He looked around a hundred and eighty degrees, like every house on the road belonged to kin.

"Frankly, I think he's full of shit. Kid ain't known for saving his money or making good decisions." He nodded toward the child-mother's house across the street, as if that were the perfect example. "Got my great-great-niece in a bad way. I plan on leaving her what little I got when it's my time to go. But that God-damn great-great-nephew of mine . . . he can go to hell. What else you need to know?" he asked. "Sometimes you just live too long, you know it?"

"Some days it does feel that way, sir."

"I'd love to help you lock him up, though."

She gave him her business card. "Then this is how you contact me if you learn anything. Any idea where he's eyeballing living over on Edisto? He might be holed up there."

"No idea. The less I know about him the better." He fanned the card, slowly like it was an effort. "But I'll keep this handy."

She smiled at him. "You okay?" She had a soft spot for seniors.

He cocked his head. "Sure. Why wouldn't I be?"

She hadn't asked his name, and he hadn't offered, but she could find it easy enough. "Well, take care and call me if you think of anything. Or if you see anything. Or if you're slowed down relaxing and it makes you think of something you wish you'd said."

To that he laughed. "Lady, if I slowed down anymore, I'd be in the ground."

She returned and knocked on the Magnus address once more. After a circle around it, peering into windows just in case she could catch someone avoiding her, she returned the direction she'd come. Edisto Beach didn't need her gone for long.

On the way back, she kept an eye on the other vehicles headed in the opposite direction, hoping to catch that old red truck. It was three thirty give or take. This business in Ravenel hadn't taken long. She'd be back home in thirty minutes.

She hadn't gathered much intel, but she had learned that Magnus had an interest in Edisto. Which house was he hoping for, she wondered. And how was he gaining access to a house when he had no money and no job to pay for it?

Was he legitimately attempting to move or was this some scam? Or some pea-brain guy bragging about something totally out of his reach?

Or did the old man inform her of ideas that were no more than random thoughts collected in the corners of that shadowy old skull of his, half of them from mysteries on TV?

Just how much time and effort did she need to invest into Magnus Sims except to be on the lookout for him?

Her radio beckoned. "Callie here."

"Chief?" Marie, from the station.

"What is it?"

"Call from that new CBD store. Sophie caused a ruckus. Word has it that punches were thrown. Thomas is on his way."

Callie punched the gas. "I'll be there in twenty minutes, tops."

She should have known. . .

Chapter 9

CALLIE PULLED up to a brouhaha in front of Edisto Calm. Pockets of folks huddled in spots around the store with Thomas's cruiser parked right in front. She parked behind him, thankful he had sense enough to take whatever this was inside. She could hope all was done and over with, but with Sophie involved, the odds were slim. Drama was like protein to her.

Inside the store, Thomas stood on one side of the small showroom with, of all people, Malorie. One hand rested on his utility belt, the other, closest to Malorie, jutted out and partially in front to stop or protect her, no telling which.

She'd changed clothes, wearing jeans and a long-sleeve Edisto tee, her hair mashed and askew. Sunglasses. A meager effort at a disguise.

Across from them, about six feet distant and far enough to avoid fists, were Kitty, Sophie, and Amos. Amos looked his usual self, but Kitty's freckled complexion flashed red, especially on one side. Sophie stood with that signature cocked hip thing she always did, her hands fisted so tight her knuckles were white.

All the usual characters from when the store opened, from when the picketers did their thing, had gathered to share enough feelings to draw the cops. There were no customers in the store, with quitting time not for two more hours. Callie looked at each person, seeing nobody without blame.

Something had perfumed the air in a big way from the display laying broken on the floor, its soft, blue-bottled vials and creams scattered in a six-foot radius . . . with red spray paint misted across it all. Callie surmised from the pattern that the spraying took place after the display was shoved, kicked, knocked, whatever. Almost like the damage from overturning the shelving wasn't enough to express the proper degree of anger.

One of the broken bottles had scented the room.

Callie asked the obvious. "What happened?"

A cacophony of accusations ensued. Finger pointing flashed from all directions, physically and verbally. Thomas looked at Callie and slowly shook his head.

"Stop!" Callie said in her best crowd-stopping thunder, and the room quieted. She studied each party. She then noticed the shape on Kitty's cheek being that of a handprint.

"Kitty. What happened to your face?"

Kitty pointed again, hand shaking, in Malorie's direction, her other hand instinctively covering the cheek like it suddenly hurt again. "That woman came in here, accused us of dealing drugs . . . you ought to do your damn homework, lady," she said, sidetracking to Malorie. "CBD products aren't drugs."

"It's a gateway to drugs," Malorie barked.

Kitty rolled her eyes. "You are dumb as dirt."

A man poked his head in the doorway, but upon seeing the drama disappeared outside.

"Kitty," Callie said, loud enough to stop the noise. "Start at the beginning."

Sophie did a mild stomp of her sandaled foot. "I want to say something here."

Callie shook her head at her friend. "You'll get your chance. Kitty's talking now." She returned to the store owner.

Having the stage, Kitty rounded her shoulders back and tilted her head like her neck had kinks in it. Great. Callie had two drama queens on her hands. Maybe three once Malorie took the podium.

"I was simply running the store. The traffic was down to just a couple. That's when Malorie strode in uninvited—"

"Since when does one need an invitation to come into a store?" Malorie said, voice rising and falling, emphasizing every two or three words like they had periods behind them.

"Hush, Malorie," Callie said, "or I'll have Thomas take you to the station to take your statement. We'll never get through this if everyone keeps interrupting."

Malorie blushed. Sophie didn't give a damn. Kitty puffed like all this delay had raised her blood pressure. Amos watched, uncommitted, almost entertained.

Callie noted a wide-brimmed sun hat that looked straight out of the Edistonian gift shop, now flattened by someone's feet. How seriously had they tussled? And how many had taken part? With Amos so chill, she felt sure she could rule him out.

That made her think *cat fight*, which she tried to mentally toss aside because she might inadvertently say it. "So, Kitty, you were running the store . . ."

The owner continued. "That woman came in and loudly accused me of dealing drugs. Slipped in on me all disguised like that. But I tried being nice. I tried being educational. My two customers watched, probably thinking this was some poor ignorant soul who didn't know any better, but they might learn something by listening. That is, until this bitch yanks out a paint can and directed it at me like it was a thirty-eight special."

Interesting. "Then what happened?"

Malorie yelled, "I did not—"

Callie pivoted. "I told you to remain quiet until your turn."

Kitty smiled like she'd scored, pausing long enough to ensure Malorie saw before starting back up again. "She said the CBD products were a front. She went to the closest display and kicked it over, then sprayed it with paint. I'll never get that paint off the floor, not to mention the loss of the product."

Sophie hunched and stepped forward, like she hated to interrupt. "I can take that product off your hands if you want to sell it to me at cost."

Callie's laser stare put Sophie back in line and a bit closer to Amos. He had sense to keep his mouth shut, but that lazy grin of his remained.

"Of course, my customers took off," Kitty said. "I asked Malorie to leave, but she refused. I said I'd call the cops since she'd vandalized my store and now was officially trespassing. She said I could go right ahead, and she'd ask them to search the store for drugs. I laughed at that. Then she shoved me out of the way, trying to get behind my counter where she called herself hunting for my *stash*." She gave the word air quotes. "I ordered her to stop. She went anyway. I caught her shirt and pulled her back then stood between her and the counter, in other words, my money, and blocked her. That's when she hauled off and slapped me." She touched her face. "And I mean hard."

Callie could see that. She studied the scene. "Sophie? Did you see any of this?"

"I was outside with Amos. After seeing the customers flee for their lives, we went in, and the display was already down." She paused before adding. "I heard the slap all the way outside, though."

"Fact not drama?"

She looked stunned. "All fact, Callie, um, Chief. Customers literally ran. Went I entered, the display was broken, the paint everywhere. Kitty was standing next to the counter, blocking access, just like she said. She held a hand over her cheek where she'd been hit."

"Did you see Malorie hit her?"

"No, but I'm not dumb."

Callie turned to Malorie to allow her to finally have her say. "Care to add to this?"

"I heard drugs are often sold behind the scenes in these types of stores. I wanted to look for myself. She wouldn't let me. I couldn't call the cops without proof, could I?"

"So you committed an assault."

"No," Malorie said, shaking her head harder than necessary. "It was just a slap. No weapon. Didn't even take her off her feet. Not like Sophie did to me yesterday."

Sophie flared up. "What? You tripped yesterday, you lying bitch."

Malorie came right back. "But you were trying to push me. You just missed."

"Stop it!" Callie said, throwing her outside voice. "Kitty, do you need medical attention?"

Kitty touched the spot. "No. I'm okay."

Callie went back to Malorie. "What about the spray paint?"

The woman pouted. "It was spontaneous. I might have lost my temper."

Spontaneous. "You always go around carrying cans of spray paint? Just in case of a *spontaneous* urge for graffiti art? You disguised yourself, for God's sake."

She had no answer, but her eyes narrowed.

Without a doubt, Callie could charge Malorie with four or five assorted violations. From the obvious assault to criminal trespass, destruction of private property, and disturbing the peace. She peered at Kitty, that handprint fading on her left cheek. Then she cast a glance over the rubble. This was not Malorie. She could be an irritant, and she perpetuated a holier-than-thou comportment, but she'd never been like this. She'd sown arrogance and flashed snootiness that scorched the unsuspecting, but nobody would ever expect a resident with decades of tenure on the beach to haul off and strike another human being.

"Make her pay for the damage and ban her from the store," Amos suggested. "Shouldn't that compensate for what had to be an impromptu fit of temper?" Amos saw it. A side of Malorie that wasn't the norm. It made sense him being the peacemaker, too. Callie had never met a pothead who didn't like the world to remain mellow and even keeled.

Instead of cuffing the woman, she pulled Malorie from Thomas and off to the side. "I could charge you with so much, Malorie. What got into you?"

Anger still shined in the woman's eyes. Callie had hoped Amos's suggestion had softened her and made her think of the what-ifs.

Shaking herself like a bird settling feathers, Malorie threw back her shoulders. "Sophie and Amos traipse through this town with everyone knowing they do pot, and nobody does anything about it. Why don't you arrest them?" It was a half fussy, half whiny question, but the two in question couldn't help but notice from her manner and heavy nod in their direction. Sophie whispered to Amos, who leaned in, listened, and chuckled.

Moving herself in the way of everyone's line of vision, Callie thought for a moment. South Carolina had lightened up on what constituted a misdemeanor or a felony in the last couple of years. As long as someone wasn't smoking in public, Callie didn't care. No harm done. There were far worse issues like speeders and domestics. Even the golf cart law-breakers were worse than someone chilling with a smoke. That made Amos and Sophie a non-issue. The lines of assault and property damage, however, weren't quite as blurred.

"Malorie," she asked up close, so the others didn't hear. "You are the worse problem here. Can't you just let Kitty alone?"

Tears welled in her eyes. Not exactly expected. Callie turned her around, back to the others, to give her a moment. "What is it?"

"My sister went from marijuana to harder drugs." Malorie sniffled. "She drove her car off a bridge, leaving behind two teenagers who still haven't gotten over it."

There it was. Malorie didn't grasp the chasm-wide difference between her sister the addict, and Sophie who sat on her own secluded screened porch with a joint. Callie was sure other factors floated around the sister scenario but now was not the time to tell Malorie that her sister likely harbored had way more issues than Sophie and Amos.

This was one of the many cases of a resident having left their muddy, messy past on the other side of the McKinley Washington bridge, the lone entrance to Edisto Island. It was understood that people had skeletons in their closet, and so many had escaped to Edisto to forget them. So much so that everyone who took up an Edisto Beach address was assumed to have a tale they preferred untold.

"Somebody ought to burn this place down," Malorie said, in a low growl.

Callie moved in closer. "Say what?"

But Malorie abruptly changed her tune. "I mean I hope it loses money," she said. "Hope it goes broke. Hope it goes bankrupt. Hope people—"

"You need to shut up while you're ahead," Callie said, flat-lined and stern. "Are you coming back here?"

"For what?"

"To picket, to vandalize . . . to maybe burn it down?"

Malorie sucked in a breath. "I didn't mean that."

"The jail is forty miles away," Callie continued, "but Thomas gets paid whether he's writing parking tickets or escorting your sourpuss self to lockup. Which is it going to be, Malorie? Leave Kitty alone and cover the cost of damages? Or jail? If you throw the mention of arson in there, we're talking hard time. Your choice."

The woman gave a snort. "You wouldn't lock me up. You're a beach cop. You and your people barely know how to write traffic tickets. You can't even stop burglars, from what I've heard."

Well, guess it had already gotten around about the two burglaries.

But this was not a time to compare notes on Callie's bad-ass abilities. Malorie and ninety nine percent of the beach were not aware of who she'd saved, who she'd put down, who she'd arrested . . . and who she'd killed with the broken end of a beer bottle.

Callie had lost a husband, father, boyfriend, and loyal officer, each thanks to something she'd had a hand in. The kind of history that kept her awake a lot of nights.

Now, however, was not the time to brace and compare battle scars. All Malorie would relate to be her own loss.

"Are you seriously trying to talk me into charging you?" Callie said instead.

The huffing continued a few more times, then slowed. "I can't win here, I take it?"

"Depends on what you call winning, but I'd say not going to jail is a win-win for everyone." *Good Lord, this moronic lady wasn't going to be happy no matter what, was she?*

"Are you taking the deal? Paying and staying away?"

Malorie was way more bullheaded than Callie had given her credit for. Harassing town council was one thing, but this . . . she'd lose all credibility on this island if she got arrested. Maybe not so ugly sounding in the short run, but the next time she tried to challenge town council, they'd be looking for paint cans and posting a guard. She'd lose invitations to bunko nights. No more invitations to be a docent at the fall plantation tours, something Malorie not only enjoyed dressing up for in hoop skirts but also was good at reciting history and enchanting tourists.

The advantage of policing a small town is that you were familiar with the quirks, the skills, the positives, and the negatives of most of its residents. As much as she deserved the charges, Malorie going to jail served nobody.

"Still waiting, Malorie," Callie said.

"I'll pay her," she finally replied. "And I'll stay away. I'm sick of this place anyway." She breathed out once heavy. "You wouldn't arrest me would you? Really?"

"I've arrested people for less," she said.

Malorie started with a retort then changed her mind. Guess she had some semblance of sense after all.

"That's great," Callie said. "I really appreciate your cooperation." That was about the nicest thing Callie could think to say.

She turned to the others, leaving Malorie alone in the corner of the room. "She doesn't understand CBD, and she lost someone to drugs. With that in mind, do we want to make a major issue about this?"

Kitty did a slo-mo sweep of her hand over the mess and mayhem strewn across her floor, waiting for the obvious to be addressed.

"Yes, she'll have to pay for this," Callie said. "How much?"

"Five hundred dollars," Kitty said, apparently having taken her time of silence to run numbers.

"You sure that's enough?" Amos asked.

Callie eyeballed him for interfering.

"My offer still stands on the damaged product," Sophie said. Odd Sophie being so obliging, with her not wanting the store to exist in the first place, but despite having a retired, financially enhanced NFL player as an ex-husband, she loved a deal.

"What's with you helping all of a sudden?" Callie asked.

With a bobble of her head, Sophie said, "I don't know. It's an economics issue for me, I guess. Plus, I hate Malorie more than Kitty."

Sophie's logic ran different than most, for sure. Callie would have a chat with her another time, to put Malorie's personality into perspective. She returned to the waiting guilty lady and relayed the deal, which was accepted.

Callie held out her hand for the paint can. "Can you make good on this for Kitty tonight?"

Malorie nodded.

There. All saved.

Retrieving the mashed straw hat from the floor, Callie handed it to Malorie and escorted her to the door. Under her breath, she reminded her of their deal. "Let me know when you've paid her. This is outstanding until you do, okay? I can still make the arrest."

From the store's porch, she watched the woman all the way to her car. Watched her get in and watched her leave the parking lot. When she returned inside, all of them, to include Thomas, attempted to tidy the place.

"Nail polish remover," Sophie was saying as they analyzed how to get that paint off the floor.

"Turpentine," Amos said, very old school.

"Rubbing alcohol," Thomas said. "Used that to get spray paint off a fence one time. Remember that guy, Chief? We locked him up. Left us to help the homeowner out being they were a million years old and couldn't do it themselves."

Being fall, dusk descended faster than in regular tourist season, and with nobody waiting outside to come in, Kitty sighed. "Guess I ought to go ahead and close for the day, huh? A fantastic Grand Opening." She repeated the sigh. "In case you didn't notice, that was sarcasm."

"Leave the Grand Opening banners up," Callie suggested. "Just act like tomorrow is Grand Opening all over again."

Then Amos, in his notorious aim for the positive, said, "But did you make good money before this mess? I mean, how was your first day really? You sure had a lot of people in here, and not too many of them left empty handed."

Sophie jumped on the optimism wagon. "People saw your light blue bags all over this town, I bet. It can't have been totally ruined. Plus, now you are news. That attracts a lot of people."

Kitty held one of said bags, one of the larger ones, and started filling it with the red painted bottles and boxes. "No, wasn't too bad, I guess. A little better than expected, to be honest." The others jumped in, and once the unbroken products were collected, Kitty handed the bag to Sophie. "Guessing about two hundred dollars there . . . at cost."

"Can I get it to you in the morning? Cash?" Then in afterthought, Sophie peered at Callie, like she was contributing to some low-level law breaking.

"Not my business, y'all," Callie said, just glad the ordeal was over with nobody in jail. "Anyone care to meet me at El Marko's?"

Everyone answered in the affirmative.

"Including me?" Thomas said.

"Of course," Callie replied, feeling generous. "Dinners on me."

She would've invited Malorie if she were still around. She could have rebuilt some of the lady's crumbled reputation. Instinct, however, warned her that would not be the case, plus Mark didn't need another bout of temper tantrum in his place of business.

The radio bleeped. It was too late for Marie to still be at work, so it had to be the Colleton County dispatch. "Chief Morgan here."

"Break-in in progress on Mikell Street," said dispatch. "House across the street reported."

Again? "On it," she said. Then to Thomas, "Let's see if we can catch them this time. Come on."

Sophie would spread the news of the third burglary before Callie and Thomas had the chance to even get to the scene of the crime.

Thus turned the world of Edisto Beach.

Chapter 10

THE AUTUMN SUN had begun to sink, the sky still blue with tinges of purple and orange, a scene that usually eased Edisto Beach into a gentle night. Callie, however, shot like a bullet up Palmetto with way more urgency to reach this burglary than the others. The first held no danger with the culprit contained, cuffed to the flagpole. Nobody reached the second until after the culprit was gone, chased away by a second party before the first could do damage.

This time, however, Callie itched to lay her hands on Magnus Sims. She was gut-sure this third attempt was his, and if she could, she was nailing his sorry behind.

Mikell Street was a crossroad between Palmetto Boulevard and Myrtle, but with nothing in her way until she had to turn onto the street itself, she made great time. Both hands on the wheel, she reached the right corner and turned, barely hearing her tires on the asphalt. Thomas appeared from the opposite end, the Myrtle Street side, just in case they could box the burglar in.

Both had their eyes peeled for Magnus's red pickup the whole way there.

Surely one or the other of them would see him.

But neither one did.

Please still be there.

They arrived, no truck in view, much less a red one. Neighbors from both sides of the house and across the street had already accumulated in the front yard. Two women in their sixties sat at the foot of the outside stairs in the circle of a porch light, waiting for the cavalry to arrive. Streetlights popped on in places.

"You're late," said one of the women in jeans and a floppy sweatshirt, flipflops on her feet. "You missed him. He's gone." For some reason, nerves, probably, she had to say it three different ways to make the point that the police missed their mark.

"Which one of you is the owner?" Callie asked.

The one who hadn't said anything raised her hand. "That would be me."

"Are you okay?" Callie knelt before her, wondering if she was getting cool in her capris and sandals, a long-sleeve tee from a 1985 Chicago concert.

"I'm fine," she said, not on the verge of tears, not angry, nothing.

The other woman spoke up, more rattled. "She's calm as a rock in a tornado. Nothing phases her. Me? I freaked out hearing she walked into *this*."

Callie peered over at Thomas. *What is this?*

"Excuse my friend," said the homeowner. "She's just worried for me. My name is Dorothy Calloway, and I own this house." She held out her hand for Callie to shake. "I'm a retired attorney out of Spartanburg, but I've lived here ten years. This is Frances Fairfax, my long-time neighbor across the street." She gave a mild wave at the group of people along the road. "And those are the other neighbors."

Callie appreciated having to deal with the calmer lady who had her act together. "What happened, Ms. Calloway?" She'd never met this particular resident, but she'd heard of her. Her husband, also a retired attorney, died last year.

"I was over at the Fairfax's house, having our afternoon wine. I usually come home by dusk, but I was tired, and the wine wasn't setting with me. Could be I just wasn't in the mood. Yesterday was the first anniversary of my husband's death, and I tied one on then, so as you may know, nothing tastes good on the day of a hangover. I slid out an hour early. Five thirty-five, to be exact."

This woman recited details like they were out of a file. "What kind of law did you practice?" Callie asked.

"Criminal law," she said, and smiled. "Wondering why I'm not a puddle of tears and snot, aren't you?"

"Sure am. Yes, ma'am," Thomas said before Callie would explain to him that after that type of career, Ms. Calloway would be accustomed to all level of surprises coming at her from out of the blue.

"So—" Callie began.

"What happened?" Ms. Calloway asked.

Callie nodded.

"I came in and threw my keys on the credenza. The man was going through my desk in the living room, and he about jumped out of his skin. He'd already gone through my bar and my bedroom, I learned afterwards."

Good so far.

"He went to run out the back door, which he'd jimmied open, and I took off after him, grabbing the first thing in my way to have as a weapon. A baseball bat."

Callie couldn't hide her reaction. "You keep a bat handy?"

"Since my husband died. And a nine-millimeter in the bedroom."

"Good thing the thief didn't find it when he rummaged through."

"Why do you think I ran in there to check first after he took off?"

Callie liked the woman. "Back to the man."

"I bellowed 'What are you doing in my house?' He spun and looked at me."

"Mask?" Thomas asked since the last two times he'd worn a balaclava.

"No. But somebody recently beat the shit out of him. Swollen jaw, bruising around his nose and eyes, a busted lip. That stunned me. Made me wonder what did I miss? Made me look for an accomplice to pop out. Somebody had to have done that to him, and not that long ago."

Callie pictured Calloway and Magnus catching each other off guard, for a second just eying each other. "So he saw the bat, you went after him, and he ran out the door with you in pursuit."

Ms. Calloway gave a lone nod. "Screaming."

"You or him?"

"Me. I was hell-bent on bashing in his skull. I'm afraid my scream only made him run faster."

To that, Callie had to laugh. "I guess so. Please, continue."

The evening had fallen around them, and the neighbors inched closer. It was like Ms. Calloway told a campfire story.

"He tripped and fell running out the back. Cursed like a drunken sailor, because his jaw hit one of my chaises."

Someone gasped in the crowd. "Then did you hit him?"

Someone else commented, "If she had, he'd be a body, not escaped."

Nervous laughs and dittos all around.

"No, I didn't hit him, but I got another look at him. His eyes were swollen, and he had bruising all over him like someone else had gotten to him first, like I said. But he was young enough to collect his wits, and he scrambled to his feet, leapt over the railing, and bolted."

"Which way?" Callie asked.

Ms. Calloway turned almost completely around, facing due north. "He ran that way, toward Big Bay, but no telling where he veered off. I didn't go after him, if that's what you were going to ask."

"No, ma'am, didn't expect you to chase him. However, I must ask if you recognized him. Have you seen him around town?"

"Never seen him before," she said.

Callie pulled out her driver's license photo of Magnus. "Is this the man?"

Narrowing her gaze, she studied the picture. "I believe so. Like I said, he was beaten up, but that could be him. I can say this, though. He was about five foot ten, dark hair, early to mid-thirties, a mild ethnic appearance, which I suspect is a mixed heritage. Light brown complexion. Dark monotone clothing . . . not much of a disguise if you're trying to blend in on a beach." She paused, like she was shifting the conversation. A light shiver ran over her. "I interrupted him."

Adrenaline. It was catching up to her. "Did he take anything?" Callie asked.

"A small jade figurine, a sapphire and diamond cocktail ring, a diamond teardrop necklace, and a gold piece my husband inherited from his grandfather. The figurine was beside the jewelry box, and, of course, the other three items were in it. I have no idea what all that's worth, but it could bump five figures. Those pieces haven't been appraised in ages," Ms. Calloway replied.

Guess the third time was the charm. Magnus had finally snared some loot, and he'd picked one of the better houses to accomplish that. "Any pictures of the items? I'm sure your insurance company will be asking for them. I'd appreciate copies, too."

The shiver was gone, but Ms. Calloway's posture had melted a degree, like the excitement had ebbed and reality set in. Maybe even some of the what ifs, too, like what if the burglar had turned on her. Or what if he'd come in while she was there.

"Let me take a look inside," Callie said, standing. She needed Ms. Calloway to walk her through the experience again. Thomas would come with them, taking notes. She looked to Ms. Fairfax to come along, to be at the ready for any unexpected emotional fallout.

She had DNA from two balaclavas and now the chaise on the back porch. Thomas could see to collecting it from the chair.

The two head covers were already entered into evidence, still stored in Callie's locked cruiser. She needed a more thorough background run on Magnus, and if he was in the system, they'd have something to compare to. With positive identification, however, she wasn't sure she'd go through the expense. Such tests weren't cheap, and Edisto's coffers weren't very deep.

Small-town police weren't like *CSI*, *Dexter*, or *Law and Order*, where forensics were performed at the drop of a hat without regard to budget. *Put a rush on this* was ordered in every crime fighting show on television. Callie could do basics. Very basic basics. But she usually went to the Colleton County Sheriff's office when in need. Anything serious went to SLED, the old agency Mark retired from. In both cases, however, she sat in line for results, and unless she had bodies and serious time constraints, she waited behind other small towns like hers, and that didn't count SLED's own needs.

Hell, she had just hired two more officers after two years of begging for them. To spend slim funds on what amounted to a lone burglary since the other two came up empty in terms of items stolen didn't make a whole bunch of sense.

The public wouldn't understand that.

The town council did.

If she got her hands on Magnus, she would back him in a corner and still solve all of this though. She did have eyewitnesses.

She wished that the vigilante had somehow stepped in on this one, and she wondered why he hadn't. Magnus was ballsy going from a beat down in a failed burglary to another heist in a matter of hours.

She couldn't believe she wished for the vigilante to be more vigilant.

But she had, and there was a reason she wished him present. A strong sixth sense and the glimpse of the walker on Jungle Road had her wondering if Bruce had stuck around Edisto, having no place else to go. Being bored, at least she hoped he was bored and not into anything criminal, he traipsed around looking to be needed. That would be his way.

Lots of loose thoughts pinging around her head and a concentrated dose of wishful thinking.

This burglar, who by all accounts sure sounded like Magnus Sims, had hit one, two, three . . . one house right after the other while the police were occupied with the CBD store two miles away. Edisto Beach wasn't big, but one end was distant enough from the other to perform a crime while the authorities were occupied on the opposite.

Three houses. The same burglar. All three instances occurring during activity at Edisto Calm. Made Callie almost wonder if Magnus and Malorie might know each other. Almost.

They took the necessary report from Ms. Calloway. She was more upset over the gold piece than anything else with its historic value atop what could be decent monetary worth. Callie thanked the woman and promised to do what she could to recover the valuables. Ms. Calloway said she'd look for photographs and email them to the department.

Outside, Callie walked Thomas to their cruisers. "How about checking out the pawn shops and regulars in the area and forewarn them. Some are still open. Call those, then handle the others in the morning. Let's get ahead of this man unloading his loot. Tell them to inform us if Magnus comes in. Give them a good description of his wounds. He won't be difficult to identify."

Thomas had a better grasp of these types of people than Callie. "Call Don if you think he can help." Don was Deputy Don Raysor, a Colleton County Sheriff's deputy who on more days than not was on loan to Edisto Beach as another uniform. He was born and raised in the county and kin to ten percent of its residents. He'd fished every creek, hunted every patch of woods, walked every foot of marsh, and understood the people and history. Along with Marie, the two of them knew Edisto's souls inside and out.

"On it, Chief."

They stood there, paused, her still thinking and him waiting for the results of said thought. They'd worked together long enough to have the habit down.

"We need another body on duty tomorrow," she said.

"Just what I was thinking," he replied.

"I'll deal with Janet Wainwright." She said it almost to herself.

"Pardon, Chief?"

"She's already called me out," Callie explained. "She thinks crime is rampant now."

Thomas lowered his head and exhaled. He didn't have to say it. There was no pleasing everyone. If they didn't arrest enough people, if they didn't write enough tickets, they were allowing crime to escalate. If they held crime statistics to a reasonable level, giving the public the sense that all was good, they ran the risk of losing staff and budget, the town council labeling such as unnecessary.

But when they, whoever *they* were, experienced crime firsthand, they expected the entire force, a tank and a chopper to stomp out this huge surge of crime and corruption.

Janet, a major Edisto entrepreneur, would call this a crime spree. She already had to Callie. She'd now mention her concerns to town council, and one of them would come to Callie. Here lately, they'd taken advantage of the newest council member to act as the go-between, to preliminarily express their concerns rather than air out the laundry at meetings. On one hand, Callie appreciated that. On the other, it gave Donna Baird, the newest councilperson, the one who replaced her old adversary Brice LeGrand, the upper hand. The powers that be were using her, much as they'd used Brice. With him, they'd courted his hate for Callie. With Donna, they capitalized on her friendship.

Brice had dated Callie's mother forty-five or more years ago, before Callie's time. He lost Beverly to Lawton Cantrell, Callie's father, and had never gotten over it, regardless that he'd married someone, regardless that Callie had nothing to do with any of it. The result was he had remained a thorn in Callie's side, forever seeking ways to complain in open forum and suggest Callie be dismissed. He'd come close to suc-ceeding twice.

Then he'd started pulling over speeders, figuring that him doing it was indicative of Callie and her officers falling short. She told him that wasn't his job, and if he and his buddies on the council would give her a couple more officers, the speeders would be handled more efficiently. He enjoyed the strut, the braggadocio behavior of being in charge though, but he pulled over the wrong party one night and wound up dead from two bullets in his chest.

That's how she got two more officers, for a total of eight now. Nobody put words to the thought, but Brice's life was a huge price to pay for them.

Now council danced around her, not confronting her head on. They'd used Brice LeGrand to the point of it blowing back on them. With Donna chosen hands-down in a special election to replace him, the council switched tactics in addressing their chief.

Callie liked her well enough. The retired veterinarian loved Edisto and had lived in town for a few years after she sold her practice and acclimated well. She ran alongside her Great Dane, named Horse, the two having become popular with citizens and visitors alike, making her and her noble dog memorable goodwill ambassadors.

The council gentlemen, Donna being the only female, assumed the new *woman* could handle the prickly police chief *woman* better than they could. As simple as that.

The concept was insulting to both Donna and Callie, but they re-spected each other. The delivery system interfered with their relationship, though.

Three damn burglaries though. Callie expected something to come at her from council any time.

She watched Thomas walk back to his car, to begin his canvas of the beach in search of the red truck or Magnus Sims himself. She'd do the same for the next hour, but no doubt that man, if he had half a brain, had found his ride and booked it out of town. Ordinarily she would have Office Manager Marie jump right in studying cam footage from the causeway, hunting for signs of that truck, but she'd gone home. That meant Callie could hunt for Magnus or study hours of cam footage.

No, Marie could do the cam work tomorrow, covering the previous two days. The thing was, they knew he'd been here. All the footage would do was confirm his vehicle, and therefore, him, and paint time frames.

This was Magnus's third strike, and she wasn't cutting him one inch of slack. She would notify the Charleston Sheriff's Department, as well, in addition to the BOLO she was putting out right now. She couldn't believe this man didn't already have a record of this behavior.

Magnus was either gutsy or naive. Or both. Something, however, seemed to have motivated him into these criminal actions of late.

Funny how it was the stupid ones that made you look bad.

She and Thomas toured the streets, and in the middle of their perusing, two more officers arrived on duty, so for a little while, they had a lot of ground covered, but no joy.

Instead of eating dinner at El Marko's, she went home. She wasn't in the mood for a room full of company, even with her tucked away VIP table, and she'd had Mexican for the last four nights. She craved seafood.

Mark kept saying he was getting her an air fryer for nights like this. He appreciated that she couldn't eat tacos and burritos three times a day. But her birthday and Christmas, both in the same month, were only weeks away. Out came her age-old cast-iron skillet, her smaller one, and she seared herself up some flounder. Salt, pepper and lemon was all she needed.

She'd just turned the fish out onto a plate when someone hit her doorbell. The house wasn't a year old thanks to it having to be rebuilt after a crazy woman set it afire once upon a time, and Mark had made sure security was inherent in this one.

She lifted her phone to open the app he made her get, too. A big black nose was up against the doorbell cam.

Wow, it hadn't taken Donna Baird and Horse very long to get their marching orders from town council.

Chapter 11

Bruce

"SERE," BRUCE WHISPERED, the unknown visitor banging on the front door a second, then a third time. Finally, she stirred.

Bleary-eyed, she brought the recliner upright, blinked, and fought to collect her wits.

"I didn't want to answer the door," he said.

"Aunt Sere," hollered the visitor, now clearly Larue. "Let me in. It's me and my friend."

That told Bruce all he needed and what he needed to do. "I'll sleep outside tonight." He hustled to the bedroom to grab his two bags. They were packed. They stayed packed. Habits learned during deployment stuck to a man when being ready could mean keeping your life or not. No need to wait for her approval. This was best for the both of them.

Larue wanted in, and this late probably meant he needed a place to sleep . . . or hide out. Bruce guessed both after the day's events. He was a hundred percent sure the friend was the good-old-soul he'd punched up pretty good earlier in the day, too.

He hurried out the back, slid his two bags and shoes beside the shed without missing a step, and hustled light and bare footed around to the front, just like he had two days prior. With his back to the side of the house, he listened as Sere opened the door.

"Hey, Larue . . . boy, what happened to your friend!"

No secret as to the friend now.

"He got accosted, Aunt Sere. Can you tend to him?"

The rusty hinges creaked. "Of course I can. What's your name again, baby?"

"Magnus," he said, hesitating. "You forget me, Miss Sere?" The door shut, the hinges going back to sleep.

Had she just asked his name for Bruce's ears, because she was too sharp to not recall.

Lace sheers, the Walmart kind, hung on the living room windows. Bruce hadn't been fond of them upon first examination that week he moved in. They could be seen through. Sere loved the sun coming in, she said, but she felt something was needed over the glass as partial privacy. A compromise for her. Exposure to him.

However, at this moment the curtains, especially at night, enabled him to peer in yet not be seen. Sometimes fate decided what you needed.

Bruce recognized the cuts and bruises of the man he'd cuffed at the first house and smacked around at the second. By now that meant that the police chief of Edisto Beach was fully aware of him, too. If that couple had not come home at the second address, Bruce would have tied Magnus up for her yet again, hoping to God this time she charged him. She was tough, but then, she was a political entity in that small beach town. Economy and efficiency, not to mention public impression, mattered.

Bruce had interceded such that nothing was stolen, though. That had to be it. Why else would the guy be running loose?

The voices mumbled, but the house was too ancient to be tight. Every window, door, flue and vent allowed noise. In the middle of the night, when he couldn't sleep, Bruce had listened to the natural, and sometimes vicious, sounds of nightlife in the woods and on the marsh, guessing which species died and which did the killing.

Maneuvering not to be seen, he positioned his ear to hear through the unsealed base he'd seen Sere put rolled up plastic bags against inside. Hopefully he'd learn how long these boys were sticking around and what their game plan was. Apparently Larue was wingman for Magnus. After the second break-in, Bruce had trailed Magnus to where Larue lay waiting for him, in that beat-up pale blue Toyota that the nephew drove.

"Can I stash something in the closet again?" Larue asked, grocery bag in hand.

Of course, Sere let him, and once he was through, she motioned to Magnus. "Now, come on to the kitchen, and I'll fix up your face." She led the way, *tsking* to herself down the hall. A wink was exchanged between the men before they disappeared.

Bruce didn't think long about what might be in the bag. More pilfered junk. Right now he wanted to hear more of this dialogue, so he shifted to the rear of the house and hunkered on the porch beneath that old kitchen window that let him stare out over the swamp when he did dishes.

He liked being hidden out here off Raccoon Island. Away from common travel while being able to see incoming from road and water long before they could see him. The balance quieted his system, one that

had come to stand stiffly on guard for almost as long as he could remember.

Hunched down, he heard little more than water going on and off at
the sink as Sere cleaned cuts and rinsed off her rag. He heard humming
from her and ouches from him. Bruce heard more noises from the
marsh, honestly, and he would spend his night on this very porch if not
for the chance of discovery. The shed would have to suffice.

This place had offered him more mental peace than he'd experienced
in years. No pressure. No cohabitation short of Sere who was the easiest
person in the world to share a house with. She respected personal space,
sometimes going hours without conversation, letting the outdoors be
their background music. Maybe that was why he hadn't left. That and
the purpose he felt he was finding there but hadn't quite named.

The refrigerator opened, then cabinets, the two men searching for a
free meal.

"Damn. Since when do you stock this much food, Aunt Sere?"

"Someone was charitable," she lied. "Saw me put items back I
couldn't afford and decided to bring me a couple bags to tide me over.
Awful nice of her."

Bruce smiled at the masquerade.

"Who was it?" Larue asked. His ilk would want to know the who,
where, and how of getting anything free.

"A tourist, if you can believe that," she lied again. "From up North."

Magnus snorted then winced. "Since when does that happen?"

"Yankees can be nice," she said.

Bruce's foster home had been in Hartford, Connecticut. He'd never
labeled himself a Yankee, but he guessed someone could hang that on
him if they wished. The military had sucked geography out of him. He
had belonged to nothing but the U.S. Army, and now that he was out,
he belonged nowhere but where he happened to be at that point in time.

"It's late," Sere said. "What're y'all's plans?" She'd be wanting to
know for Bruce's sake, and he silently blessed her for asking.

"We'd hoped to hang here a day or two," Magnus said. "I need to
heal."

"You do stand out, boy. Don't you have a home?" she asked. "Won't
people be worried about you?"

"Called them," he answered, most likely lying. "Said I was staying
with my best bud here."

"Not at his place, though. Nephew, won't your momma wonder where
you're at, too?"

Larue tried to play the innocent loving relative. "Called her. Said I wanted to spend some time with you." Then he grunted. "She don't care where I'm at. She kicked me out the other day, remember? Aunt Sere, I could fall off the edge of the planet and she wouldn't miss me for a week. She's too busy with her *man*."

"Oh, dear Lord, not another one," Sere said. "That must be her fifth this year."

"Seventh," he corrected.

Sere scrunched her lips, her forehead knitted. "Well, you don't need to be exposed to that. Y'all go decide where you want to sleep. Just stay out of my bedroom. There's no sheets except for what's on the one bed besides mine. You'll have to share or settle for blankets."

"We're good," Magnus said. Then the kitchen light went out.

Bruce wasn't sure where they'd gravitated to until he heard Magnus fuss loudly about the limited channels on the TV.

So back Bruce returned to the side window. Sere took to her recliner, Larue knowing better than to do so himself. While she dragged a knitted blanket over her lap, one that had to be two generations or more used but baby soft from use, Larue and his partner took to opposite ends of the sofa. The nephew bent double a thin throw pillow like he'd sat there many times before. Lights low, the blue screen reflecting in their eyes, they finally found a show and turned zombie-like, unblinking.

Bruce was about to creep away and make his bed in the shed when Sere spoke up. "You didn't accomplish anything yesterday, did you? To-day, either."

For a split-second Bruce thought she was talking to him.

"No, we didn't," Larue said.

"At least you didn't get caught," she added.

Larue laughed. "Look at Magnus, Aunt Sere. He got caught. Got his ass handed to him. Someone beat the shit out of him."

"But who?" she asked. "A tourist?"

Bruce waited, eager to hear how that would be explained. These were unruly, disobedient guys, petty thieves who saw themselves better than they were. Yet here Sere was, appearing to stand halfway on their side. Again, the kin thing, maybe. When someone is yours, you tend to make excuses for them. Bruce wished Sere had better relations than this or at least had options from which to pick a favorite.

"No idea who he was," Magnus grumbled. "Bigger than me. Quicker than owl shit, though. Had me thinking of nothing but hauling ass."

"But now you've been seen," she said.

"I guess so. Yes, ma'am."

Funny how they didn't go into the first time, when Bruce had cuffed Magnus to the flagpole.

Bruce shifted, his left shoulder against the planks, his ear about a foot from the crack beneath the window, his listening on higher alert. This conversation seemed to be taking a small detour from what he expected.

Sere continued with her questioning, making Bruce start to wonder why. "Who else saw you?"

"Today? That guy who hit me, for one. And the two people I assume are renting the place. The other guy ran off just like me, like he didn't want to be seen either. Funny thing is I saw him at the first house, too, believe it or not. I don't get how he knew where we'd be."

"So the cops didn't see you?"

Magnus looked at Larue.

"Tell her," Larue said.

"Tell me what?" she asked.

Magnus gave a long breath. "This mysterious dude cuffed me to a flagpole so the cops would find me on the first one."

"Meaning they know you now."

He quickly spouted, "But they let me loose since I didn't take anything."

Scoffing into the air, she leaned back in her chair, not believing what she was hearing. "So they had your ID, and they were able to show the renters at the second house. Did they see your face?"

Magnus paused, afraid to speak up now.

Sere smacked the arm of her chair. "Well, that's a yes. Son of a bitch, boys."

"But we got away," Larue explained. "Cops didn't see us, and, trust me, they got there quick. Magnus here got away though."

"And how would you know that?" she queried.

"What?" Larue asked.

"That the cops got there quick?"

Proud, Magnus explained instead. "Since we were in Larue's car, not mine, we drove by. Don't worry. We were all clandestine like. Like we lived around there."

"Idiot," spat from her mouth in a tone Bruce had not heard before. "Neither of you drives a vehicle that any of those well-heeled renters would dare sit in, much less own, so why would it be tooling up and down the road?"

Larue piped up. "Then we were, like, contractors. They drive old cars and trucks. And we didn't go back and forth. We just drove by once. Just slow like."

"Most of those contractors are on a first name basis with the realtors and the cops," she said.

Magnus attempted to appease her. "I'm not from the area. They wouldn't recognize me."

"My very point!"

"Oh."

Everyone sat still for a moment, the men not daring to cross Sere, and Sere thinking. "Yet now they have your name, address, and make and model of your truck." Under her breath she grumbled, "Dumber than a box of rocks."

Larue leaned forward, reaching out to touch her, then changed his mind, as if he'd get scalded . . . or scolded . . . or both. "We did a third house, though, Aunt Sere. Hit pay dirt on that one. That's what I put in your closet."

She cut a gaze at him, as though he had one last chance to justify living.

"Got gold and jewels and other treasure," he continued like he'd been called on stage to perform. His one chance. "If you want, I'll take it to a Charleston pawn shop, instead of that one in Meggett. Better yet, McClellanville. They'd never think we'd go there. The police would be checking Meggett since it's so close, like we're too stupid to know better."

"Heaven help me," she uttered. "Stupid's your middle name, boy."

Nothing else was said for a few moments, and when Bruce peeked in to judge the air in the room, Sere was holding out her hand for the remote. She didn't speak until she was holding it. "Larue, go to that pawn shop in McClellanville." She was using the remote like a teacher wielding a ruler.

"And Magnus," she said and shut the television off. "You've compromised my nephew and compromised me because of your pudding head. You can't stay here longer than tonight."

"But . . ." he started to say.

Larue stepped up instead. "He's the one who nabbed everything. He deserves his cut. Plus, he can't go home."

"Because the authorities know his name and now his address," Sere said.

"He has no place else to go," the nephew pleaded.

Sere gave a mild shrug. "Not your problem and definitely not mine."

"I'll tell them you put us up to doing this so you could find the money for your property taxes," Magnus said.

The recliner eased straight up. "And I'll be the poor defenseless woman you took advantage of. You took money from me. Made me hide you. Who do you think they'll believe? I've been known in these parts twice as long as you've been alive, son. And my people go well over a hundred years prior. You didn't think worth a damn when you picked those houses and went in them. I can't wait to see how your dim-witted skull can talk your way over me."

Magnus's voice rose half an octave. "Larue will vouch for me."

Sere didn't say anything. Funny, Larue didn't either.

"I'll just kill you then," he continued. "He'll get the house, which will make him take my side."

Bruce stiffened. He would disappear that one without an ounce of regret.

"Who says I haven't left the house to his mother?" Sere said, her tone low and way more controlled than his.

Bruce wasn't stunned by much, but Miss Sere had morphed into something he hadn't seen before. He wasn't sure what to think about that, but the only way to understand was to listen harder. She wasn't scared. She was solid.

Just leave Edisto. He could do that. He didn't do drama. He didn't do relationships. And he damn sure didn't do silliness like this.

He would camp out in the shed, maybe further in the woods, then strike out at daybreak to find himself a low-key eatery, plug in his phone to charge, then decide whether to head north, south, or west. East put him in the Atlantic.

Something told him to hear this to its end, though. Magnus was showing some backbone here, and he might have the guts to follow through and kill the other two if he felt he could benefit financially. The dumbest cop could read him, though, even with his face busted up like it was. He wasn't that bright.

But such people didn't make the best decisions. He'd become a low-level loose cannon, so to speak.

"Who says I left the house to anyone?" Sere said. "Who says I didn't leave it to the Edisto Island Open Land Trust?"

"What's that?" Larue asked. As kin, he probably assumed all these illustrious assets would be his one day.

"It's local people who preserve this damn island is who they are." The chair creaked as Sere shifted forward. "People either give them conservation easements or just give them the land." The chair creaked again.

She was hammering home a point. "My people have had this land a long time, you little shit."

Magnus wasn't interested. "Wait a minute. I'm not family, but I'm the one who is risking his neck to find money—"

"Shut the hell up," she said.

"Dude, let her have her say," Larue mumbled.

"Little shit," she repeated, lower and more under her breath, but then she continued. "Four generations at least. That long proves my people had enough moxie to fight for this dirt, pay for it, maintain it. People used to have more respect for their property, and it's up to me and my kin to be grateful for that and have the foresight to continue that legacy. You don't just live for yourself. It isn't just about you."

"Who's it supposed to be about?"

Damn, Magnus didn't have the sense God gave a gnat.

"Don't you have anybody to give a damn about?" Sere was having a preaching fit. Larue didn't dare say a word. Magnus was dumb enough to keep talking.

"I have a kid," Magnus said, like it took a PhD to accomplish that. "Yeah, a baby. With my cousin next door."

Sere reared back. "Well, look at you all grown up and manly. Let me guess. You didn't marry the girl, and she has the baby."

"Maybe."

"She lives with her parents."

A pause there. "Maybe."

Her belly laugh rebounded, coming loud and clear to the outdoors. "And she's your cousin to boot."

"Our mommas are second cousins, so it don't count."

She only laughed harder.

Bruce would be downright entertained if the subject matter wasn't connected to three thefts and endangering Sere. He didn't like her not being surprised at what the two guys had been doing, but that didn't remove her from the threat.

"I so pegged you right," she said, a hint of a growl in the words. "I can read people, but since you're friends with Larue and he doesn't have many of those, I got stuck with you as well. Without the money for the taxes on this place, we lose it. Larue? If you don't want to inherit this place, then the two of you just go about your business. Leave here and do your own thing. Otherwise, get me some money. Be smart about it or don't do anything at all." She let that sink in. "And I'll just leave this place to the trust. They've already been asking me. My ancestors might appreciate me doing that instead of leaving it to family. At least the family I've got."

This was a whole other side of Sere that Bruce hadn't seen. Should he stay or go? Care or not?

A night in the shed would suffice. That was enough time to come to some a conclusion. His heart nagged at him, the feeling contrary to the conversation he'd just heard. He'd come to like the old woman, but suddenly she'd exposed a side he wasn't sure about. Was she just show-ing off in front of these two men, saying bold and intimidating things to redirect them? Or was she the kingpin of two dudes robbing houses?

The horde of *loot* in the dining room and nearby closet warranted a study. He hadn't gone through her things, not seeing the need, assuming they were a collection of historic pieces, hand-me-downs from relatives, and items she could not bear to let go. His intuition told him otherwise, now. He wasn't so blind as to believe robbing these houses had been a recent, short-lived plan to pay this year's taxes.

How had she paid for the other years?

The only reason Magnus hadn't been successful at the first two houses was Bruce, that and a poor selection of where to rob. The only reason Magnus had been successful at the third was there being no Bruce.

And to think he'd almost defined his purpose as being an altruistic mission to befriend Miss Sere. He assumed Miss Sere needed shielding. Hell, he wouldn't be surprised if she didn't have a rifle, a shotgun, and a couple of handguns hidden in that living room and around the house. And had used them. He kicked himself for not having checked.

"Tell me," she continued, when Bruce thought all had been said and done. "You hit three houses on the same end of town, right?"

"Yes, ma'am," Magnus said, like he was in high school. "A good strategy that I still stand by."

Sere did this little wave movement, not discounting him, but instead urging him to continue. "School me, little man. Convince me you have more than a chicken brain."

The thirty-year-old clouded over at the insult but quickly recovered, apparently confident in his decisions. "I—"

"I gave him the idea on which houses to hit," Larue spouted before Magnus could plead his case.

"I orchestrated the details," came his partner's reply.

Sere pointed at Magnus. "He's the one in jeopardy right now. He's the one who broke in. He's the one got beat up. Let's hear his plans,

Larue. Your so-called orchestration has fallen rather short, wouldn't you say?"

Magnus scooted to the edge of his thin, concaved sofa cushion, fueled to take a stand. "You see, they have this new store that opened up. A CBD store. Got everyone all worked up. People protesting. People wondering if there's pot in there. The cops are watching it hard."

Sere scowled but listened, Magnus waiting a second to get her permission to continue.

"Go ahead," she said.

"We hit places where the cops aren't. And we hit fast, with them thinking we wouldn't return to the scene of the crime. It was a smart plan, Miss Sere. Really smart. We just didn't count on that guy coming out of nowhere."

"Yea, the guy," she said.

"Well, and you'll like this part," he said, grinning. "We figured if the cops didn't think we'd steal back-to-back like that, we figured this new guy wouldn't either." He slapped his leg. "And we were right. That's legit wealth in that bag in the closet. You gotta admit, that's sound logic."

Bruce wasn't severely disappointed in Sere. Deep feelings had abandoned him years ago. He lived day to day, as internally secluded as possible, but had he let his guard down? Some, maybe. He'd deemed Sere close to harmless but shrewd enough to be self-sufficient. Now he understood more as to how she achieved said self-sufficiency. The first time the boys had come by, she'd acted a role. . . for Bruce. A ruse for whatever reason. To test him, shoo them off, whatever.

The poor did what they had to do to survive.

"Any money to be made in that kind of store?" Sere asked. "It's not drugs, right? So no real money involved?"

"Oh, they make money," Larue said. "Everyone thinks CBD shit is magical and a kissin' cousin to marijuana, so they think it's cool to buy it. After just one day people have been coming and going like they were giving the junk away."

"So why aren't you hitting that store?" she asked.

The men, whom Bruce had come to envision as boys, looked at each other stunned.

"That's what I told him!" Magnus exclaimed, proud of himself.

"Cops are around in the day," Larue said.

"And that means what?" Sere asked.

Magnus answered. "That we rob it at night." He sucked in a breath and grinned like he'd won the lottery. "Tonight. Like they wouldn't expect us to hit three houses so close together, they wouldn't expect us to hit the store the same day." He hit Larue in the arm. "Genius, right?"

Sere sat back in her chair, like her mission was done. She even clicked the television back on. "Well, you know where I'll be if you get by with it."

The two men, however, kept talking, composing when and how to do whatever needed doing.

Bruce scurried through the woods versus the walk path, making his way to the road and checking which vehicle they'd come in. He found both. The dilapidated blue Toyota and the faded red pickup. They'd been driven up the narrow, rutted drive and hidden in the trees halfway between the road and the house.

He removed a wire from under the hood of Larue's car, leaving the red pickup's engine intact. They'd take off in the only vehicle they had, not taking time in the dark to figure out what was wrong with the other.

After they drove off, he would repair the car, hot-wire it and follow.

Chapter 12

THE TOWN council woman and her escort, the Harlequin Great Dane, stood patiently waiting for someone to answer the door at *Chelsea Morning*. The overhead porch light popped on, triggered by the diminishing evening sun, and both human and beast looked up at the same time.

This Callie knew from peering at them on her phone from a few feet back in the hallway. She could see them, but they couldn't see her. She almost didn't want to answer. Horse mashed his nose against the smokey etched glass, attempting to see. He could tell she was on the other side.

It damn sure hadn't taken Janet Wainwright very long to inform council, had it?

Callie decided to answer. She wasn't ready quite yet to justify her department's actions when it came to three attempted burglaries on Edisto Beach, but nobody could ask for more. Some people, however, like Janet Wainwright, thought that police should have eyes on every street corner and in front of every house, deterring crime before it happened.

"Well, hello, Donna. What brings you here?" Callie asked upon answering, backing up to allow both inside. She'd given permission for Horse to come into her house two months ago. He was trained well, and as long as you didn't dangle food in front of him or let him get too hot, he didn't drool.

"Can I get you something to eat? I just took flounder out of the skillet," she said. "At least let me fix you something to drink."

Donna clicked her tongue and beckoned Horse. She escorted him to Callie's side porch, which was screened and contained, then returned inside alone. "Now, you sit down and have your dinner," she said. "I'll have whatever you have to drink."

That was the thing about Donna. Standing there all nice and simple in her khakis, Hoka walkers, and boonie hat, she could disarm most anyone with her gentle firmness and people skills. Horse's sweetness only clinched the deal.

Give her a year or two, and she'd be mayor.

What made her even more disarming for Callie was the fact she lived with Stan Waltham, Callie's old Boston boss. He'd come to prefer the deep South to the cold North, yet he was never ever losing that thick accent that gave away he came from Bean Town.

While Callie had broken her nose during the recent hurricane, poor Stan had broken his leg. Stan had come home after surgery to an empty house. A sea of people had been willing to check in on him, but only Donna went the extra mile. Since she owned the only house that had lost its roof, she offered to provide live-in caretaking services for Stan, for as long as it took. Funny how seven weeks later she still lived there. Her roof had been restored a week ago. Callie was waiting for Donna to put a For Rent sign up on it.

Callie's department and a few more natives had an ongoing pool on whether she'd leave Stan and return home. Callie had bet on January 5. Long enough to enjoy the holidays then realize they were no more friends. Thomas had bet by Thanksgiving. Mark put his money on the end of the year.

From all the interest and jocularity around her, obviously one couldn't dislike Donna, and her moving in with Stan had almost made her family in Callie's circle.

Callie liked Donna so much she wished they had become friends before the politics. Instead, they'd connected during the recent hurricane, the council woman having gotten stuck at Callie's place during the storm.

Donna had even met Bruce, the man Callie was almost sure was living in Edisto's jungle. But she would only remember him as the man who saved Stan and dressed a wound on a missing girl's arm.

Which meant Callie wasn't about to bring up seeing who she thought might be Bruce. There'd be no explaining why he'd still be on the island. Hurricanes usually chased off visitors, convincing them to vacation more inland next time.

Callie placed the water with lemon before the woman and brought her own plate to the table as both took their seats. Via remote, she put on some background jazz. Mark had suggested speakers when the house was rebuilt, and she'd come to enjoy the indulgence.

"You eat and I'll talk," Donna said, leaning elbows on the table, the drink between her hands. She wasn't as old as Callie's mother, but she was old enough to feel motherly. Her hands held no rings, the weathered appearance natural and pleasant.

She suited Callie.

"There's been a complaint to council," Donna started, pausing to let that impact settle on her hostess.

Callie went on with her fish, not wanting to guess the subject since Donna might be addressing something minor and totally off base from the expected Wainwright gripe. Callie wasn't a believer in kindling fires. Let others talk and show their hand first.

"Kitty Ingram," Donna said. "And the chamber."

Callie stopped mid-bite. That was unexpected. "What was her complaint?"

Damn that was fast, too.

"You did not provide enough protection to stop the destruction of her shop. Particularly on its grand opening day. Council feels a little embarrassed that the Edisto Chamber of Commerce held a ribbon cutting that morning, then the brand-new business gets vandalized in the afternoon. Speaks ill of the town."

At least she didn't add *don't you think* on the end of that sentence. Callie hoped that was because Donna was the messenger, not necessarily the critic.

"Is that all?" Callie asked, halfway through with her dinner, having eaten faster so that full attention could be given to whatever this was.

Donna tilted her head, off put by the nonchalance. "She's rather upset about this, Chief."

Scarfing down the final bite, Callie swilled some water, got up and put her plate in the sink. "Let's talk this out from the beginning," she said, returning to her chair. "Nobody from the council was there today."

"A couple of them were at the chamber ribbon cutting," Donna corrected.

Callie gave her that and waved it aside. "We had police protection at that site most of the day before, thanks to the protesters, who got permission from *the town* to do their thing. Then the next day we were there from before the ribbon cutting to when the store closed, give or take twenty minutes here and there when we attempted to protect the rest of the town."

This grievance mattered little to her professionally but irritated her more at the time-consuming aspect. She had to meet with Kitty. Callie would then speak to her own people and endure the eye-rolling and mockery in return. Some people might even think less of Callie or Thomas, the uniforms involved. The complainer would then be on edge, watching to see what corrections the department made under duress from the council. And town council itself would lay in wait measuring.

Yet, in the meantime, she had burglaries taking place. Burglaries that might not have happened if Edisto PD had been canvassing the streets instead of standing guard at a new business.

"Donna, today's event was practically unavoidable."

Donna listened, and Callie wished she'd left out the word *practically*.

"A protester came in and struck up an argument. They came prepared with spray paint," Callie continued.

"Might as well say the name, Chief."

Callie had no problem with that. "Okay, Malorie McLauren. She has a bee up her butt about CBD. Both Kitty and I attempted to educate her, but she wasn't in the frame of mind to hear." She took a sip of her water, taking a second to select her next words. "But right there, on site, Kitty and Malorie came to an agreement. Thomas and I mediated said agreement. Malorie would pay Kitty for damages, and Kitty would overlook the issue. Sophie even offered to buy the ruined product, to keep Kitty from losing even more." She gave Donna a side-eyed look. "So, what happened between this afternoon and now?"

Doing the math, that meant Kitty hadn't wasted any time. Her problem had been settled, so why did she feel the need to kick up dust?

"Just when did she contact council?" The more Callie thought about it, the more she sensed Kitty filing the grievance not long after Callie drove away to that third burglary. If that was the case, she hadn't given Malorie a chance to pay.

Donna gave a soft shrug, smiling gently. "She said it wasn't about the payment. It was about anything being allowed to happen in the first place, and a fear of more happening in the future."

"Jesus Christ, Donna . . ." and Callie blew out a long exhale. "I cannot afford to plant an officer in her store full-time, which is what it sounds like she wants. That's about the only way we can prevent something like this."

But then another thought hit her, which might explain why Donna seemed to be patiently waiting for more. "She wanted Malorie arrested, didn't she?"

"I think so," Donna said, even and steady.

Callie gave a *humph*. "Well, nothing I can do about that now, and to be honest, I would not have changed how we handled things. Miss Kitty can get over herself. I am sorry she had some damage, but I'm not functioning on the whims of the populace, Donna. I make these calls, not town council, and definitely not a citizen. Especially one who told me she was made whole before I left. Between Malorie and Sophie's compensation, she said she was good."

Donna held up two palms. "I'm just the messenger."

Callie reared back. "Um, actually you're not. You are town council right now. You speak for them. That means you are the town of Edisto Beach sitting there in my chair, in my house, assessing one of its employees and giving a mild warning that this sort of thing better not be repeated."

"I'm trying not to be as you say," her friend said. "It's difficult."

"Sure it is, but it's politics. I have to play it. You have to play it. But there has to be some common sense in here. We cannot bend to every complaint. We make the hard calls."

Silence fell between them. Callie may have let it drag longer than necessary, but this visit felt wrong. She had hoped Donna possessed the fortitude to stand up to the desires of those men. Of course, that was assuming she felt differently than they did.

"Forget the council," Callie said. "What do you think?"

Donna exhaled heavily. "The complaint indeed may be a little hasty on both hers and the council's parts. But . . ." and she stopped.

Callie waited, gaze held, sensing another shoe ready to fall.

"Kitty Ingram felt she didn't have the option of waiting to see if you and your department could protect her store tomorrow. Especially if the culprit was not charged. Any tempted culprit who saw how today was handled might see opportunity for tomorrow."

Oh, wow.

"And especially in light of the burglaries . . ."

Ah, here it comes. Callie lightly shook her head but said nothing.

Donna rubbed the underside of her fingers across the placemat before her, following the lines of its weave.

"The request for us to watch the store took us away from other duties, like patrolling," Callie said. "My bet is that someone saw us concentrated at the store and capitalized on the burglaries." Who couldn't see that? "We cannot be in two places at once, Donna."

"We gave you two more officers," she said.

All that did was allow two uniforms per shift, with more on the busier days. Before, they'd often resorted to a lone officer. Three shifts per day, seven days a week, with a limit of forty hours per week per officer. . . assuming nobody took off, was sick, had court, arrested someone and spent the day in Walterboro processing them. She already had one officer talking of leaving. An older one who'd put in six months and decided it was time to hang up the badge. That was common. She almost hated hiring anyone over fifty anymore, but then she had to remind herself that she was going on forty-three.

If she told Donna about the pending retirement, Callie risked being accused of not being able to hold onto employees. They might refuse to refill his slot as a penalty, like that would even make sense.

"We've had someone else complain about the burglaries," Donna continued.

Callie didn't ask who. That sounded childish. The burglaries had happened, and who had a concern was not an argument to have.

"Janet Wainwright," Donna said.

That would've been Callie's guess. She'd been ticked enough after the second. By now she'd have heard about the third.

"You don't drink, do you?" Donna said.

Callie knew good and well that Stan would've told her about Callie's past with alcohol. "Nope. Don't keep it in the house either."

"Just thinking now would be a good time for it. Might let us talk easier."

To have alcohol around for guests only made temptation come out and tap dance on Callie's deep-rooted thirst on evenings like this. Mark didn't drink often, and total abstinence under *Chelsea Morning's* roof became the norm.

She'd promised to remain sober since he'd come into her life. Promised her son as well. Almost every resident on the beach knew of her previous problem, so you could almost say she'd promised them all to live a dry life.

But, damn, a gin martini would taste luscious right about now.

Time to bring this issue around. What was the point? What did council expect of her and her department? "I assume you came with suggestions? Preferences? Changes in routine?" There were a hundred ways to ask what they wanted her to do differently.

"Three officers per day shift," Donna said. "The main shift, when people are watching."

"We only have eight officers, for God's sake. You're asking for five on duty per day. Not counting the night shift, to which we assign only one."

A lone night officer wasn't uncommon. Problems didn't occur then. Officer Russell Wiley even preferred those hours and had held that particular watch for at least four years. Sure, he'd been caught napping a half dozen times, but nothing had happened on his watch. Edisto Beach went comatose after dark.

"Add the deputy from the sheriff's department," Donna said. "And that makes nine."

Callie was so disappointed. "Do the math, Donna. Y'all should've done the math before they sent you to me. It's just not doable."

She hated being told how to run her shop. She wasn't agreeing to the *suggestion*, and this was not the end of the discussion. She had to admit, however, that the least abrasive manner in which to address this was what they were doing right here, across the table from each other.

Sure beat in the middle of a public council meeting like before.

She got up. "Need a refill? All I have besides water is tea with stevia in it."

"Water is fine."

Callie did the refill and took a bowl out to Horse, setting it down before handing him a treat. She'd learned to keep something for dogs around, particularly in the cruisers, thanks to Donna. Callie hadn't paid much attention to how many dogs were on the beach until Donna joined the council.

"I'm not locking up Malorie," Callie said, coming back to sit. "And I'm not reporting to Janet."

She thought for a moment, and Donna let her. "I could keep an eye on the CBD store but not park a full-time uniform at the door. That's not fair to the rest of the beach. Just one officer in that vicinity, in that commercial area. And trust me, she doesn't want an officer in the store. That makes customers nervous, like there's trouble waiting to happen."

Donna relaxed. "Well, I've delivered the message."

"But you are not getting three officers per shift, day in and day out. It's not feasible unless y'all want to come off the taxpayers' hip and find me another officer."

"Not happening. They told me to tell you that, so I assume they expected you would ask."

Enough about the store. "What's Janet wanting out of all this? An officer patrolling just her properties? Answering to her a couple times a day? Escorting her contractors?" She could go on with a half dozen other inane suggestions but saying them out loud only demonstrated how ludicrous it was to appease each and every business owner in town. "What about McConkey's? What about Pressley's? What about the Pavilion?"

"Janet just wanted to bitch," Donna said. "Just keep crime down."

"Sounds like just as much a town council problem as a PD problem,"

Callie said. "I know Janet. She'd make your life more miserable than mine."

Donna inhaled and held it a moment before a long release. "So I've been told."

Donna had done her job, and Callie had exhausted her replies. "Sure wish we could have that drink."

"You and me both," the retired veterinarian said. "I hate drinking alone."

Good, they were off duty and back to the personal. "Can I ask you a question?" Callie asked.

"Only seems fair."

"You moved in to assist Stan in recovering from his broken leg. Though he's still mending, he's much better. How long are you staying with him?"

As close as Callie was with her old boss Stan, she hadn't delved into his personal life. At least not of late, no more than praising him at each step of his recovery. He walked with a limp these days, occasionally with the cane, but he'd come a long way, much of which was due to Donna's tending.

"Listen to you," Donna said, narrowing her eyes. "Probing and without much discretion either."

"Seems to be that kind of night," Callie replied, then just leaned on the table, waiting.

Donna had gone back to channeling the weave on the placement with her fingernail.

"Stan is close to me," Callie said, like that gave her the go-ahead. She didn't mind being protective of him. He'd been there for her for a decade, going on two. But when Donna didn't say much, and hesitated to look her hostess in the eye, Callie recognized that the veterinarian had crossed the line from neighborly caregiver to sharing a bed. She'd bet a month's pay on it.

Donna never did answer the question, but they still managed to speak late into the night, breaking once to walk Horse in the back yard to do his business, then returning inside to continue their chat. Horse made himself home on a comforter Callie puddled on the floor.

By eleven, they'd talked out each character on the council, and those who ran all the businesses. Callie'd confirmed the natives who thought they ran the show and the ones who really did. Then there were those to trust, and those who'd never be satisfied with how Edisto was managed. The ones with sway . . . the ones nobody listened to.

Theirs was a conversation Callie had to admit wouldn't have happened unless Donna was on the council. Callie could work with this woman, in front of council and behind their backs . . . just like they thought they'd acquired a secret weapon to use against, with, or despite Callie. The balance seemed fair enough.

Mark came in around eleven thirty, the guest a surprise but not unwelcome. Horse followed him around like he had treats in his pocket, wanting attention until Mark kissed Callie good night and disappeared into the bedroom.

That's when the two ladies, voices raw from talking, weary from a long day, called it a night. Donna stood and waved a hand for a droopy Horse to heel. He was ready for bed too.

Callie walked the two to the door, and a coolness slid over them from the drop in temperature outside. November at the beach. There was no car in the drive because Donna and Horse walked everywhere, and Callie was about to ask if they needed a lift home . . . still to Stan's, when an odd light caught her attention off to the east. Nothing big, but brighter than normal in the commercial area, like there was some event she wasn't made privy to.

Her phone lit up as did her radio, not a split second before she heard a siren in the distance. Not one of her people, but a different siren, from the fire station. Then a police car a couple of blocks away.

Fire. Her heart leaped into her throat. She hated fire. She feared fire. Her husband had died in a fire.

"Gotta go, Donna," she said, leaping back inside for her weapon and car keys. All reports were telling her something was on fire down Jungle Road.

The radio said one building, but one building was bad enough. If it spread to the rest of the commercial entities, the loss would be devastating. And that was assuming nobody got hurt.

Mark suddenly appeared. "Fire?"

"Yes," she said, not happy at the weakness in her voice.

He lightly shook her by the shoulders. "You got this, Sunshine. I'm coming with you."

About the time she was ready to hit the stairs, he was, too. "You'll rock it, Callie. Just do what you do. You're good at this."

Bless him, he tried.

It's not about you, she had to keep telling herself as they bolted out the door. *It's not about your fear of fire.*

Chapter 13

Bruce

BRUCE HAD TO wait until close to eleven before Larue and Magnus got off their asses and followed Sere's suggestion about the CBD store. This loose sense of coordination between the old lady and the two younger men was a new dimension, which told Bruce he might need a new perspective.

That didn't mean he wasn't disappointed. He was. Most of all in himself, for not reading her better. Sere was a survivalist, not unlike him, and he'd missed that.

Sometimes he hated being a civilian. Check that. A lot of times.

He should've seen her for what she was, a senior woman alone and afraid of an empty house. She came from plain folk. The two men were plain folk, too, with an unbaked way about them, making them believe they were deeper than they were.

Bruce had retrieved his shoes from the shed and donned an Army green ball cap, throwing on a dark lightweight jacket that held no personality. He wore no logos. Then he returned around the house and through the woods, where he assumed a squat somewhat behind and partially beside a large oak to watch and wait.

The wait would let him question what he was doing and why. Uncertain he would even follow the two men, he pondered the whys of doing anything but leaving Edisto.

Sere had treated him well. He'd felt her rather smitten with him, and he'd pitied her solitude, maybe had hoped to teach her to embrace it like he did. Only she'd been the one to influence him, teaching him that sometimes it was nice having another person around.

He'd repaired her house, and she'd cooked for him, bringing him drinks outside while in the middle of chopping wood for the fireplace. He'd chopped a lot of wood.

Becoming a vigilante on the beach had just happened. He wanted to keep her nephew out of trouble because he seemed all she had. Bruce didn't like Magnus taking advantage, though.

Damn it, he'd underestimated them all. He didn't normally do that.

But in all this misunderstanding and bent judgment, another thought stuck in the recesses of his brain. One that he had not wanted to tease out and analyze. Was Sere part of their wayward behavior?

The front door of the house opened and slammed shut. Nothing clandestine whatsoever, but then, who would hear them out here? But being clandestine, even when unnecessary, was a habit Bruce maintained, not understanding why anyone else would not.

Dressed in dark clothing, the two men still made enough noise to be heard a half mile away. Bruce could count every footfall made from the front steps to the car, even across nature's damp, leaf-covered floor.

They'd hoped to go in the old Toyota, as Bruce had predicted. They'd talked too much about Magnus being identified and his red truck being known. But when the Toyota wouldn't start, after ten minutes of arguing and messing with something they weren't sure how to fix, they defaulted to the pickup. They could never be labeled unpredictable.

They cranked up. Magnus driving, they turned around in the silted street, one and a half cars wide, and headed toward Laurel Hill Road, which would take them via Pine Landing Road to the main thoroughfare. From there they would either go left to leave the island, or right to head toward the beach.

Bruce let them get a head start, then started the car. Grateful for a three-quarter moon and a cloudless night, he took the road without headlights and came within a half mile of the truck. Close enough to see it turn right.

From there they took off, speeding like they had a deadline to meet. He, however, knew where they were going. He couldn't get lost.

He drove a tad under the speed limit. There hadn't been much time to think about the change of events, and he decided he ought to give it thought. The changes in these people, for instance. No, more like the reality of learning who they really were. That was on him.

Freaking out had been trained out of him years ago. Events and people impacted him or they didn't, but they didn't devastate, upset, or depress him. They happened. He dealt. His blood pressure maintained a steadiness in time of crisis, a talent derived from his survivalist up-bringing as a child and military necessity as an adult.

What he needed to wrap his head around was why he bothered. Why was he still on this island? What did he think he was doing following these two nitwits, two men with no more sense than God gave a potato? His allegiance to the old woman had been tarnished, proven somewhat wasted. So, again, what was he doing?

The moonlight gave everything a sleepy, artistic feel. It was like it gave him permission to relax, think, and appreciate the details of where he was. Lone coach lights and solo streetlights appeared randomly in country yards, like they stood guard against potential peril, protecting the sleeping islanders inside. Everywhere else was dark. Coal black dark.

He was on guard one moment, alone in obscurity the next. Not part of anything, but he wasn't sure being part of something was worth the investment.

Yeah, he'd had a lot of time in his life to ponder existence, but he'd never come up with an answer, so he decided it wasn't about having an answer. It was just about survival. That's what he and Sere had in common.

That still didn't seem like enough of a reason for him to be here, though, at this place, in this moment . . . driving in someone else's car to somebody else's business.

He never had to ponder these thoughts when he was with the guys, but his guys weren't deep thinkers, either. He was more alive now, yet he wasn't sure what that meant.

Good thing he didn't get depressed, but suicide never made sense to him either.

He lived, almost thrived, in this limbo, not limbo hell as some called it, but just an in-between with him not caring to put a foot on either side.

A shrink would have a label for somebody like him. He didn't care about that either.

He passed the island post office. In his few trips back and forth, mostly on foot, he'd committed the route to memory. Three miles tops in front of him now. The two buddies might even be there at the rate they drove. Still, he had time.

His thoughts arbitrary and incomplete, he sank back into them for the remaining minute or two he had. Something niggled at him. Subconsciousness mostly, but in his search for purpose, a tiny ember of something told him there was a reason he stayed. He didn't want to know, really. He wasn't sure he wanted to put a name to it.

Though he knew the name.

Her name.

He almost wished he hadn't met her. Almost.

The causeway appeared in the distance ahead, the moonlight accenting high tide on either side of the road.

He crossed the bridge, like crossing into another dimension, and instead of turning down Jungle Road where he suspected the two idiots could be found, he continued straight, Highway 174 having become Palmetto Boulevard. After eleven, in most towns, a bar or two would remain open, but in this sleepy community, activity diminished. Nothing moved.

He had driven slow enough to glance down Jungle Road to his right in passing but didn't see the truck. They likely cased the area, like he would do. To avoid them running into him and recognizing their own vehicle, he slowed, ticking off house options. He found an unoccupied rental on the land side of Palmetto, the side not on the water, because everyone who drove Palmetto looked toward the sea.

The house was unimpressive and stained, not painted a pastel color like so many of the others. He backed into the slot under the house, shut off the engine, pulled down the visor, and blended in.

They never came by though. That told him they continued past Edisto Calm down Jungle Road, like they belonged there. It was a long road, so they had time to inspect the area and talk about how to proceed, because from the sounds of things back in Sere's living room, this act was entirely impromptu.

He waited another few minutes. He gave the two men twenty, long enough for them to get their nerve up, return to the CBD store, and make their approach.

When Sere made her suggestion that they tap that venue instead of someone's rental, Bruce had to admit surprise. Not shock, though. Low-level thieves thought like that. *Let's try this, or let's try that.* If a place made money or sold anything, it was worth breaking into.

He hadn't expected to see her in their ranks, though. She'd registered more as the benevolent aunt who tried and failed at turning her nephew into a better soul. Had she started down that path and gotten sucked into their ill-conceived methods of finding money? Or was this something new? Or was she in charge most of the time? Or had she just directed them this time to keep them from screwing up on their own?

Bruce still wanted to tether himself to the concept that her involvement was one of making ends meet, not of greed. Her speech to the men about land, legacy, and forebearers held a level of fidelity.

He also liked her warning she might commit her property to the land trust. That idea made sense and held purpose, something her predecessors would've appreciated versus turning the place over to the likes of this nephew. If she wasn't somewhat tending to Larue, Bruce would help rid her world of him. From the sound of the boy's mother, she wasn't worthy of the inheritance either.

Time was up. He left the vehicle and trotted between houses, just a few degrees east of due north, his internal compass placing him within a hundred yards of the targeted venue.

The truck wasn't there, but he was sure he'd spot it sooner or later. In his analysis of the area, he labeled his first choice of hiding space to be behind the real estate office owned by that Marine. A quick detour noted the truck hidden behind a palmetto tree between the building and the marsh.

They hadn't even thought about cams, and if that Marine didn't have exterior cameras everywhere, then she fell far short of what he'd expect from a retired jarhead. She was wealthy from the looks of things and posted her name on a quarter of the houses in town. She had savvy and intelligence.

But not his problem if she recorded them being there.

He returned to near the road, Edisto Calm not a hundred yards away. Nothing looked out of sorts, but then he caught the movement of a flashlight inside. They'd already breached. He'd give them a moment to feel comfortable and to collect whatever it was they thought they'd be able to steal, then he'd make his call. No sound business owner left cash in the register overnight, so he expected them to hunt around a few more moments.

The flashlight went out.

Done so soon? Had it been that easy? The owner of the place had been that dumb to leave a day's earnings so readily found?

Bruce scurried, bent over and quick, to the side of the building and peered inside. The two men stood in the dark, shaking a flashlight. One tried messing with it, then the other took it from him. They only had one between them, and nobody had checked the batteries.

It appeared each man was one chromosome short of a slug.

Coming up short with no more batteries or a correction of any kind, Larue went to feeling his pockets, while Magnus searched behind the counter. The latter came up with a box of matches, probably used for the ambience of scented candles with this being the type of enterprise it was, all hippy and sensory. But he also held a cloth-looking bag.

Bag slipped under his arm, Magnus struck a match, only then looking around for something to light. Larue stood nearest a candle, a rather cumbersome one about the size of a Mason jar, and he grasped it two-handed, holding it for his partner to ignite.

But in lighting it, they seemed dissatisfied with the results, so Larue went for another candle. Two had to be better, right?

The cumbersome antics between them, one with matches, the other with candles, made them second guess who did what and when. Larue set down one candle in a clumsy move, his other hand occupied, but he turned too fast. Magnus went to light the second before Larue had the first set safely on a table, the edge of it tipping, sending it to the floor.

Larue high-stepped backwards. Magnus reached to catch, burning his hand on a lit match. He bumped a table, lost his balance and fell into his cohort, both going to the floor. The commotion was easily heard outside.

That's when Bruce lost sight of them, unable to stand high enough from his ground position to see inside and get the full picture. What he managed to see, however, were the flames that accented the room bright enough to tell him they'd touched off something combustible.

He pulled out his phone and dialed 911.

"Um, someone is inside that new CBD store on Edisto Beach, and they caught it on fire. They might even be on fire, because they're still inside." He hung up before the operator could ask his name or tell him to stay on the line.

Suddenly shouts carried through the air, loud and panicky. Having exited like they entered, out the back door, they fell to the ground but quickly scrambled to take off running.

Bruce started to go to them but held himself back. Watching from around the corner, he convinced himself they'd escaped serious harm before he bolted off to a neighboring property, some type of outdoor sports rental shop. Taking up residence behind a stand of oleander and myrtles beside the set of stairs to the entrance, he squatted and watched.

A siren screamed in the distance, then two. First police, then the fire department from the sounds of them. Larue and Magnus tousled over each other like roaches outed in the light, hunting for a rug to crawl under. They rose and sprinted, headed toward Bruce.

He hunkered down, invisible to these two idiots, and watched them run within eight feet of him. Magnus held something in his hand, protecting it against his body. The bag. Canvas.

They passed by Bruce's hiding place and continued across the street.

Bruce hustled from one hiding spot to another, taking a final stance behind a rack of kayaks. From there he spotted the two thieves headed behind Wainwright's office. Magnus threw the item he had protected into the red truck before climbing in. They turned the vehicle around, kicking gravel and shells, and headed past him again, this time to the causeway, leaving town.

They couldn't go to Magnus's house. They wouldn't go to Larue's mother's place, not unless they were even denser than original conjecture. So that meant they were headed back to Sere's.

Bruce returned to where he was hiding before, near the outdoor rigger's stairs. He decided against fighting the fire. He had no tools, no water, and the authorities would be there with better resources before he would make any kind of difference.

Not his problem, either.

That line of thought, however, didn't work as well as it normally did. Not his problem, but it was somebody's. This time it weighed on him more than he cared to admit, because the problem was hers. For some unexplained reason, it mattered to him that this incident fell to Callie Morgan.

Instead of following the two men, he remained in place, drawn to watch how this excitement played out, and how she handled herself.

A police cruiser arrived, and he tucked back into the shadows. The fire truck appeared, not thirty seconds behind. The proper people leaped to work. She wasn't among the first responders.

Bruce navigated the darkness and flora to return to Palmetto Boulevard and the Toyota. He eased it out, telling himself to cross the causeway like the two idiots and just leave town. Avoid the crowd. Avoid being seen. He wasn't a regular here, and strange people stood out when analyzing a fire. Nobody would remember him from the hurricane days because they had all abandoned ship, but why hang around to test fate?

But he didn't leave, couldn't leave. He eased off Palmetto onto Jungle Road. He parked across the street and down from the activity, just not under a streetlight. Cap on, nobody would see his face.

It didn't take ten minutes, maybe less, for more cops to appear, along with a zillion people who poured like ants out of a stomped hill. Then there she was.

Chief Callie Morgan, dressed in civilian clothes, maybe even called out of bed, now functioning like she was made for this line of work. She talked with people, gave orders, interviewed, gathered intel, and studied what happened, analyzing what may have occurred that she couldn't tell on her own right away.

He admired her. He had no idea why.

He'd been married. It didn't work. She hadn't understood him, thinking PTSD was little more than an excuse to avoid people.

Callie Morgan, however, had controlled him during the hurricane.

She had made him save her friend. She had done her job and never lost her mind. Even after breaking her nose, she'd collected her wits and ordered him and others to do what needed to be done . . . in the middle of a damn hurricane.

She had suspected he'd been one of the kidnappers, but in light of the disaster at hand, she had rationalized, put the crime into perspective, not without a small amount of second-guessing. She hadn't turned him and his cohorts in. There was something about all that that made him walk away from the other two, almost like she awakened him. She'd taken him on the medevac chopper to put distance between him and the other two men, and he had to believe she was giving him a chance to start over. He'd helped her. Then she'd helped him.

In his prior life, they'd never hurt anyone in their crime spree. They'd kept ransom at a minimum, well within reach of the wealthy they targeted to entice them not to call the authorities. The other two would've kept on with it, but he chose not to. They'd disbanded over it. Correct that . . . he'd disbanded the group, no longer attracted to their *adventures*, as they called them, that would one day, in one way or another, get them arrested.

She'd suspected. She'd put pieces together. She'd realized nobody got hurt. She'd also seen that not a single victim could say what happened. They could not be identified.

She had no hard evidence, but she also didn't bother to cobble together the circumstantial evidence that could have been molded into a case given the right judge and the right district attorney. Some hardcore detective might've sunk his teeth into such a case and played the odds, but she seemed to think twice.

He wouldn't have pursued them with so little evidence, either.

Something told him that she'd gone against her normal grain by not going after him. Maybe because she'd spotted enough redemptive value.

He understood.

Something about that . . . something about her . . . made him hang around Edisto.

He rather enjoyed being the vigilante to her cop.

Chapter 14

CALLIE PARKED where she could, which still meant fifty yards back from Edisto Calm. Exiting the cruiser, the stench of the burn and the stinging smoke registered immediately, urging her to fight whatever internal flaw this was of hers that stopped her from confronting fire. She broke into a run. Sucking in the foul air, she pushed herself to make up the distance, leaving Mark on his own.

"Excuse me. Coming through. Police. Let me get by." Again, her size compromised her, most of the people heavier and taller than she, and while she tried not to shove people aside, she was forced to, apologizing as she did.

Half the town had to be there, crammed on Jungle Road and in the Food Lion parking lot, wedged in every parking area for a two-block radius. Thank goodness the fire truck reached the scene before the path had blocked.

Officer Russell Wiley, her night guy, attempted to keep people back.

"Keep them away," she told him, in essence telling him to just keep doing what he was doing.

The fire didn't seem as critical up close. Thank goodness for efficient government employees. Them and whoever called 911. Which made her think . . . who *did* call 911?

Callie scanned the clusters of people, not seeing anyone hurt. At the same time, she hunted for her counterpart, Fire Chief Leon Hightower. Weaving in and out, she found him on the west side of Edisto Calm, directing his guys, a total of three.

"What do you need?" she asked him.

"Just keep people away," he said, like he even had to.

"Anyone hurt?"

"No, not that we've seen. Someone drove by and called it in. Found nobody yet who knew anything, but I've kinda had my hands busy."

She understood. "Talk later."

He nodded and stepped closer, redirecting one of his fighters and the hose in his hands.

The fire had been contained to the interior, making her wonder how much the store's inventory had fueled the flames. The outside, lightly smoked up, maybe.

Her heart slowed. She hated laying eyes on flames, but they'd just about been doused.

Thomas arrived, then Annie, then Ben Benoit, all three officers in civilian clothes, their badges anchored on them, their holsters in place. She ordered them to hold off the public, even push them further away, because they'd inch back in at any opportunity.

She did so as well, but with more interest in watching people, seeking any person overtly interested, who didn't make sense to her, who might be the firebug watching their handiwork.

Scanning the faces, she wanly smiled and waved off those awaiting the latest update. Moving in front of them, past them, studying deep inside the throng behind them, she wasn't seeing anyone who set off alarm bells in her head.

Until she looked past them all, to the clearing. There, in front of Janet Wainwright's real estate office, a tall man in his mid to late thirties stood in front of a faded, dated, blue Toyota. A sixth sense told her to study him harder. A deeper sense told her to approach him versus the three hundred other people.

His gaze connected with hers, and he held it.

Bruce Bardot.

In the shadows, the cacophony, the movement, she wouldn't be able to stand with her hand on a Bible and swear it was him, but she felt something about this figure. She would almost swear this was indeed the man.

He nodded once in recognition, like he knew she needed the confirmation.

Funny. She found it odd he had a car.

Seeing him, confirming it was him, was like opening a book you hadn't read in a while and attempting to reconstruct what the story had been about.

He didn't wave. He didn't approach.

Here she was in the middle of so many people, all of them familiar with her, and yet she wanted to run over there and, what. . . catch up?

But he was here, at a fire. Who said he hadn't seen something? He'd have a keener eye than the average Joe standing around wondering what happened. If he'd been a vigilante for burglaries, why not here as well?

Regardless, she needed to speak to him.

She pushed through people, harder than before. She'd stood around long enough for people to see her, recognize, and be curious.

"Chief!"

Callie turned to that voice. Janet Wainwright. Of course she would be present. Her real estate office was too close for her not to worry about its safety. "Just a minute, Janet."

"No, right now is good. I might not catch you otherwise." The tall Marine, an angular woman in her sixties, blocked the path. She wasn't one Callie expected to easily slide around.

"We know nothing yet," Callie said, hoping that appeased her for now.

"Who started it?"

Callie halted and stared. "That sort of falls under the category of *we know nothing yet*, Janet."

"We need more cams on our streets," Janet said, speaking loud enough to turn heads. "May I count on you to bring that up to town council? If we don't have enough officers, then we might as well use technology."

If wishes were horses. . . flashed across her mind, something Callie's father would say when she would ask him for something out of reach. *If wishes were horses, beggars would ride.* But now wasn't the time to speak in verse.

"I need to see your cams, now that you mention them, Janet, and if they solve this case, then who better than you to bring it up at the next council meeting."

Callie tried to look past Janet as she spoke, but a few people had gathered around her, seeing that someone had detained the chief, and was hopefully getting answers. . . or gossip, depending on what you wanted to call it.

"Would mean more to the residents if their police chief pushed for more means to make the community safer," Janet said.

"Seeing your footage and possibly the culprits would make you everyone's hero, wouldn't it?"

"Yeah," said someone in the crowd. "That would be awesome, Janet."

The real estate broker glanced into the horde for who the stranger was using her first name.

That was interruption enough. With each word came another ear, and Callie watched helplessly as people gravitated from watching the now-controlled fire to Janet who was totally milking this podium she'd occupied.

"I agree with you about the cams, Janet. I hope to see you at the next town meeting where you can bring them up. Might not hurt to have a price tag in mind when you do." There. Ball back in her court, and Callie could slip away.

"I'd be willing to come to that meeting," said someone to Janet's right.

"I'd be glad to be there, too," said a woman. Before long, Janet had a circle of minions willing to take up the cause. Their conversation increased, positioning where said cameras ought to go and who should be in charge of managing them. Like nobody professional would be consulted for those types of decisions.

Callie pushed past the real estate broker, brushing against her and receiving a disgruntled mumble in return.

But once past the small conclave, once she could make her way across the street, Callie found nothing. The car was gone. Bruce was gone.

Why was he even there to begin with? And why had he stuck around for her to see him, which she wholeheartedly believed. He wouldn't be seen unless he wanted to be. As an ex-Ranger, and a highly trained and keenly aware individual, he knew when to be where and how not to be seen. She shouldn't be surprised he left once people gathered. He couldn't afford to be seen.

Why was he still here though? Maybe he had no place else to go. He'd mentioned he liked Edisto once upon a time.

You could fit all of their conversations into a thimble from back then, but she still gathered he respected her. Maybe even liked her. He'd assumed Mark's place at the hospital until Mark could get there, giving her and a few others a taste of charisma.

He spoke of living solo, but now she began to wonder if he preferred living solo on Edisto Island.

She wasn't sure what to do with that if he was.

But she understood enough about Bruce Bardot to know that he did little without reason. He might've been propped against that piece of crap vehicle as a sign to Callie that he had seen something.

She walked to the street and glanced around; in case he'd just moved somewhere close by, while not expecting to find him. He'd find her when he chose. The fact he was here, making eye contact, said he would soon.

Or so she wanted to think.

She walked around the exterior of the crowd, to return to the scene such that she wouldn't see Janet again. She'd about made it back to Thomas when someone hit her shoulder. With a fist.

She spun, ready to take someone to the ground.

"This is the protection I get as a new business owner in this town?" Kitty Ingram.

Mascara ran down her cheeks, hiding half her freckles. Her hair had lost its composure, standing in wild disarray. Somewhere she'd lost her shoes, and her clothes were covered with soot.

The hardness in her relaxed, and Callie forgave the fist. "Are you all right, Kitty?"

"Why did you let this happen?" Kitty cried. Amos appeared out of nowhere, putting his arm around her, cooing something under his breath. Kitty wasn't listening.

"Someone broke in and set it on fire," she cried to him, tears flooding her words.

Callie remained steady. Kitty could sling all the accusations she wanted right now. Her one-day-old, brand-new livelihood had gone up in flames, literally.

"Do you know how it started?" Callie asked.

Kitty shook her head, sobbing.

"Did you see anyone strange around before you left? Did you see anyone after you closed?"

More head shaking as Kitty searched the tissues in her hand, seeking a dry spot to use. Callie looked to Amos. "She lost a lot," he said. "Money behind the counter, for one. The bank wasn't open by the time she closed, so she put it in a bank bag, one of those canvas things with a lock on the zipper. I slipped in to check. They ran me out, but I saw enough to see it was gone."

Now was not the time to tell Kitty that nobody left money in a store overnight, whether you lived on Edisto or in Charleston or Chicago. Nowhere was this safe.

"How much money?" Callie asked. Most people paid with plastic and cards saved on digital wallets and watches these days, especially on vacation, so surely there wasn't much cash in that bag.

"Three or four hundred dollars," he said, talking over his shoulder while consoling Kitty.

"What will we do? We owe people," Kitty cried. For a moment Callie wasn't sure who *we* were, but she caught on when Kitty repeated herself to Amos. "What do we tell them when we can't pay?"

Callie thought that Edisto Calm belonged solely to Kitty, but okay. Amos's involvement wasn't Callie's business, except to ask him who he thought may have jeopardized *their* business. Surely three hundred dollars wouldn't break them.

Amos caught the shift in pronouns and noted that she noticed. He was almost holding his breath.

"Can you think of anyone who might break in, Amos?"

"No, ma'am," he said. "Not unless you want to consider the obvious."

Callie waited for him to put a name to that.

"Malorie McLauren," he said.

Callie had been the only one to hear Malorie say under her breath that someone ought to burn the place down.

Kitty nodded like a loose bobble-head. "You're a hundred percent right."

"That doesn't sound like her, Amos," Callie said, while pondering whether Malorie was capable of doing what she'd said.

"Does spray painting an innocent store owner's shop sound like her?" Kitty wailed. People turned at the raised voice. Great. They had an audience now.

Callie tried to ask low without the gawkers hearing. "She paid you like she was supposed to, didn't she?"

"Yes, but she wasn't too happy about it," Kitty said. "Called me a bitch."

Callie started to ask Kitty what she called Malorie in return but didn't see the point. Not with her business destroyed in the background. Not with listeners. "Has anyone seen her tonight?" she asked instead.

"No, but why would she stick around?" Kitty was on a roll, eying the crowd like she had a growing sea of allies.

Was Malorie's comment coincidence or foreshadowing? On the other hand, Amos had thrown out Malorie's name rather quickly. Kitty's dramatics had interrupted him and drawn too much attention for Callie to question him further. This was not the place to pick his brain.

"Kitty? Did you call 911?" she asked.

The woman looked up through tears. "No. What does that mean?"

"It means you didn't call 911, Kitty. Did you, Amos?"

He shook his head and Callie believed him. Usually someone came forward in situations like these, professing to be the hero. They would come out of the crowd and tell Hightower or her. That hadn't happened.

"We'll need to interview both of you in the morning," Callie said, not wanting to do more here. "Separately." She'd have to risk them brainstorming tonight to get their story straight, but no avoiding that. Her interview skills ought to be able to tell who lied and who told the truth. Honestly, her instincts already told her to expect little truth from them.

There was something they weren't saying already.

"You better interview Malorie, too," Kitty said. "Assuming you want to be fair with any of this. You cops might not like a CBD store either. When you choose not to arrest a vandal, you can't help but wonder if she was left loose to finish the task. What do you think?"

"Nine in the morning okay for you two?" Callie asked, not taking the bait.

But Kitty wasn't ready to end this. "So, you won't answer, huh? Are you letting her off the hook for arson, too?"

"I'll investigate the fire, Kitty. So will Chief Hightower." She didn't want to mention Malorie and arson in the same sentence. She had to get Kitty off these accusations. She motioned for Kitty to come in closer, and Callie spoke low, for no other ears to hear. "If they decide this was arson, then your insurance might not pay for the damages, so I wouldn't shout it around, if you catch my drift. Somebody might report it."

Kitty froze, eyes wide and stunned.

Callie didn't have to say more.

Amos came up. "What?"

But Callie didn't want to discuss this with him. The hint that Amos might be partial owner was little more than that, a hint. It was up to Kitty whether or not he needed to hear the insurance side of things.

Instead, she motioned with a hand for Amos to take Kitty off. Kitty was willing and Amos curious, so they obliged.

Callie slid off in the other direction to find the fire chief. There was no talking to anyone tonight. Not until everyone settled down. She expected Malorie to lose her mind, though, after somebody on the Edisto grapevine told her that she'd been accused in front of an Edisto mob of setting a fire.

As the fire had disappeared, so had most of the crowd. The fire was totally out, and maybe a dozen civilians remained, and even they looked to be leaving. Everything was soppy wet, the air filled with a thick, musty stink. Callie went to find Leon Hightower, locating him inside the store, analyzing the destruction.

"Figure out what happened?" She stayed in the doorway to avoid stepping on evidence, or anything Leon might not want disturbed.

"The fire started here, in front of the counter, with something flammable. Turpentine, alcohol . . ."

"Nail polish remover?" she added, remembering the three items that Sophie, Thomas, and Amos had recommended to clean up the red paint. "Someone sprayed paint in the store, and I believe the owners were trying to clean it up. I was here right after it happened, and conversation centered around options on what solvent worked best."

"So, they could've tried all three," he said.

"Or more," she added. "The rags used would've burned up, right?"

He stooped and pointed to a black object. Maybe a can. "That would be the turpentine."

Callie wasn't so quick to blame Malorie for this fiasco now. Could she have broken in and seen the solvents and spontaneously decided to wreak havoc? Possibly. Doubtful. Or could the owner, or *owners*, have just mucked up what they were doing in the clean-up? After all, Amos loved his smoke. Something had to light his joints.

They'd still crown Malorie with this, blaming her for them having to clean up in the first place. There was also the chance that someone else, totally unrelated to any of these players, broke in and robbed the place, using the solvents to cover their tracks.

"We'll rope the place off for now. I'll come back during daylight to look closer," Leon said, then he peered over at her. "I'll try to get you something of a report tomorrow. You have any idea who made the 911 call?"

"No. I'll call dispatch and see who did. I'll check with the owner and a few others tomorrow and see what I might be able to uncover." She gazed around the room that only hours before had been so clean and neat, before the paint, and now, the fire.

The curiosity of who called 911 clung to her like the scent of the smoke. She called dispatch, identified herself, and asked if they could pull up that call and play it for her. It took a few minutes, but the operator came through.

The caller didn't identify himself and ignored the dispatcher's request for information. *Um, someone is inside that new CBD store on Edisto Beach, and they caught it on fire. They might even be on fire, because they're still inside.*

Bruce's voice.

What had he seen? Why hadn't he stopped the arsonist, thief, whomever was inside?

Had he waited around to tell her? The man seemed to function with a code. Callie assumed he'd hung around waiting to make eye contact on purpose. She was almost sure of it. Maybe he'd driven by and just called, but he hadn't tried to save anyone. The timing of the 911 call proved he'd been there rather conveniently for someone who preferred to live in shadows.

He knew the something that had happened, or the someone who did it. She was sure of it. She just hoped it wasn't him. But why would it be?

Surely there were better ways to get her attention and inform her that he hadn't left Edisto.

Chapter 15

CALLIE COULD SEE her patrol car from the CBD store now, no longer blocked by the crowd. The fire department rolled up hoses. Her officers strolled around, studying damage, probably waiting for her to tell them they could leave. Officer Wiley, the only one officially on duty, had taken off already, probably before she could give him some real work to do. Every police department had one or two Officer Wileys. As she walked back to the burnt building, she told one officer to tell the others that they were no longer needed.

Chief Hightower roped off the building with tape, his last task before heading back to the station. Callie wandered over to him. "About done?"

He nodded, smiled briefly. "Yeah. Accelerant for sure. Being it was after hours leans me toward arson, but from what you told me, it could also be carelessness on someone's part in trying to clean up."

"The fact the solvents were on site complicates things," she said, keeping Kitty in mind. This was not a case of the owner burning down their own place for insurance money, but even if someone else did it, there was the insurance payoff dilemma. Arson had to be absolute fact.

"Whether arson or nonsense or simple accident, the guilty party isn't going to want to raise their hand and claim the blame," he said.

"True that." An insurance company would want proof that the owner wasn't involved, that someone other than the owner broke in and deliberately caused it. To demonstrate that would require finding said person.

She wanted a culprit to hang this on before ruining a store owner's life.

These last two hours she'd watched the onlookers, taking note of who came and went and who tried to slip in closer to see more. Who tried not to be seen. Who seemed to care too much. She'd listened to snippets of conversations, giving the appearance she wasn't, hoping to hear a word or two from someone needing to brag. Callie saw and heard nothing to take note of.

The only exception was Bruce Bardot. Some armchair detective would consider him a very likely candidate for arsonist. He was the suspense movie character who watched the fire, measured how everyone reacted, and analyzed how well the fire department did their work. But he'd be more likely to watch the arsonist, in her opinion, with the arsonist never having a clue. That was more his style.

She needed to talk to him not only to rule him out but also to ask what the hell he was doing with the burglaries. How did he know about them in time to intercede, and why did he bother getting involved? Why did he make his way to two of them and not the third?

Why was he here tonight? He'd made himself known to her, then left. What did that mean?

She had zero idea how to find Bruce, though. The standard methods of looking someone up would lead to dead ends, because he didn't leave traces of himself. If she asked around Edisto, people would not know his name. She had no doubt he lived someplace where he wouldn't readily be seen, much less remembered.

She bet nobody even noticed him tonight but her.

Thomas moseyed over in jeans, badge on his belt, not too worse for wear from the mud and the soot he'd managed to collect from his shins down. "Can I ask you something?"

She held up a finger. "Wait, first, have you seen Mark?" He hadn't come over, and surely he hadn't walked home. The restaurant had never been in jeopardy.

"Yeah," Thomas said, and he pointed to her car. "He said he'd be catching a nap waiting for you."

Looking in that direction, she couldn't see him in the front seat, but she liked knowing he was there. "Okay, good." She turned back to Thomas. "As to your question?"

"What does Hightower think about all this?"

"Could be arson but nothing confirmed." She made him recall the solvents, and the plan to remove the red paint. "Trying hard for it not to be arson," she added. "Insurance jackals love hearing that word. It's an easy way to refuse to pay."

He scowled. "But if she could prove she wasn't there . . ."

"The word *arson*, Thomas. Just depends on who ensures her place as to whether they'd cut her a check or shut the door in her face, using *arson* as an excuse."

He gave her a knowing look. "Speaking of doors, I took a look at the back . . ."

"Yeah," she said. "Someone might've broken in."

"Doesn't that clear the owner since she has a key?"

"What if she forgot it . . ." Callie waited for him to come to more of his own conclusions.

"Lots of options," he finally said.

"And we can't plant seeds for ideas used by others to evade the truth, Thomas." She sucked on a lip then caught herself. She had already told Kitty to keep her mouth shut about the A word, just for this reason. "You're free to go home and try for some sleep. Are you on in the morning?"

He shook his head. "No, my day off, but all that wasn't what I wanted to ask about." He glanced across the street.

Nobody stood there and no car remained, but Callie predicted what he was going to ask.

"Earlier there was this guy over there." He nodded to where Bruce had been.

She looked over there, saying nothing.

"Tell me if I'm wrong," he continued, "but isn't he the medic from the hurricane? Not sure I remember his name. Began with a B."

Thomas had seen Bruce only a little while during that chaotic time, when they cleared the road and met the helicopter, maybe a half hour tops. That chopper ruined anyone hearing each other well, too. At the last minute, he'd seen Bruce hop on the chopper with Callie and Stan in lieu of leaving with his buddies. He had no idea about what that last part meant, and he hadn't asked. Callie had no intention of laying it out for him, either. Thomas, of all people in her life, fathomed her use of the *need-to-know* mantra.

"I saw him, too," she said.

"Figured you did." He was no dummy.

"And I was wondering the same thing about him," she said. "Why was he here? Why didn't he come over? It would be odd if that was him, wouldn't it?"

He looked at her hard and shook his head. "Quit bullshitting me, boss." Sometimes he could read her almost as well as Stan could, a credit to his people skills. He was quite the natural when it came to policing, too, and recognizing what should or shouldn't be happening. Or who should or shouldn't be around when it did.

Nobody else was near, but she gave another glance around. Thomas had proven himself as someone who could maintain a confidence, so maybe he could help her look for Bruce.

"Alright, yes. I believe it was him," she said.

"But why . . .?"

"No idea," she said. "Maybe he fell in love with Edisto. Who knows?"

He still looked skeptical. "Young couples, retirees, but not single men. He hasn't been working anywhere I'm familiar with, so what's he doing for a living? Where's he staying? But most of all, why was he here in the middle of the night? It's not like he just happened upon the fire and sat around to watch. And I recognize that car. I'm just not sure from where."

She argued with herself on whether to pull Thomas a hundred percent in on Bruce being the burglary vigilante. He had no idea about Bruce's past other than he'd been a Ranger. Anyone with half a lick of sense would value those skills, but nobody would make the leap that he'd decided to protect Edisto from harm. Hell, she didn't believe it yet.

"I'm in the dark, too," she said. "But . . ." Maybe she'd explain a little further. After all, this was Thomas. "Help me keep a look out for him, okay? I have some questions for him. Me, not you, not Deputy Raysor, not Annie, not anyone but me asks the questions. That clear?"

He looked validated at first. He hadn't been wrong in recognizing the man.

"And don't tell anyone else what you are doing."

He slid back into skeptical. "Why not? And why only you?"

"Because this fire case is mine and mine alone. He was here, and we don't know why. To tell others to look for him would mean explaining the whole hurricane experience as well as label him as a suspect here. I don't care to do either." *Need to know* applied here as much as it had at any other time.

Edisto was a beach town conducive to beat cops. The department didn't have the manpower for her officers to work investigations. Most of them didn't have much in terms of those skills to begin with anyway. If they had, they wouldn't have joined the Edisto Beach Police Department.

Instead, the department and the town were familiar with the talent Callie brought from her tenure as a highly recognized detective, which was part of why she was hired to start with. She'd solved a beach crime nobody saw . . . before they hired her. Alone she held more investigation experience than the entirety of her force.

Her silence told Thomas to back away. "I'll keep my eyes open, Chief."

Another reason for Callie to rely on him was that he lived on the island, and he also lived closer to the bridge. He traveled almost the length of the island to come to work from his tucked away two acres back down Bailey Island Road. He leased the small two-bedroom, worn out house from some legacy family who'd long ago left Edisto. He hoped to one day buy the quasi-shack affair with savings Callie worried he'd never have enough of. At the same time, he worked on a small fishing boat he hoped to one day perfect and sell for something bigger.

He covered a lot of ground every day when he reported to work. He was more familiar with the island people. He would now go the extra mile and take a different road each way, hunting for anyone who didn't belong.

She, however, was not as familiar. She'd vacationed at the beach and now lived at the beach. She was learning the island's silt roads and waterways, but nowhere near like Thomas.

With a two-fingered salute, he told her he had his orders and wouldn't question. He'd learned a long time ago that going along with the chief was worth its weight in perks and opportunities later.

Callie returned to take another look at the devastation. Hightower was packing up the truck.

The door jamb showed damage, but it had been an easy entrance to violate. Few entrances on the beach were all that secure, honestly. She tried to enter like a burglar, thinking like one, but robbing a CBD store at night? Unless someone wanted to seriously restock their lotions, gummies, and tinctures, what was the deal? Most sales took place with plastic, like Amos said. And like Hightower said, the fire seemed to start in front of the counter near the solvent containers, in particular the turpentine can. Not behind the counter, where someone would have gone to find the bank bag.

If there was little cash or anything of substantial value, had the intruder gotten frustrated and set the place on fire out of spite? Or had they screwed up? The reward didn't seem to outweigh the risk, and it almost gave Callie a sense of this feeling rather personal.

Had Kitty come in to clean up and lit candles out of habit . . . maybe? Or Amos lit up a smoke not thinking of what might be flammable? Grand opening day seemed a bit premature for an insurance fire to make ends meet.

The more she thought, the more the Kitty and Amos show made the most sense, even over Malorie setting the place on fire, but their scenario was rather lame, even for them.

After their nine o'clock appointment, she'd address Malorie. And whether she liked it or not, Sophie, because she was in with the first two.

She kept her feet in both worlds . . . the hippies and the normal. That was Sophie. She fit in everywhere because she wanted to take advantage of any perks she could grab from every friend and customer she could. Hell, she hadn't paid for anyone to fix her house in years. Or to remove raccoons from her attic. Or repair her mailbox when a tourist hit it. The list went on and on. She stayed in everyone's good graces for a reason. She had connections. She carried good karma. Everyone couldn't help but love her, even as quirky as she was. Even Malorie, believe it or not.

Callie would bet a week's pay that Sophie had already smoothed things over with her, playing both ends against the middle. Yeah, always throw Sophie on a list of people to interview about anything amiss on the beach. Whether at the station or not, whether a formal interview or not, she always had some flavor to add to the pie.

Chapter 16

Bruce

THE TRUCK'S DASHBOARD read two thirty in the morning, yet Bruce took his time on the road back to Sere's. Despite the night's plethora of awareness and activities, Bruce rode one hand on the wheel, the other elbow on the console to his right, thinking. His heart rate remained steady. He'd learned to control that long ago, in far worse scenarios.

Without question, he was headed toward a confrontation. How deeply he would get into these two men and their pursuits was yet to be determined. The answer depended on who he did any of this for, which was what he really struggled with.

Was he protecting Sere? Maybe, regardless of her misdirected allegiance to the dead-beat nephew. She was alone, money-poor and land-rich with no means of keeping her life afloat without scraping here and there. Her age and lack of resources and relatives lent her toward a rather forced trust in Larue, trust being a rather loose term.

Bruce saw that he had been a welcome distraction for her. For a few weeks she'd been able to pretend she wasn't lonely and wasn't locked into Larue and his petty theft ways of supporting her. One could say she was lucky to have Larue, but the harsh reality was she had no choice. Bruce had become that wishful option. No wonder she doted on him so much. As temporary as he was, which he had professed from the outset, she had held onto him in a way that made more sense to Bruce now.

He saw himself as a breath of fresh air for her, but what ran through her mind now? He'd run out. Where had he disappeared to? Had he heard what she was up to? She'd sent Larue and Magnus off on a quest, a rather foolish quest in both theory and, ultimately, practice, in hope the idiots brought back more than trinkets that would be pawned for pennies on the dollar, but Bruce hadn't returned.

He imagined her looking for him, calling his name, limping outside and wandering around beckoning for him like a dog on an adventure and not wanting to return to its owner quite yet. Hopefully not gone for good.

He felt her disappointment from here. She wasn't a bad person, just someone who had to make ends meet any way she could.

Yes, part of him headed back to see Sere through to whatever end she needed, but he also felt a deeper purpose from another direction. One that could come to no real conclusion other than an altruistic sense of duty. He hadn't felt that feeling since he left the Rangers, but this still wasn't the same.

The police chief had respected him during the storm and given him the benefit of the doubt that there was more good in him than criminal. In an odd form of demonstration, he'd gone solo and left his bad influences right in front of her, almost like he wanted her to be aware.

Their moments at the hospital, after she was treated for the broken nose, remained vividly etched in his mind. That one-on-one represented the genuinely most humble moment he'd experienced in years, talking to someone outside the small Ranger circle. In a way that was damn sad, but in another way had proven . . . comforting. He hadn't realized how long he'd been on alert. That night he'd hitched rides back to the island and then crashed for twelve hours beneath the front porch of an unoccupied house off a silt road, allowing years of vigilance to melt off of him and into the Edisto Island ground.

She stood vigilant for Edisto Beach in a manner he admired. Her community, the economics, the property . . . she stood fast for them all, theoretically standing on that wall that protected her people. That tiny package of power bore the onus of Edisto's safety and did so at a level that Edisto probably didn't fully appreciate. God, he understood that. He admired that. He could almost love that.

While he wasn't the type to welcome love, much less do it justice, he could assist her. Though he'd tended her nose, she'd tended his . . . soul? Regardless, their connection that day instilled in him an odd sense of obligation.

Was that why he'd taken up the torch of dealing with Larue and Magnus? They threatened Edisto in addition to taking advantage of Sere. His so-called obligation hadn't a name yet, but his participation in whatever this was felt more right than most things in his life.

The original commitment, however, to Sere and her two guys, clashed with Callie Morgan and her mission. He was the conduit between them . . . or could be. To do nothing was to not assist the chief. To do something would rob Sere of her nephew. It wasn't like he and Magnus had just taken a bag of dollar bills. They'd left that store on fire, not giving a damn whether it got a little scorched or reduced to ashes.

Without him, Callie wouldn't find the two men. Without him, Sere would be affixed to the shenanigans of what these idiots did, maybe even go down with them since they'd already demonstrated insufficient sense to think. They'd never keep her name out of their work.

Nobody saw them . . . this time . . . and time would tell if they were caught coming or going on camera. In the shadows of night, they'd worn dark colors in the form of hoodies, and they'd parked away from the site. His surveillance of the beach spotted few cams of much worth.

They were dumb enough to get caught eventually. Question was what else would get burned or damaged in the interim. Who might get hurt?

Turning off the main highway, he reached Laurel Hill then Raccoon Island Road. It was two thirty in the morning with the moon still bright enough to see the road like the sandy grains held onto bits of neon.

He pulled up in the old blue Toyota, behind Magnus's red truck, knowing full well that Larue and Magnus would've noticed it missing. His choice of nabbing the Toyota had been to make Magnus drive his pickup, giving the chief some type of connection to the man she sought, particularly on the cam at the entrance/exit of the causeway into town limits. She no doubt had his license, and therefore, his DMV intel.

He exited the car, letting the door slam shut. This time he didn't skulk along the house's wall nor peer in windows. He didn't return to the shed to check on his bags. He waltzed right through Sere's front door.

He'd committed.

Larue and Magnus sat perched in the living room, reliving the night to Sere, seated across from them in her recliner.

"What the hell?" Magnus said, rising to his feet, his chest puffed like he intended to do something about the intruder who'd cuffed him at the first attempted burglary and beat his ass at the second.

Bruce's tight smile kept Magnus from taking a step forward. "Nice seeing you again," Bruce said in his low voice, edged with poised tension. He'd take on Magnus if the man wanted to tangle, but in these few short seconds, the odds became clear that wasn't happening.

"You missed me on that last house," Magnus said, his upper lip tight and daring. "Best haul I've gotten in quite some time."

Bruce regretted missing that third break-in, a break-in he hadn't been aware of until he'd listened to them brag to Sere earlier about the loot. However, he didn't dignify the comment with a reply.

Sere stared at Bruce, and he wasn't sure what he registered in those eyes. Torn allegiance and lots of unspoken secrets hung in the air.

"Wait," Larue said. "Who the hell are you?" His frown deepened.

"And what the hell are you doing in my aunt's house?" Turning to Sere, he seemed to find it odd how she said nothing, not disturbed in the least at this stranger who entered without knocking.

"I've been living here," Bruce said. "Thanks to the most gracious hospitality of your aunt."

The clash of realities stunned Magnus into silence.

Larue exchanged looks between his aunt and this intruder. "What the fuck?"

Not a man for speeches, Bruce left the room to retrieve a glass of water from the tap. He was thirsty, and his sudden appearance had done what he wanted it to. Still uncertain how all of this would conclude, he'd leave his belongings in the shed, not sure where he'd lay his head tonight. He wasn't so sure he wanted his bed to be in this house. Not with those other two there.

Voices escalated in the living room. They'd have to talk for sure, and no telling for how long so he took his glass out back to the porch. The old metal chair, once painted a Miami aqua, sat in its same spot, faded with rust around hinged bolts, giving him the best view of the marsh. The light in the night sky would allow him to see parts of the water, maybe even some wildlife. He thought it might be going on high tide. He hadn't become adept at the instinct of knowing where the water level was at any given time of day. Not like Sere. Probably that police chief, too.

This time of night, though, sounds were far apart. The occasional predator interrupted the ambience by taking down prey, the noise echoing into the distance, but everything soon turned back to silence.

He'd nearly finished his water, and he had about decided to disappear when the screen door creaked. Sere came out, aiding the door to fall softly behind her. She reached for a table, a railing, then a chair, using items in a rote manner to stay stable as she found her porch swing.

He didn't speak as she maneuvered. Finally, she sat, the seat complaining until she settled. "I need money to keep this place," she said, taking some breaths to catch up from the exertion.

She hadn't asked a question, so he gave no answer.

"They don't like you here," she said, then added, "Surprise" with a light smile.

He gave her a light smile in return, but the mood wasn't lightened. Still, he didn't speak.

"Seems you like to interrupt their plans," she said, poking the bear.

He noticed she said *their* plans, omitting herself, but he didn't point that out. Not important. A waste of words.

A creature slapped the water to the right, and Bruce didn't flinch when a bird squawked at being caught unawares in its sleep.

Neither did Sere. "The boys think you're dangerous."

"What other people think about me is not my concern," he said.

"You aren't going to ask me what I think about you?" she asked, trying to be tough.

"Again, no—"

"Concern of yours," she finished for him.

She swung like many nights before, only this time the visit didn't seem so peaceful. Her loyalties were challenged. Besides, Bruce would soon be gone. He'd made no bones about that. Larue, however, had no place else to go.

Pragmatism was the order of the night. Each of them could see that in the other. In a lot of ways, she thought like him.

"I'll stay elsewhere," he said.

"I told them you were welcome here. They don't like it, but I feel like I owe you with my not being honest and all." She breathed deep which made her take an equally deep hacky cough.

"No need." He stood to go put his glass in the sink.

She reached to take it instead, a small reminder that she could still be hospitable. "What's your plan?"

"Making it up as I go," he said, letting her have the glass. He stepped down off the porch.

"Where are you sleeping?" This time she sounded like she really cared.

"Not in the house." He started to go around the side of the house, a totally different direction than she'd expect if he were staying in the shed forty yards away. He was also wondering if he ought to return to the shed he had hidden in before he came here. It wasn't but a couple miles up the road.

"Wait," she said.

He turned.

"You don't say much about how you feel, do you?"

He gave her a light shrug, more of an answer than he'd give most folks. He still liked her, but she had a leak in her loyalty that could not be plugged. Nobody was perfect.

She seemed to sink deeper in the chair, peering down. He gave her more time in case she had more to say.

"They were only taking care of me," she said. "Don't hold that against them."

Sorry, but she wasn't their main focus. Surely, she knew that. "I listened to your speech about land and legacy and ancestors' expectations," he said.

She looked up and raised a brow. "You heard."

"I heard."

Time crept by as he stood there, honoring her as she tried to think of what to say. He was used to people letting him down. She, however, had let her guard down for him and let him in . . . and mucked it up.

"Feel like I lost my knight," she finally said.

"You just woke up from the dream," he answered, and left.

He strode around the other side of the house and kept walking, feeling eyes on him. He circled around and found a comfortable spot in the trees, hidden behind a myrtle he could see through, where they couldn't make him out in the dark. Once all the lights went out, he waited twenty minutes more. Then he made his way to the shed, prepped the ground behind it, and immediately fell asleep.

Chapter 17

CALLIE HAD PLANNED to sleep an extra thirty minutes, but the banging on her front door nixed that hope. Nine times out of ten an early morning interruption came from the neighbor next door. Callie didn't even have to throw on a robe. Mark would remain in bed. That's how familiar Sophie was to them, practically family. There were worse friends one could have.

Callie didn't say a word as she answered, and Sophie strode in like she held a standing invitation. She started babbling two steps across the threshold. "I would've asked you what happened last night, but I had an early yoga class this morning. Just got out."

Her fuchsia-colored tights weren't sweaty, and she'd thrown on a loosely knitted lavender shawl with fringe over her white tank top, one of her more conservative outfits. Sophie didn't set foot in public without all aspects of her image in place.

"Edisto Calm burned," Callie said. "The inside, not the outside. Kitty's inventory is hundred percent toast." She shut the door.

Sophie made her way to the bar between the kitchen and living room, facing through the opening toward the kitchen. "Can you get me something to drink?"

Like a kid coming home from college, she expected to be waited on. "I'm here for you, Callie, and you're here for me, like we always do. Ask me your questions, and then I'll ask you mine. You know you had planned to talk to me before the day was through. You always do. You know I know things."

Jesus, the speed that woman could talk. Callie blinked to make sense of the kitchen clock. It was seven thirty, and she was meeting Amos and Kitty at nine. She needed caffeine.

"Let me fix my coffee, Soph. You're too much of a jolt to the system for me to absorb anything without it. You want a cup?"

Sophie laughed with sarcasm. "You can be so funny sometimes. You're like this dry comedian I used to watch on Saturday Night Live."

"I asked if you wanted coffee," Callie asked, blinking, trying to decide how to make hers. No milk. Black and potent this morning.

"Already had mine," Sophie said. "One cup a day limit. You know that. Fix me something else."

Callie retrieved one of the carrot juices out of the fridge, kept there for surprise moments just like this. She slid it across the bar to her friend then returned to her coffee. She listened to it drip as she leaned against the counter, now wishing she had her robe on after a shiver. The machine gurgled its last drops as Sophie went on and on about who was there last night, and how she'd called around early this morning to *educate herself*, before she came to meet Callie. Sophie hated anything happening on the beach without her presence.

The bedroom door opened. Mark dragged himself out dressed only in sleep pants, Callie's robe in his hand. "Figured you needed this," he said, dropping it over the back of a chair and pointing to the coffee maker. "Think I'll have one of those, too."

"Aww," Sophie said. "You didn't have to get up for my sake. I was just here for your lady." She then smiled wide. "But thanks for the view, Cajun Man. Love the chest hair."

Mark cut a slow smile at Callie, inferring there was no way to sleep in this house with Sophie's mouth turned on. They'd have to go to bed earlier tonight. Callie slipped on her robe then came to the bar, throwing a banana at Sophie, something she always ate without fail. Mark remained back at the coffee pot, his forehead against a cabinet door, eyes shut.

"Well?" Sophie peeled the banana. She'd do so halfway then save the other half for later, taking it with her. She ate less than a bird.

"Well," Callie repeated, stealing a couple sips before having to carry on a conversation. Sophie's interview was on her agenda today, but she preferred prepping for it fully dressed and after breakfast, her brain engaged. "The fire was set with an accelerant," she said.

Sophie sucked in a deep breath, full of drama. "Arson?"

"No, Soph, and don't you run around town spreading that, either. You'll screw up Kitty's chances of an insurance settlement if that word gets around."

Her demeanor changed on a dime. "Oh, I wouldn't."

"Actually, you would, so remember me right now, this morning, sitting here in my robe, telling you not to say that word. To anyone. Okay?"

"Rude."

"Realistic." Callie sipped more coffee, feeling the energy seep in. "I was going to call you to come in, by the way."

"I sensed that. It's why I came over."

"Of course you did."

Sophie felt she could predict things, see the future, and talk to dead people. There'd been a few times Callie had seen moments that made her ponder the truth of those assertions.

Even from her bar stool, clad in her robe, Callie went ahead and questioned Sophie. Informal was more productive when dealing with her anyway. If she could see a talk as more gossip than interrogation, the more cooperative she was.

Callie started with something to pique Sophie's interest and hold it there for a while. "Kitty said something I feel might've been said by accident last night."

Sophie sat up straight. "Ooh, what?" Her mouth gaped then shut, then opened again. "You're asking me to confirm someone's secret, aren't you?" She was totally interested now.

Lowering her voice, Callie asked, "Kitty thinks Malorie started the fire."

Sophie reared back, patting the air with a hand. "No way. Malorie's all mouth. She was already calling me this morning, hoping nobody pinned this on her. She wasn't even at the fire. She was at Whaley's on a date."

Callie couldn't see Malorie on a date. She couldn't picture the kind of guy who'd want to, unless he was a male version of her, in people's business and stirring trouble. "Anybody we know?"

Sophie gave little shakes of her head. "Nah. He's from Mount Pleasant. A real estate agent but not a decent one. Sells houses under half a mil, and that's chump change in Mount Pleasant. I hope she dumps him. She could do better."

That was debatable.

With Malorie having a confirmable alibi, Callie leaned in, taking this to the next level. "Kitty said something else, too. Are you aware of Kitty and Amos being partners?"

"As in . . . sex?" Sophie asked. That would be where her mind would go first.

Okay, they could start there. "Sure. As in are they seeing each other?"

The giggle answered for her. "Yes, aren't they cute? And how funny is it she sells CBD, the fake stuff, and he—"

"Sells the real stuff?" Callie finished. "As in what kind of *stuff*?"

With a pucker, Sophie tried to blow off the slip. "Even I've bought weed from him. I mean, not all the time, because I can get it cheaper . . .damn."

"I'm not after pot smokers."

Sophie's shawl slid a hint as her shoulders eased. "You had me worried there."

"What does he sell?" Callie asked again.

Sophie repositioned, like she had this. "Weed."

"What else?"

"Things I don't use."

"What would those things be?"

Sophie's eyes narrowed. "If I've never bought or used them, how would I know?"

"You know. You know people who know. People talk to you about things they wouldn't say to God."

With a cock of her head, Sophie took that in. A smile spread. "Thank you, Callie. That means an awful lot!"

"You're welcome. So what else does Amos sell?" Hopefully the third time was the charm.

A manicured nail went up. Coral. Already repainted this morning. "If I tell you, you cannot say where it came from, okay? Otherwise, I lose my confidante status."

Guess it was okay for her to rat as long as Callie didn't mention the rat by name. Made sense in Sophie's world. "Promise. Cross my heart," Callie said.

Tucking her feet under her rock-hard bottom, Sophie leaned an elbow on the bar, the other hand left to talk with. "He prefers pot. That's his main market, which we all know is meaningless anymore. That silly man has good product, and he's likely to light up right there with you, you know?" She laughed. "You gotta love him."

"Good salesman," Callie said.

"Yeah, right?" Sophie giggled, probably in memory of her latest high with him.

"And his other products? I'm sure he's just as good there, too. The reason people love him so much."

Sophie's light dimmed a tad. "He doesn't do pills, though, if that's what you mean. But he does offer. . ." She looked over at where Mark stood in the kitchen, busy over the stove making something. "Is he making us breakfast?"

"Maybe. Focus, Sophie. Finish your sentence. *But he does offer . . .* what?

"Coke," she said, with a turn to face her friend, more serious than before. "Not my thing, and when I hear anyone taking it, I try to talk them out of it. Nothing good comes of any of that."

"On that we agree."

"Sad the people on that crap." She jerked upright. "And don't you go after them, either."

Callie relaxed on her bar stool, for Sophie's benefit. "No intention to. Besides, you gave me no names."

"Right," Sophie said, sniffing, smelling the bell peppers and onions sizzling in a skillet.

Callie saw her opportunity. "Mark, would that omelet happen to be for Sophie?"

"Maybe," he said, having heard everything, pretending he hadn't. The acoustics in the kitchen area were damn good. "She want anything else in it?"

Sophie turned to Mark. "Do you have spinach?"

He shuffled back to the fridge to see. "Yep."

"How do you connect with Amos?" Callie asked.

"Most of us call him. We used to meet him just about anywhere," she answered, attention still on Mark. "No meat, okay?"

He raised his spatula in acknowledgement.

"What do you mean *used to*?" Callie asked, not reminding Sophie that an egg was a cousin to meat.

"No butter either. That's animal fat," Sophie added, then without missing a beat said to Callie, "He's at Kitty's store now, silly. Just makes sense, doesn't it?"

It did. Malorie McLauren hadn't been too far from wrong. What, if anything, had she known as fact about Amos's activities? Were her accusations speculation or rooted in experience?

"Is he who you're protecting, Soph?"

"Don't want him caught, is all. It's best he not have a headquarters, you know?"

Good heavens. Callie wondered how she'd been so slow with what was right in front of her. Then there was Kitty's remark in a fit of dismay outside the fire . . . *We owe people.*

Amos had commented about how she kept money under the counter. What if that wasn't the only thing stored under the counter?

Amos, you idiot.

"Give Sophie your best super-duper breakfast, Mark," Callie said. "What would we do without her?"

Once asked to perform, Mark's breakfast presentation would indeed merit a cover feature for *Bon Appetit* magazine. With a kiss of appreciation, Callie left him entertaining Sophie while she showered and dressed, eager to pull three more people aside for questioning at the station.

The fire investigation drove her, but Amos's purported drug dealing ranked a close second, though. Fire would be the thrust of her efforts with these people, the obvious. She leaned toward talking to Kitty first. She didn't appear as put-together as Amos, and despite his cool nature and nothing-rattles-me behavior on the exterior, he must have some level of business acumen to be handling coke on Edisto. She prayed his activity was no more than a sale to the occasional tourist or the infrequent resident.

She liked Amos, but he didn't live high enough to indicate he made much from his drug endeavors, leading her to believe it was little more than a hobby to help him earn a living. He was a long-time resident of the island. He wouldn't want to mess up that legacy any more than Callie would. Someone on the outside looking in wouldn't understand that. He was comfortable.

But Kitty might've been a tempting means to something more, something that he'd never had access to before nor given much thought to, and with the store not his, she presented a fresh opportunity. Callie nor anyone else she'd spoken to on the town council or in the community thought of Edisto Calm as anything more than Kitty's dream, and the products no more than items that were a hundred percent legal.

The fact that Amos carried the pot-head reputation while dating the legitimate CBD saleswoman only added to the ambience of the store with its colorful paint job and hippie vibe. Customers were able to feel a tad naughty going in, with the peace of knowing they were perfectly legal, part of the vacation feel. The location being what it was and too many eyes on the store's business, Callie doubted drug dealing would've gone too long without being noticed.

She needed to think more about Amos. What was the opportunity that drew him into Kitty's business? Just the money? A business partner with perks?

She came back out to find Mark cleaning up and Sophie gone. The woman never stood still in one place for long. Even when working at El Marko's as Mark's afternoon and evening hostess, she couldn't just seat people. She chatted to the regulars and straightened chairs, refilled glasses and made suggestions to those not familiar with the menu . . .

anything short of clearing a dirty table. Not with those nails.

"Did she say anything about the CBD store business?" Callie asked, coming to Mark, adjusting the firearm on her side.

"Not about Amos and Kitty," he said. "That's something, though. What's your next step?" As a retired investigator, he would be interested, and Callie welcomed any and all suggestions. She'd hire him if she could, but he much preferred his restaurant by day and being the random consultant by night.

After listening to Sophie and thinking in the shower, Callie had changed her mind about interviewing Kitty first. "I'm going with Malorie if I can arrange that this morning. After talking to Soph, it makes more sense. Also, I don't want Amos to get wise and lawyer up, and even if he does, I don't want him to tell Kitty to lawyer up, so the order is Malorie, Kitty, then Amos, with no time in between Kitty and Amos for them to collaborate."

"Sounds like a plan," Mark said. "Especially since Malorie damaged her reputation and established doubt. Her threats atop her confrontations with Sophie and Kitty, then the paint . . . she'd be high on my list. Not too bright a criminal, but she ranks up there in terms of suspects. Knock her out first."

"Good, then I'm off," she said. "Don't let Sophie talk it up at the restaurant, okay?"

He shrugged. "I'll do my best. She's like a bottle rocket, you know. Pretty to watch but no telling where she'll go."

Leaving, she grinned at that visual. In the car she checked the time. Five after nine. She'd told Kitty to show up at nine last night but wasn't sure she'd heard or would bother. Instead, she called Donna Baird, the only person she could think of who might have Malorie's phone number.

When Donna picked up, Callie heard birds in the distance. "Are you already outside walking Horse?"

"It's what we do," she said, then in an aside said hello to someone in passing. She loved working the people of Edisto, now twice as much as she had before the election.

"Stan with you this time?" Donna had gotten him to do therapy for his broken leg via her walks, once he could maneuver the stairs on his own. Horse had learned to slow his gait to that of Stan's, walking alongside him, just in case. For a man who'd never had a pet before, he'd come to love this beast.

"As a matter of fact, he's right here," Donna said. "Want to talk to him?"

"Let me talk to you first. Do you have a number for Malorie McLauren?"

"Ooh, that woman . . . I'm sure I do. A week doesn't go by . . . give me a second."

Callie waited. Malorie loved staying atop of council's activities and sculpting an opinion on whatever they had on their plate. She deemed it her role as a resident to stay keen on everything, and with Donna being the newest council member, and a woman, of course Donna would have her number. She went out of her way to assimilate and that included hearing out the residents. Malorie liked to be heard more than most.

Donna texted Callie the contact.

"You made her one of your contacts?"

"Yes, after the third call I figured it inevitable. What's up?"

Callie didn't want to spread word about the investigation, but the fire was already headline news. "The fire last night."

There was a hesitancy before Donna replied, "I can see that." And she was smart enough not to ask more. "Now do you want to talk to Stan?"

"Sure." Callie put her phone on speaker and started the car. She was late enough as it was.

"Hey, Chicklet. How's it going?"

"Investigating a fire," she said.

"I assumed so. I hate that place burned. You ever tried gummies before?"

She had to contain the laughter. "Can't say I have. Now you're a fan, I take it?"

"Slept like a baby last night. Didn't help the snoring, per my favorite council lady, but I went coma-like and stayed there 'til morning. Damn fine discovery, in my opinion."

She released a funny humph. "Glad you like it. Just don't overdo them or you'll wind up like Amos."

This time she got a humph in return. "Ain't happening. Guys like that are trouble, just in slow motion."

"You just confirmed you're sleeping with Donna, old man."

"Never said that."

"You all but said it. Go ahead. Own it. I think she's good for you. Horse has given his approval."

Some silence before he said, "Baby steps, Chicklet."

"Not what you'd say to me. Anyway, thank Donna. I'm pulling into the station now."

"Late start?"

"Thanks to the fire last night. Talk later."

She hung up, gathered a couple of things from her passenger seat, then looked up, doing her usual canvas of the area before leaving the locked vehicle.

Malorie waited outside, arms crossed, a cigarette going and a scowl across her face that would stop traffic. Guess she was going to be Callie's first interview after all.

"How's it going?" she said, approaching the woman.

"Thought you were supposed to be here by nine?" Malorie said, throwing down the cigarette only half smoked, crushing it beneath her leather flat. When Callie raised a brow at the littering, she stooped over and picked it up, looking lost as to where to put it.

"Just bring it in," Callie said, taking hold of the door handle. "There's a trash can right inside the door."

"I thought—" Malorie started, hesitant to cross the threshold while Callie stood waiting for her to do so.

But then Callie understood why. Inside both Kitty and Amos waited, seated on the old leather sofa against the wall.

Extracting real answers from these three would be like pulling teeth, and Callie told herself to dig in and just do the job.

Chapter 18

ONCE INSIDE THE station lobby, Malorie spoke first. "Kitty said you said to be here at nine, Chief, but I'm not waiting with them. And I wanted to tell you, in front of them, that I had nothing to do with that fire. I haven't even returned to that damn store since that. . . earlier incident. Except to drop off the money." She pivoted toward Kitty and pointed. "Tell her. Tell her I paid you. I don't want this hanging over my head."

Kitty had already told Callie earlier, but Callie let her hit replay. "Yep, she paid me," Kitty said, droll.

Malorie spun back around to Callie. "See?"

"Yep," Callie said, not telling Malorie that Kitty had complained to town council.

"So I can go now?"

"No, ma'am. Let's go to my office and have a chat."

She stiffened, even taking a step back. "But I paid her."

"There are a few other topics of discussion, and out in the open is not the place to address them." Callie moved toward the swinging door that would take them past the counter to her private office.

The office manager Marie remained attentive to her work on a screen, having heard such controversial conversations so many times under this roof. If Callie needed her help, she'd be there, but otherwise, discussions between cops and civilians were background noise.

Malorie hesitated to follow. Callie held the swinging door for her, moving it back and forth a couple times to make her point. Finally, with the room's attention on her, Malorie proceeded.

"Have a seat," Callie said once in the office, motioning to the two chairs before her desk. Malorie chose one, and Callie shut the door, removing the temptation for Kitty and Amos to eavesdrop from the lobby.

"Why didn't you ask me to come here this morning?" Malorie asked as Callie retrieved her recorder from the top drawer and arranged it on the desk. "Why did you have Kitty tell me?"

"I didn't ask Kitty to tell you," Callie said. "I was going to call you once I arrived, but there you were on the doorstep. I appreciate you being here, though." She pulled out a notepad for thoughts and prompts. Only took a minute to set up having done this so many times before.

"Wait," and Malorie looked at the door like it had a window in it. "Kitty told me you required all three of us to be here at nine."

"Again, I'm glad you were here." Callie clicked on the recorder, noting the time, place, and names of the people present. That stopped Malorie from rattling on, shutting down any complaint against Kitty. There was something about words being on record that made people think twice before saying them.

For five minutes, Callie did a rehash of the previous day at the grand opening, preserving on record the details leading to the fire. Malorie had a way of wrinkling her nose at the parts focused on her.

"Yes, I did spray paint a display," Malorie confessed. "In hindsight I wish I hadn't." But then she was quick to add, "And I paid her five hundred dollars for what I did, though, to cover the product and the work to clean up the paint. It wasn't that bad, and I think that figure was more than sufficient to do the job. Sure, I wrote a check, but I promise it's good. By then the bank was closed, and the gas station's ATM limited me to two hundred dollars." She then repeated, "The check is good. Honest."

Malorie fed the recording with lightning speed comments and recollections, Callie letting her. Her ramblings and utterings spoke of who was present, the time of day, what was said, even the weather. All of it was accurate. Little of it needed explanation. Not only would this word vomiting prove more efficient, but Malorie might say things Callie hadn't planned to ask.

"I think it pissed me off that they wouldn't let me see behind the counter and in the storage room," Malorie said.

"Why would you think they should?"

"In case that's where they kept the real drugs," she said, without a blink. Malorie seriously thought drugs were handled in the store, whether out the back or under the counter or upon request. Obviously, she felt someone familiar with any form of weed was into all forms of weed. A shallow, naïve belief, but she owned it, and it justified her behavior to a certain degree. In her mind she protected Edisto Beach from the rest of the town that would've approved, licensed, and issued a grand opening for a venue to sell illicit substances.

Callie let Malorie go on a little longer, and about the time she wanted to cut her off and redirect, Malorie ran out of steam. "Did you see illegal drugs?" Callie asked, wanting to make a final point regarding Malorie's obsession. "Did anyone else tell you they saw drugs? Did you see anyone make such a purchase?"

"No."

"Was that a no to all three questions?"

"Yes."

Then in a moment of pity for the woman, as if the recorder wasn't even on, Callie asked, "Why are you pushing the drug side of things so hard if there isn't any proof?"

"Because like I told you, marijuana is a gateway drug. My sister was the perfect example of it, and she died."

"I'm sorry about your sister, Malorie. I really am."

"Thank you."

"But like I told you, CBD isn't marijuana."

"Same plant."

"Not really," Callie said. "But we need to move on. When was the last time you were at Edisto Calm yesterday?"

"When I gave Kitty the check. She didn't like getting a check, but that's how it had to be."

"What time was this?"

"Between seven and eight. They were in there scrubbing the floor."

Callie jotted details down in addition to the recording to get details and timeline on paper. "They?"

"Kitty and Amos."

"Nobody else?"

"Not that I saw. Not unless they were hidden in that storage room. A drug client would've hidden themselves, though."

Callie didn't bite. She did, however, stop and lean elbows on the desk, like the next question made a big difference. "Did you go back after everyone went home and start that fire?"

Hand clutching her collar, Malorie exclaimed, "No!"

"Did you go back and steal anything?"

She inhaled, stunned. "Of course not."

"Did you not tell me yesterday, when I pulled you aside from your confrontation with Kitty, that you hoped the place *burned to the ground?*"

This time the inhale choked her, and she coughed hard, like she'd sucked down a mouthful of spit. Once finished, sniffling from the effort, she cleared her throat. "I. . ."

"The question calls for a yes or no answer, Malorie."

"Yes, I did say that, but I meant someone else, not me. I wouldn't dare break the law."

Callie laid down her pen. "Other than vandalism with a can of red spray paint?"

More throat clearing. "That was . . ." and she stopped, hunting for the word.

"Unintentional?" Callie asked. "No, you meant to do it."

"I don't have a word for it," she admitted. "Because it wasn't a nice thing to do. Any other day I would not have done it."

They went round and around, Callie asking questions in different ways to see if she got the same answers. She did. She also acquired the name, phone number, and address of Malorie's date, and which waitstaff at Whaley's could cover where she was and who she was with last night. Problem was that the fire was set after all the restaurants were closed.

"Any chance you slept with the boyfriend?" Callie asked. "Had him over for the night? You know, giving yourself an alibi?"

Even middle-aged, Malorie blushed. "He didn't stay the night. He left around midnight. I went straight back to bed."

Callie didn't bother emphasizing the *back to bed* part.

"Bottom line, Malorie, is that I believe you. But you do need to come up with someone to cover you between the time your beau drove away and one o'clock in the morning."

The woman thought hard, mumbling to herself while walking through her evening, searching for the alibi she so desperately wanted to leave on record. She wanted, as did Callie, for her to cover herself, walk away, and be deemed innocent of anything criminal. "I just went to bed," she said meek and sad.

"Anything on your phone during that time? People often lay in bed and text, comment on social media, and send emails. Maybe even make a call?" Callie wanted to remove her from the suspect list almost as much as Malorie wanted to be off it.

Yanking the phone out of her purse, Malorie scrolled here, punched there, starting and stopping and changing direction until she found her conversation on Facebook with someone about a certain kind of makeup on sale from a celebrity in Hollywood. She spun the phone around to show Callie. The time said eleven hours ago, which would fall in the time frame. But that could have been done on the way to setting the fire.

"I'm sure there's more," she said, returning to scrolling. "Yes, here." She pivoted the screen toward Callie, showing her an Instant Message conversation with her niece in Tennessee who'd just come off a date of her own.

"You wouldn't have to be home for that either," Callie said.

Malorie reddened again, flashing embarrassment. Callie had no idea why. Slowly, Malorie turned the phone around again, only this time peering down, not wanting to see Callie's expression.

The selfie showed shadows of suggestive lighting. Malorie lay across a disheveled bed wearing a pink lace nightie that bulged her arms and boobs too tightly. Her hair was unkempt, and her chin and cheeks rubbed raw from the lovemaking. She'd donned a fresh coat of lipstick, still wore false eyelashes she'd never be seen wearing in public, and grinned like she'd just conquered her man. Callie slid her finger up, revealing the meta data. Time 12:45 AM.

Close enough.

Malorie began to tear up. "Please, please, please don't show this to anyone. Or tell anyone."

Callie fought to maintain a grip on as serious an expression as she could manage. "I wouldn't dare do that to you, Malorie. I just need to remove you from suspicion. I may have questions later, but for now I'd say your bases are covered."

Malorie sniffled and put her phone away, shame coating her like suntan oil in July.

"Don't lose that picture, though," Callie said.

Her guest shook her head, still not making eye contact. "Is that all?"

"We'll be needing your fingerprints, but we'll be in touch for that. So sure. Go on. Thanks for coming clean with me on . . . you know. Our secret. I promise."

With a slight nod, Malorie eased out.

She'd lost her sizzle. Her public appearances wouldn't be so loud for a long while.

Callie didn't ask her to tell Kitty she could come back. She didn't think Malorie was all that excited about being seen in the same building as Kitty right now, her shame flashing off her like a motel no vacancy sign.

Callie came out to the counter, seeing that the woman made it through without incident. Both Amos and Kitty rose.

"Just Kitty," she said.

Kitty looked at Amos for him to argue. "But we're a team."

"Not in my office." Callie turned, emphasizing this was not up for discussion.

Divide and conquer was a real thing. At a minimum it made for less drama.

Like Malorie, Kitty wanted exemption from suspicion. She would also want to see all of this mess trussed up neat and tidy and clean enough for her insurance company to rubber stamp the claim.

Callie shut the door like before, Kitty grimacing like being confined was insulting.

"For privacy," Callie explained. "And to avoid interference on the recording. Nothing sinister, I assure you."

Kitty sat poised, so unlike the hippie vibe she gave off at the store. Her age came through louder without her cool and tranquil air sculpted for the public. There was nothing easygoing in her eyes anymore.

"Let's start with an idea of what's damaged or missing," Callie said, once the recording started. Best go with a factual topic that didn't require opinion. Callie had seen the site and could estimate the damage, but best she hear it from the owner.

Kitty seemed to like how this was starting, like this was an accident claim. "The fire was limited to between the counter and the front door. Six displays are ashes, and two displays damaged. The counter is smoked up and may need replacement. I hate that, because Amos built that himself. I really need Amos to account for what else is ruined."

"I'll get to him in a little bit. The register was behind the counter. Anything missing out of it?"

Kitty shook off that possibility. "Looked mauled to me but no matter. I didn't leave any money in it."

"That's good," Callie said. "But I thought you said last night you were missing several hundred dollars."

Looking at Callie like she totally missed some point, Kitty explained with her hands and a little piece of drama. "I had a bank bag missing from under the counter. It held the money and a couple of checks. Can't believe people still write checks, but with the bank closed, we left the money under the counter. There's a lock on that bag that's next to impossible to get into. Amos keeps the key. But with most sales paid with plastic, it isn't much. Better?"

This was a totally different Kitty than the one so distraught last night, the one talking about how they were supposed to fulfill some financial obligation after all this damage. She stated the bank bag was missing. But without much in it, the theft appeared minor in relation to the rebuilding and restocking required for Kitty to get back on her feet.

This event could be anything from a sloppy theft to something malicious. A thief having no clue what was valuable in the store, maybe. Or a person angry about the store's existence and wanting to burn it down, with that latter scenario having Malorie's name all over it to the average person. That rumor might stick to her for a long time, too, because she wasn't about to reveal her alibi.

Then there was always the suspicion of self-destruction for insurance purposes. But who burned down their new business on grand opening day?

"Let's go back and create a timeline," Callie said. "Start from when I left you with the red painted floor to when I saw you at the fire last night."

Kitty took Callie from the store to dinner at El Marko's to going home, but without giving the address of where home was. Of course, Callie asked. Honestly, she had no idea where Kitty lived and had, therefore, assumed it wasn't within the town. Kitty hadn't been seen much around the beach but for the last six months.

"Amos's house," she said, almost whispering, then glanced up waiting for a reaction she'd have to respond to.

Callie was familiar with Amos's place. She wasn't surprised they lived together and honestly didn't care. Few behaviors surprised Callie anymore. One had to confess stabbing five people and eating them for dinner to astonish her.

"Go on," Callie said as benign as she could, leaving the topic comfortable. "You live with Amos. You went home with Amos after dinner. When did you go back to the store last night?"

"When a friend called. A friend of Amos's anyway."

"About what time?"

"After midnight."

"Who called?"

Kitty shrugged. "You'll have to check his phone or ask him."

Callie gave her a thoughtful pause. "Y'all didn't scrub the floor somewhere in that timeline?"

Her posture perked up. "Oh, yeah, well, we did do some of that after dinner. Made some good headway, too."

"So you left the solvents in there?" Callie asked.

"No need carrying them home."

"And the rags you used?"

Kitty nodded. "Sitting right there in a coffee can." She froze. "You're not saying we might've started our own fire, are you?"

Callie wanted her to think about that for a second. "Did Amos light up while he was working?"

Kitty literally had to think about that, like she wouldn't have told him not to or he wouldn't know better. "No. He had his hands full."

"Y'all light any candles?"

Her guest scrunched her nose. "Not wasting my scented candles like that. You'd never be able to smell them over that stench."

"What time did you leave the store to go home?"

Head tilted, Kitty seemed to be adding the hours. "I guess I'd say nine. The fumes were giving me a headache."

There was nothing there to turn into suspicious activity, nothing to hang one's hat on. "Okay," Callie said, changing the topic. "Once you were called about the fire, did y'all go to the store together or separate?"

"Together, in one car. Why does that matter?"

This might sound trivial to Kitty, but an accurate timeline was the foundation for any crime. "What time did you arrive?" Callie asked, letting Kitty's question go unanswered.

"Twelve forty-five. They wouldn't let us inside at first. They got it under control quickly . . . just not quick enough. Guess we ought to be glad the building didn't burn down." She teared up. "It only just burned everything inside."

Callie passed the box of tissues. "Do you know anyone who would want your shop destroyed?"

"Malorie."

"Besides her."

"No."

Callie shifted subjects, because discussing Malorie would only draw out the ire in Kitty. "Let's move to something else. Who are you in debt to?"

"I have a car payment. I don't have a house payment."

"No," Callie corrected. "Just regarding the business."

With a tip of her chin, Kitty acknowledged she understood better. "I have a line of credit with the supplier of my product. Amos invested in the start-up costs. You know, painting the inside, constructing displays, installing the lighting, building the counter, which he did, like I said. You remember the inside, right? It had been a real estate office."

Callie remembered indeed. Last February a fresh personality in her thirties had sashayed onto Edisto Beach and set up shop in that little building thinking there was ample room for one more real estate expert. Her naivete cost her big time as the lack of interest sent her out of business by September. Nobody asked what happened because everyone understood that Wainwright Realty was what happened. All because she'd dared cross the causeway into town without asking. The official license came from town council. The unofficial approval, however, came from the residents for any enterprise to succeed. Kitty was learning that.

"Whose name is on the license of Edisto Calm?" Callie asked.

"Mine."

"Not Amos?"

"Just me."

"Whose name is on the lease?"

"Mine."

Callie was already aware that in a fit of arrogance, Janet had acquired the Edisto Calm building once she ran that other agent out of town . . . and Callie always bet she regretted the purchase. It sat empty for almost a year before Kitty came along. Now that Callie was aware how active Amos was in the business, she guessed it only took a quick mention in Janet's ear by him to get that lease approved.

Speaking of Janet, she'd soon want the ins and outs of when the building would be free for repair, even if she held several months' rent in advance for times just like this. The Marine was rarely caught on her back foot.

Amos had hung around the building and assisted often, once Callie thought about it. He'd hung around the picketers, presenting himself as one, but on second thought, he'd wanted the business to succeed, drawing attention while diluting the animosity by inserting his jovial nature into what could have gone sideways.

They chatted about who else might have made snide remarks about Kitty's choice of enterprise, but no one had much of a problem with CBD. Not anymore. Vacationers maybe sampled them for the first time on Edisto, thinking it was a fun way to experiment with the chill, but CBD stores dotted the country like drug stores now.

In the end, the interview took no longer than Malorie's. Kitty was shocked, hurt, and scared. Genuinely and understandably so. Not sensing any insurance fraud or other concocted scheme to make a buck, Callie wrapped up.

"I think we're good." She rose. "You can scoot home, if you like. I might be a while with Amos."

Kitty seemed puzzled. "Why interview him? He would tell you nothing different than what I told you, Chief. We're a team."

"Procedure, Kitty. He's in on the store with you. I can't talk to one and not the other, and we're not allowed to talk to people together.

Interviews are strictly one-on-one." She shrugged. "My hands are kind of tied thanks to procedure." A small fib, but close enough to the truth.

An open-mouthed expression of slow understanding hung a moment. Finally, she nodded slowly. "I can see that."

"Appreciate it," Callie said, escorting Kitty to the lobby, not giving the two a chance to exchange ideas before Amos came back.

Slowly but surely, Callie sensed another side to the Amos she thought she understood. What was his attraction to this tiny business? Was it a matter of assisting his new lady friend in the name of love, or was the business something he saw potential in, with Kitty just a perk on the side?

Something also told her this next interview wouldn't be so quick. She would suspect Amos to be savvier, and he would suspect the discussion to be more than about the fire.

Chapter 19

AMOS FLOUNCED in like the middle-aged, lackadaisical islander he was with no stress sticking to him at all. "How ya' doing, Chief?"

He didn't get two feet inside her office before Marie poked her head in. "Town council said to call one of them when you can." She darted attention to Amos, Callie getting the subtle, silent hint it was about the fire. "They said if you didn't have time, maybe Thomas could come by—"

"No, ma'am," Callie replied. "They can wait to hear from me."

They already wanted an update because their phones were probably ringing from business owners. Edisto Calm hadn't been open long enough to establish a following. The council had already hit up Chief Hightower for his insight per a text she'd received from the fire chief.

Edisto's small-town ivory tower never missed the opportunity to appear loftier than they were. None of this was their call to make. A building had burned, lives weren't lost, the fire department did their job, and now Callie's people were doing theirs. It hadn't been twenty-four hours, and they wanted to be able to brag to the constituency that *they'd* taken care of business.

They could wait. She had an investigation to complete.

For a split second she expected Brice LeGrand, the dead councilman, to push his way into the station demanding answers, then she caught herself. No. Those days were over.

She wouldn't put it past Donna Baird to do an impromptu drop in, though, asking for a lunch partner to accomplish in her subtle way that which Brice used to demand.

Marie left.

Opening a new file for her recorder, Callie explained to Amos that the conversation would be on the record, and this was part of an official investigation.

"Amos, trace your steps from the time Malorie sprayed red paint inside the store to when you arrived at the fire last night," she said.

"Whatever Kitty said is good with me."

She narrowed her gaze. "You sure you want to go with that?"

The nonchalance in his demeanor slid a little. "Why, what did she say?"

"It's just easier to tell me where you were during those hours, Amos. Unless she lied and you're trying to match up your story with hers."

"No, no," he said, not so laid back anymore, but attempting to show he wasn't rattled either. "Start when?"

"When Malorie spray painted the store."

He gave the right time since, after all, others were there with Callie having come up on them right after it happened.

"I left," she said. "Take it from there."

They went to dinner. They scrubbed the floor. They went home. He didn't hide the fact Kitty was living with him. He'd had women live with him before. During Callie's tenure, she was aware of at least three others, but none of that weighed into anything.

Everything matched Kitty's report.

He got the call from a friend, and Callie made him name the friend, someone she was aware of and who could easily confirm Amos's statement. So far his timeline matched Kitty's.

"Let's talk investment," Callie said.

"What do you mean?" he asked.

"Kitty stated she didn't have the money needed to fully fund the enterprise. Is that true?"

He did a little mouth shrug thing. "Yea, pretty much."

"She states you've been involved almost from the outset of Edisto Calm. That you are very educated in the whole venture, top to bottom."

He chuckled. "She's lived and breathed this store twenty-four seven, so I ought to be. Woman has breathed this store since I met her."

"Which was when?" Callie asked.

"What, when I met her?" He didn't seem comfortable with the shift off of the store.

"Sure. You jumped on this train when you met her, I take it? She hasn't been local but maybe six months, Amos. How'd you two meet?"

Easy question, or so that's what his expression said. Callie would decide if it was the truth or not. Amos had a lazy way with that as well, so often full of himself and dodging anything that let you see inside him. She'd always wondered what his own story was. Everyone on Edisto had one.

Note to self: ask Sophie. Then get the other side of the couple's story from Marie. Between the two, Callie would have a better picture of the real Amos.

"She came to the beach to scout it out about eight months ago," he said. "Met her at Coots one night when she couldn't find anyplace else open to hang at. We closed the place down . . .with a few others, I might add. She told me her plans, having decided she wanted her shop on a beach, but wasn't sure which one. I asked her out again, we chatted, and I sold her on Edisto." He swept out his hands. "Just call me an ambassador."

"Good for you," Callie said, his animation easy to smile at.

He smiled back, all pleased with himself.

"And just like that you decided to invest in her business?"

The smile thinned a bit. "Not exactly," he said. "We sort of fell in love. Wasn't until she couldn't find a place she could afford to lease that I offered my assistance." He'd mentioned *in love* with a waggle of his brows.

"Go on," Callie said.

"I put a bug in Wainwright's ear about the building. It was empty. Janet needed someone to buy it, lease it, use it for something other than an empty landmark. Once I nailed that for Kitty, everything went green light."

"Are you part owner?"

He acted like he'd tasted something sour. "No need to be."

"I heard you invested your own money."

He turned positive on that note. "Sure did. Guess that shows how she has her way with me, doesn't it? Ain't love grand?"

Callie pulled up a grin for him. "Seems to be." She wrote in her notebook something that really didn't matter. She just needed time to think. "Mind my asking about how much you invested in Edisto Calm?"

The question didn't ruffle him. "I didn't invest in the store. I invested in Kitty. And I sort of lost track because I'm not really expecting it back. She'll earn a living from it. I already have my little gigs as well as a small retirement. It's a contribution to the cause . . . the cause being *us*."

His little speech didn't sound as genuine and loyal as he thought it did, but he made it sound bigger than life with his gestures and inflections. But Amos made going to lunch sound that way. Life was to be lived, he'd say, and his antics made it seem more memorable and important.

Amos played to his crowd, but just how much of his *love* was playing to Kitty's crowd of one? It really wasn't Callie's place to question his feelings for the woman, and she walked a tightrope in asking him about how much he had invested in the business. The fact he had was one thing. How much, well, just say he had dodged that answer.

"Did you have to borrow any money?" Amos's involvement with even a meager pot business meant he had clients and a supplier, and money changed hands. He could have had enough money of his own, but what if he hadn't? "Kitty made mention of others you owed money to. You were there."

She stared at Amos like she already knew the answer, pressuring him to cut to the chase.

"I have wealthy friends," he said. "They owe me favors, so they gave us a small loan. I don't care to tell you who and when. Don't have to."

"Don't really need to know . . . right now," she said.

His smug grin bordered condescension. "That's right."

"Are they investors?" she asked anyway.

"Just friends," he said, hammering his point again.

She shifted gears. "Amos, do you sell weed?"

"Maybe," he replied, just as level as you please.

"Do you sell harder items?"

This time a move with the eyebrows, but no verbal response.

"As in drugs, Amos," she said with sarcasm as big as his pretense that he didn't understand.

"I try not to," he finally said.

That was a fresh response she hadn't heard before. "Rumors say you do, and that you might be dealing out the back of Edisto Calm."

"Chief." He wanted to wind up his story. "People are gonna hate. And those like Malorie are going to exaggerate to be heard and get their way."

"Wasn't Malorie." She could see him dialing through the Rolodex in his head of potential snitches.

Smart enough to realize the chief of police would not reveal her sources, he went another direction. "How would anybody even know if I did? We'd just been open that day, and not even a full day at that with the spray paint incident."

"So you just help inside?"

He laughed. "I don't even do that. Can't run the register and staying pent up inside don't sit with me."

Indeed, he had been outside for the better of the day, with Callie and Annie having watched him and his dancing, hooping, and hollering. He socialized with everyone coming and going, like he was no more than an Edisto Beach fixture.

"Any idea who set the fire?"

"None at all."

"You were in there with Kitty cleaning up the paint. Maybe you spilled one of the solvents you were using, and it caught fire?"

"We left for dinner, worked on the floor, and left, not coming back until I got the call about the fire," he corrected. "Hours later," he added.

She wrapped up the interview, seeing it as no more than checking a box with what little she got from either one of them, Kitty or Amos. Odds were they were purely victims.

Callie remained where she started, with the same question of whether some fool tried to rob the place and caused the accident, or if someone had deliberately lit up Edisto Calm. She'd already instructed Thomas to attempt to collect prints off the counter area, to include the register. The fire hadn't spread back there, the counter giving enough of a barrier long enough for Hightower and his people to stop the fire. She could hope that the thief, assuming there was one, left prints all over the register. If they were inane enough to think they would find enough money to make a break-in worth their while, maybe they were thick-headed enough not to have worn gloves.

She had an uneasy spot inside of her, though, that told her Hightower's report would say the fire was started by a solvent, which leaned toward something intentional, meaning Kitty would have an uphill battle trying to get her insurance adjustor to pay without using the A word. At least the police report could state no proof that the two owners were anywhere near the building at the time. Maybe that would help Kitty's cause.

Callie would, however, keep a keener eye on Amos. He didn't necessarily need a CBD store to run drugs. He was a mainstay on the beach. His territory was wherever he was on Edisto.

Chapter 20

Bruce

SUNLIGHT WOKE HIM. Heading to the marsh, the tide rising, he handled his morning ministrations, rolled up his belongings, and stashed the two bags. One being his clothes and minimum needs. The other was his medical bag from his days as a medic, the one used to save the police chief's friend during the storm. The one kept such that he never had to ask for medical help.

He made a wide, rounded search of the area, to take stock of who was there and who wasn't. Back around to the shed, he parked himself on the porch again, knowing Sere would come out sooner or later.

The sun set over the water of this property, so he couldn't watch the morning sun fill the sky. It didn't take long, however, for birdsong and shadows to tell him the time. He'd lived here long enough to recognize how this worked.

Before long he smelled bacon. It wasn't Sunday. Sere only cooked the good groceries on Sundays.

The screen door opened. Out came Magnus and Larue instead of Sere. One parked himself in a regular chair, the other about to park himself on the steps, then changed his mind. Instead, Larue hiked a butt cheek onto the railing, such that he could look down upon Bruce.

"You took my car last night," Larue said.

No question. Bruce resumed scanning the water.

Magnus tapped his booted foot on the floor near Bruce's rocker. "Answer the man."

"He didn't ask a question."

The two buddies looked at each other, Magnus trying to make an inconspicuous nod to his partner.

"Where'd you take it, then, because I know you took it," Larue asked.

"To the beach."

Again came the knowing looks between each other, before Magnus decided to take the reins. "You left after we did and returned after."

When Bruce said nothing, he remembered to reword his remark in the form of a question. "Why did you come back?"

"To return the car. It wasn't mine."

"You didn't ask if you could borrow it," Larue said, going for a snarl which fell short this early in the morning. "Why not?"

"You weren't here to ask."

The two kept exchanging looks like they could read each other's minds, facial expressions indicating they were totally unable to. But they were too fearful to speak openly in front of Bruce who let the routine play on, somewhat enjoying the comedic nature of these men who thought they controlled the dialogue.

"What did you do at the beach?" said Larue. "Moon bathe?" He laughed at his own joke, not noticing he laughed alone.

Bruce shifted crossed legs. "I watched a fire."

The laughter ceased. "What kind of fire?"

"A building."

Larue's nervousness filled his eyes, and as hard as he tried, he couldn't help but shoot a worried glance at Magnus. When Magnus didn't give him guidance, he asked Bruce, "What building?"

"Edisto Calm."

At first the location didn't register. Larue couldn't recall the name of the store. Then he seemed to add up some of his thoughts, and he asked, "Is that on Jungle Road?"

"Yes."

Magnus, however, tired of the game. "Did you see anyone go in there?"

"Sure did."

"Son of a bitch," Larue whispered.

"Did you see us leave?" Magnus continued.

"I did."

"Now what?" Larue yelled. "He probably thinks we set it on fire on purpose! Who's he gonna tell?"

But Magnus sat back, staring at Bruce, like he attempted to peer through his skull and predict what was inside being tossed about unsaid. "I don't think he would tell anyone. Otherwise, he'd already done it."

Honestly, Bruce hadn't made up his mind on that, unsure whether he fell on the side of Team Sere or Team Callie. He wouldn't make for a very good witness for the chief. He would be a horrible person to place on a courtroom stand.

But if she were half the quality detective he suspected, she'd get these two to confess in enough detail for their attorney to beg for a plea deal. No courtroom required.

That would mean leaving Sere on her own, robbing her of this piece-of-crap balancing on the porch rail.

Maybe these guys would decide this for him. "What did you get in the bag you took?" he asked, and Larue about toppled off his perch.

Magnus was the one who saw the opening. "Why, you want in?"

"Depends on how much you're talking."

At a moment when Magnus ought to feel potential taking shape, he blew it. "Not enough to share, that's for sure."

"What about the blow?" Larue whispered, asking as if in the quiet nobody would hear but Magnus.

So there were drugs in the bag. "How much?" Bruce asked.

"Ten eight balls," Magnus said. "Enough to make a difference on Edisto Island."

That made Bruce turn his head and pay direct attention. "That's at least fourteen hundred hits. You normally deal?"

Magnus started to swagger, a story clearly building in his head.

"Don't bullshit me," Bruce warned. "Are you starting from scratch or do you have a list of buyers already?"

"Just bought, never sold," Magnus said, his expression eager to hear more from someone who just might understand the business.

God, these two were easy. They'd scored some cocaine, by accident no less. Not a monstrous amount, but not a little bit, either. Whoever it was meant for surely had a market waiting for it. Not like in a city where his customers could number in the hundreds or more, but enough to justify its existence. He'd love to ask the chief about her experience with drugs out here.

"What do you think, man?" Magnus asked, like the chasm between them was narrowing. "You ever use?"

Bruce shook his head.

Larue used his boot toe to tap his friend's leg. "We ought to try it. See what we got. Might not even be drugs." He tried to do the same to Bruce, like they were a trio now, but Bruce shifted his weight so that Larue's toe missed. "You up to sampling?" he asked Bruce, not even noticing the snub.

"No thanks." No telling what the powder was, but the odds weighed heavily on the side of cocaine. Maybe laced with something. Maybe not.

The two studied each other without talking, imagining their next steps. Larue no doubt pondered how to taste their wares without Magnus finding out.

"Dealers don't use," Bruce said. "They are usually too smart for that."

"Yeah," Magnus said. "Dealers don't use. They're too smart to use. Hurts the profits and you don't know if it's decent stuff or not."

Larue frowned like he was denied popcorn at the movies. "On TV they stick their pinky in and get a taste to make sure it is what they say it is."

"Y'all got a talent for tasting quality stuff?" Bruce asked.

"No," Larue replied. "But it's free."

Bruce almost wished he'd go ahead, overdose, and prove he was the dolt everyone thought he was.

But Magnus came to the rescue. "He used the word *smart*, idiot. Which apparently you aren't."

"I'm not a moron," Larue said.

Bruce almost expected Magnus to come back with an *are, too*, like two brothers arguing over who got the ball. He didn't, but he was, however, calculating how these baggies that fell into their laps could be used to further their future.

They didn't give one thought to who the drugs might belong to, as in the dealer those baggies had been given to, and the supplier who had delivered them, the person who would expect to hear back about how well the product took to Edisto Island.

Bruce wondered more about the store owners. A CBD store, no less. That seemed rather in-your-face, but it probably depended upon who the owner was.

Magnus and Larue had no idea the game they'd decided to play.

The scales would soon begin to tip. These morons wouldn't be able to deal without the rumor mill coming to life. Word would get back to the original owner, and then the original supplier. They wouldn't be happy, and Magnus and Larue might be blindsided by an attempt to recoup the product and whatever money they'd collected. If these idiots got caught by either the cops or the ill-sorts who originally owned the dope, they would point fingers, hunting excuses, and, since they were living with Sere, they might spew that the robbery was for her, making her the gang boss. After all, she'd put the idea of robbing the store in lieu of more houses into their heads.

If the owners of the store were attempting to become active in this side business, the chief needed to know. The owner could develop a following overnight, right under Edisto Beach's nose. The ignorant, the educated, and the wanting-to-learn CBD buyers might decide to pull the seller aside and ask if they were aware of any real dope in the area, because they didn't know any better. Once informed, they'd return. And they'd spread the word.

But the owner's plans had been stifled, interrupted by Magnus and Larue. Even if the owners had paid for the dope, they couldn't recoup. The supplier would be aware of the heist, the failure of the owner, the spotlight turned onto the business, and the cops snooping around.

The illustrious Magnus and Larue duo would have people on their tails, and they could lead some dangerous folks to Sere's doorstep.

There was one solution to this, but Bruce wasn't holding his breath that it held a chance in a thousand of happening. "You need to return the cocaine," he said.

"What?" Larue sounded like a kid in puberty.

"You just put a light on yourself," Bruce explained, wondering why he bothered. The pragmatic Bruce would walk away and let this whole mess implode, because these two would muck it up. The only reason he didn't was because of the two women now in his life.

Sere would pay a price for these boys, and the chief would be scrutinized by her community. He couldn't walk away unless these idiots before him walked back what they had done.

"If you like, I could drop off the bank bag at the police station, telling them I found it," he said.

Magnus busted out laughing. "You must really see us as losers if you think we'd trust you."

"Yeah, you stole our car, man." Larue's smile split his face ear to ear. "Like we're supposed to trust you."

Imbeciles. Bruce would try one more time. "Then one of you take it in."

A slight hesitation then they laughed again. "That chief wouldn't let us go. And if we just dropped it off at the door and ran, somebody could steal it, we'd be out everything, and someone else would get rich. That would paint us real ignorant." Magnus stopped his rocker and with a rusty sounding creak across the old floor, he turned his chair toward Bruce. "Any more great ideas, dude?"

"Yeah," Larue echoed. "Those really suck."

Magnus furrowed his brows. "And don't think you're not part of this. You're stuck with us, dude. You know too much. You don't go along with us, we could kill you in your sleep. So, what do you say?"

Bruce had tried to show them a way out.

And he'd killed people in their beds before if that was a membership requirement. He could take them out in their beds and rid everyone of all their problems.

Except this was Sere's relation. He wished that wasn't so.

"What do you say, dude?" Magnus asked.

Bruce gave them a nod.

Game on, dudes.

Chapter 21

FIVE DAYS WENT BY.

Janet Wainwright had marched all over people's asses, demanding the fire department claim the fire wasn't arson. Demanding the police do the same. Demanding the town pay some of the loss if insurance didn't cover damages since they hadn't protected her property as a government entity should. Demanding Donna Baird, as a member of council, coerce Callie in aiding any of the above. Demanding Mark convince Callie to get the town, the insurance company, or even SLED to solve this crime and make things good financially. Janet was coming at anyone and everyone in a whirlwind with every possible argument under the sun to cover her bases.

Callie was avoiding her. She added nothing to solving these cases.

The insurance company hadn't decided yet on whether it would cover Edisto Calm's damage. Kitty's insurance company for the contents was waffling as well, considering they hadn't opened but one day. Yet Janet leaned on Kitty to clean up the place after the adjusters left. Otherwise, Janet would cancel the lease giving Kitty no chance of making up the loss.

Kitty and Amos and different volunteer personalities cleaned up the debris for the first couple of days, and Mark sent snacks and occasionally a meal for everyone. Kitty admitted being glad she got paid that five hundred dollars by Malorie and especially the couple hundred from Sophie for product, or that would've gone up in smoke as well.

That still left Callie with the open cases of a fire and the two latter burglaries. As much as she regretted the decision made at that first burglary, she had to let it go. She'd screwed up releasing Magnus. Ill-fated for sure.

If she'd nailed Magnus right off the bat, maybe none of the other events would have happened, and that included the fire. The powers-that-be needed something to hang their excuses on, so she became their biggest excuse for the new crime wave on Edisto Beach. Not that they blasted her across the airwaves, but they didn't protect her back when chatter was whispered in bars, restaurants, and assorted commercial enterprises.

She told them the owners of the second and third burglaries had recognized Magnus. That was something. And when town council decided to pin the fire on him as well, she couldn't disagree. Even she had to wonder if he had indeed branched out into robbing the store and maybe screwed up in the process.

Made sense. He'd failed in two out of three housing robberies, so his success odds weren't that great. However, in his decision to escalate and hit the third one so fast after the other, rather unexpectedly as far as burglaries went, he'd scored. If he'd felt emboldened afterwards, why not hit a store? The very store whose grand opening fanfare had enabled him to hit the houses, with the cops preoccupied. Then taking his burglary talents into the night, he'd hit a place everyone thought was locked up tight until morning.

Forget that stores rarely kept cash around anymore, but nobody said Magnus had proven to be particularly wise. Thus far, however, he'd managed to stumble in the right direction.

He wasn't getting rich, but he still took home a few thousand dollars in the last heist. Now he'd disappeared off the radar, which was smart after the identifying damage done to his face.

Once she had completed her interviews the day after the fire, she'd gone to Magnus's residence, speaking to his mother this time, then again to the eighteen-year-old mother of his child next door, but they hadn't seen him for a week. Clearly, he was lying low. The Charleston County Sheriff's Department promised to keep an eye out for his vehicle, but Charleston was a big county, and the case wasn't theirs. You could go weeks on the big island and never see a patrol car, demonstrating the extent of their interest in the remote area.

Likewise, she'd put Thomas and her other officers onto Magnus's truck, but nobody had found joy. Marie looked at cam footage. She told her favorite town councilwoman to have everyone she knew to watch for the vehicle, meaning a lot of people kept their attention open. Callie had bases covered for that damn truck.

Marie had not been able to discern the tag of that truck on the causeway cam, nor the tag of the car Bruce had driven that night. She saw them, though.

Callie likewise kept one eye out for the Toyota, the one Bruce had been resting on the night of the fire. She hadn't delved into him, where he might be, what he might be up to. He might not even be on the island anymore. Part of her wanted to run him down, and part of her wanted to keep him as elusive as the specter he liked to be. To open that door could open too many other doors. He wasn't a suspect . . . at least in these crimes of late.

There was somewhat of a kindred spirit feel to Bruce, which went against Callie's instincts . . . until the times it didn't when and she could not put a finger on what the deal was with him. She read a deep substance into the man, that he consisted of a strong sense of . . . she didn't know . . . humanity? Not the right word, but he operated on an unofficial code.

She likened Bruce Bardot to a Jack Reacher type. Military trained with a deep core of right and wrong. Maybe not how the general world interpreted the up and down, left and right, positivity and negativity of mankind, but a code he lived by. He'd killed in war, no doubt, but he hadn't killed as a civilian. That might be part of his code.

Unless he faced a situation in which he felt he had to kill, and no doubt he would do so in order to protect the right person.

She got that. She had too many notches on her own belt as proof.

She'd rise in the morning thinking yes, she'd run Bruce down, but by dinner she'd come up with reasons why not. She focused on Magnus instead. She kept telling herself if Bruce wanted to connect with her, he would. If he had something to offer, he would. She had nothing to connect him to any of this, so she told herself she didn't have the time to spare.

Though the beach was Thomas's employer, not the island, which was the county's jurisdiction, she had him assigned to traverse roads for an hour or two at a time. Methodically, he scouted for Magnus's vehicle, the map in his car marking off which roads had been covered.

Callie worried Magnus had disappeared into Charleston County and gone to ground. These cases might remain open for some time to come.

In her canvassing this late morning, the fifth day after the fire, she pulled into the Edisto Calm parking area when she realized someone was inside. Three times during the day, someone had asked if she'd solved the cases yet. Three times she had to say *open investigation* but assured whomever that they had a suspect.

"So why haven't you picked him up?" they'd ask.

"He's disappeared," she'd say.

Then she'd get the looks. On television, people who hid out were sniffed out via cams, cooperation from all the different police departments, forensics, helicopters, and satellite.

The same number of times she was asked, she bit her tongue, fighting not to spit back, *Hell, people, this is Edisto Island where most people don't know what a Ring doorbell is.*

"The way technology is, you'd think it would be easy," some even said.

Tell that to town council next time they decide the police budget, she wanted to reply.

But as the town of Edisto Beach expected her to do in her goodwill efforts with visitors and residents alike, she smiled, said they were doing their best, and reminded herself that this was a tourist community. Insulting people got neither her nor the cases anywhere.

The front door to Edisto Calm was propped open along with the windows allowing a cross breeze. Being November, there was a coolness to the air, but she smelled chemicals and burnt wood before she reached the entrance, so she understood the ventilation.

The room was singed for the most part except for one spot in the middle where the fire started. There one could see through to the ground. Kitty had done an amazing job emptying the room and was in the process of scrubbing everything down in order to judge best what had to be replaced and what was salvageable.

"It's not as bad as one would think," Callie said, wandering over to where Kitty rubbed on the frame around a window.

"You can still smell it though," she said, taking a moment to rest her arm from the work.

Callie sniffed. "Yeah, but could be worse."

"A lot worse," Kitty said, laying down the rag and capping whatever it was in the bottle she used. She pushed red hair out of her eyes, locks that were supposed to be contained in the psychedelic rag wrapped around her head and trailing behind her neck.

She studied Callie, like the chief's arrival meant news. "Caught the guy?"

"Not yet," she said, wondering which line she ought to use with Kitty about why the case was still open. "Where's Amos?" she asked instead.

Amos had kept his distance from Callie since the interview. Where Callie would see him ambling around the beach at every turn before, she hadn't seen him once since they talked in her office.

Kitty pushed hair back out of her eyes again, with Callie itching to just tuck it up under the scarf for her. "He's been helping," Kitty said. "It looks like it'll take a while to get a check to make all of this right. In the interim, he's talking with his friends again about a loan." She looked around the room, as though taking account of how much was needed. "He said he has to spend time with them to convince them, so he's been in Charleston for the last three days."

Private financing. "The same people who gave you the first loan?" Callie asked. "I can't imagine Amos groveling, but I'm guessing he has to suck it up to his friends to convince them this place can repay two loans."

"Oh," Kitty said. "We'll give them insurance money."

"I thought you only had content coverage? Janet's insurance covers the structure."

"Amos said he'd help Janet by doing a lot of the work himself. Like before."

Callie almost asked how much of a loan he was going for this time, in hope of hearing how much they'd already received, but that was crossing a line. It wasn't her business, but the fact Amos was handling all the financing with nothing in his name was suspect.

"Good luck dealing with Janet. Felt her out yet on all this?"

"Amos said to let him handle that. Janet needs us to reopen as soon as possible, not go under, so she'll accommodate us." She scoffed. "I'm not familiar with the details. He just told me to clean up the place and keep things looking like we're actively planning for a reopening. Never miss a day being here, he said. And always look busy."

No wonder the building looked so good.

"A contractor friend of his has been by twice, taking measurements. Says we could reopen in another week if we're lucky." Kitty's smile was genuine, almost beaming. "So hopefully the day before Thanksgiving," she said. "What do you think?"

The time frame seemed awfully short. The story about Amos's money friends sounded suspicious. Amos's purpose for his absence was dubious at best.

"Sounds like you've got a plan." That was all Callie could think to say to what were loose ideas at best. Amos made promises to buy time while Kitty remained clueless, just happy that her store was still a viable dream.

An uneasiness filled Callie, like a hurricane not quite on the horizon but predicted to hit land. You couldn't see it yet, and the weather hadn't made unusual adjustments in warning, but there was a sense of it. From the hints and forecasts and instinct honed from years of chasing bad guys, the hairs on Callie's arms stiffened.

The focus, however, was still on Magnus. Every Charleston County deputy who worked the island, though you could count them on one hand and have fingers left over, had received the BOLO on him along with the make and model of the truck. Thomas continued to cruise roads hunting for the truck.

She would start over, talking to people she'd spoken to before. Time made memories return.

A knock sounded at the open door.

Thomas stepped inside. "Hey, Kitty. Chief. Place looks better. Opening by Christmas?"

"Hoping by Thanksgiving," Kitty said.

Thomas looked at Callie, trying to hide his *no-way-that's-happening* thought.

"Did you catch the guy?" Kitty asked.

"No, ma'am, but I'm scouring every road, path, and deer trail for him. If he's on Edisto, we'll get him."

"Good," she said. "Who do you think it is?"

"Thomas," Callie interrupted. "What did you come for?"

"Police issue," he said. "Can you come outside?" He tipped an invisible hat at Kitty. "Sorry."

"Ooh, go ahead," she said, and returned to her rags and cleaner as Callie made her exit.

Callie took Thomas all the way to his cruiser, adding road noise to the background such that Kitty wouldn't accidentally hear. "What is it?"

"There's some new activity around the island," he said.

Callie scoffed at the ambiguity. "Not feeling a joke today, okay?"

He peered side to side. "No, Chief. I mean it. There's a new person selling coke on Edisto."

"Oh, great. How much are we talking about?" she asked.

Drugs were the last thing they needed. The island hadn't been drug-free under her tenure at Edisto, no place was, but it was cleaner than any other beach in the state. She'd been to enough law enforcement gatherings to hear the complaints and feel the concerns from other chiefs.

"Not a truckload, but we're talking dozens of sales. Different dealer, cheaper cost. I'm thinking novice," he said.

Or someone who needed quick money.

"Any sign of sales here? In town?" Always Callie's first concern. The main island belonged to Charleston County. She could not police that area. The town of Edisto Beach, however, was all hers. Any action on the island eventually made it to the beach, though. You couldn't get to the sand except through the jungle, plus the island's remoteness kept sales unseen.

Lips tight, Thomas gave her a negative. "No action heard of in town . . . yet. Looks like it's being sold to common folk. Not the wealthy. It's like it's being introduced, too, because half of the cases I heard of had never taken it before. So again, I'm thinking new dealer."

Not good at all. "Anyone describe the seller?" she asked.

"Young white men. Heard two descriptions." He lowered his voice. "One matches Magnus Sims, Chief."

"What the hell?"

"Yeah."

Instantly she thought about having let him go after that first burglary when he had been left there for her just short of having a bow on his damn head. He was a criminal who now had a partner.

Now she wanted to talk to Bruce in the worst way.

"What are you thinking?" Thomas asked.

New dealers and new users meant no established routine. People would take note and spread the word. "I need you to keep your ears open and see what else you can snare. How did you find out?"

"Prince."

Anyone not local wouldn't understand what that one word meant, but Callie did. Prince Langley, who went only by the name of Prince for cocky reasons anyone could guess, was a colorful man in his fifties who lived far out Clark Road. He rambled far and wide, though, showing up at most of the island church functions, sometimes making appearances at the beach parades or holiday fairs. A black version of Amos to a degree.

Sometimes he arrived high. Other times he was looking for how to get there. He'd outsmart anyone novice in cutting deals.

"Did they sell to him?" Callie asked.

Thomas gave a clipped laugh. "Yeah. He told me he couldn't pass it up. They were selling at twenty-five percent less than the norm, and he wanted to cash in before they figured out what they were doing. I'm surprised he didn't just buy them out."

This time Callie returned the short laugh. "First, he didn't have the cash. Second, he didn't want to take Magnus's place, assuming it *was* Magnus. My spider senses are telling me that Magnus, in his burglary ventures, stumbled across more than money and jewels and took full advantage of taking possession."

She watched to see if Thomas was reading her before she finished the thought. He wasn't. "Somebody missing their dope is also minus a hefty income, and chances are they owe money to the person who supplied them," she said.

Thomas whistled. "That idiot has stepped in shit."

"And probably has no idea he has."

Callie peered at the store, seeing Kitty periodically go by a window, earnestly working at the renovation. In her ignorance, Malorie might have pointed a finger at Edisto Calm and accidentally hit bull's eye. That is unless attorney Dorothy Calloway on Mikell Street, the third burglary address, had a stash that Magnus got his hands on. She'd have the income to be a recreational user, but this sounded like more quantity than that.

Callie's gut kept coming back to Kitty's place. Amos was known for supplying weed. Who said he hadn't supplied more than that to the tourist crowd, and that, like Malorie professed and Sophie hinted to, was dealing out the back door of the CBD store.

So pinheaded. Or was it smart? Whichever, if Amos indeed had graduated to cocaine, he was missing some of his supply. Either he was out there selling fast dope to make ends meet, having told Kitty he was working on a loan from friends, or he was coping with a disgruntled supplier.

These types of misunderstandings and sloppy business methods could result in nasty consequences. Now she wondered where the hell Amos really had been for the last few days.

"I need to talk to Kitty again," she told Thomas. "You head back to Prince and anyone else you are aware of and dig out all the information you can. Ask if they know where Magnus is staying. He's not at his residence, so that means probably on the island. Ask what car he drove. See if anyone got the tag."

Her bet was he wasn't driving his own vehicle because of her knowledge of him. Her second bet was he was staying with the owner of that second vehicle. His partner in crime.

Chapter 22

CALLIE WAS ABOUT to slide back into Edisto Calm and have another discussion with Kitty about Amos's comings and goings. When did she last see him, specifically, and when was he expected back? When had she last spoken to him and where was he at the time? While she acted awfully naïve, Kitty could be playing a role to protect her lover. Callie wondered whether Amos was already late in returning, and if Kitty even knew where he really went in the first place.

"Chief?" Thomas queried. "Anything else?" He'd been waiting for additional instructions other than snoop out the island. "Want me to call one of the others and see if they'd like to swap times with me here in town while I continue back on the island?"

"No, you're on duty, and if I need anyone else, I'll call them. Keep doing what you're doing."

He squinted, not hiding at all that he was trying to read what she had planned without him, in case he needed to have her back. He was good that way.

Personalities besides Kitty ran through her head, along with the order in which to confront them. Their main suspect was Magnus. She and her uniforms needed to amp things up a notch.

"Need a timeline, Thomas," she said. "Go back to your contacts and note where he's been and when. The vehicle . . . Like I said, you know what to do."

He left in his cruiser, his mission taken to a new level.

No doubt it was best she nab Magnus before the real owner of the drugs did. Real karma would see him caught and dealt with by the party he'd wronged, but that wouldn't exactly be proper for her to allow, would it?

She might be jumping to a few conclusions, too, but it was reasonable to assume that Magnus didn't have the means to purchase a volume of coke to sell and that he'd acquired it from his thievery. No self-respecting dealer would supply him for fear the product would go up his nose, up his friends' noses, or sold for less than necessary to maintain a standard in the region. Therefore, he had to have stumbled upon a stash. Most firearms used in crime by low-level criminals were acquired via home thefts, and the theory applied here as well.

She started to veer left and visit Mark, ever busy at El Marko's, and pick his brain. When he retired from SLED a few short years ago, he'd been involved in a drug deal that went sideways. The average person would say get his advice, but the experienced cop in her said his contacts were too old to be of value, even if he had been familiar with the Lowcountry trade. She'd speak with him about her thoughts, facts, and theories at home that night, and he'd dole out a suggestion or two, but to talk to him now would interrupt his work and make him worry for her the rest of the day.

Kitty came to the door for a breather, maybe to check on who might be outside. She was alone and probably tired of being such.

Perfect.

Callie strode from across the street, waving for Kitty's attention. "Let's sit outside where the air is cleaner," she suggested, taking a seat on the benches. Kitty joined her.

"You aren't wearing yourself out, are you?" Callie asked.

"Of course I am." Kitty put her head back and shut her eyes to feel the sun on her cheeks. "Thanks. I needed to do this," she mumbled.

"Kitty," Callie started. "I need to ask you a few more questions, if you don't mind."

"Sure," came the reply, eyes remaining shut.

Callie almost hated to interrupt the serenity. "When was the last time you spoke to Amos?"

Kitty didn't open her eyes, but a flash of a wrinkled brow came and went that would have gone unnoticed if Callie wasn't studying her. "Night before last."

"Is that unusual?"

"What do you mean?"

Callie watched closer. "I mean does he ever go a day without checking in with you? It's just what a lot of couples do."

Some silence passed before Kitty answered. "We've never been apart more than a day, so I wouldn't know." By avoiding a direct answer, she had indeed answered.

"Have you tried calling him today?"

"Yes." The word felt weaker.

"Did you try yesterday?"

"Yes. Went to voice mail."

"Kitty?" Callie asked softly. "Open your eyes."

But she didn't. Instead, a lone tear leaked out.

"Come on, Kitty. Talk to me. Where's Amos?"

When she raised her eyelids, the teardrops slid free, rolling down freckled cheeks. Kitty spoke forward, toward the road. "He cleaned for two days, made calls, then left. Said he was seeing to our financial future and for me not to worry."

"Did he say who he was seeing?" Callie asked

"No. Just said friends from Charleston."

"Did he say when he'd be back?"

"As soon as he could, but probably no more than two days."

Nobody had to say he'd stayed too long.

"Kitty, look at me."

The middle-aged hippie did as she was told, and Callie's heart hurt at the pain in the stare. "We all know Amos loves his weed."

Kitty waited for the full impact of what was about to be asked.

"And," Callie continued, "we all know that he provides a handful of people their weed when he's asked. Before you get even more worried, I don't care about his weed."

There was a big unsaid BUT in Callie's words that the densest person would hear.

"Does he do coke?" Callie asked.

Frozen, not even blinking, Kitty sat unspeaking. Callie gave her a moment until it appeared Kitty wasn't going to reply.

"I need an answer. Does he do coke?"

"Sometimes," she said. "Not very much though."

Callie continued. "Not surprised. Now, answer me this. Does he ever sell coke to others?"

This question shot life into Kitty. "No." She sat up and repeated, "No, not ever. That's a slippery slope, Callie. That's not him."

Oh, but Callie begged to differ. Amos was indeed the type to use, and since he sold weed, he was also likely to distribute cocaine. How could he not? A steady client comes to him for a few joints' worth, Amos happens to have some powder on him, and he pulls it out and asks, *Ever try this before?*

If the buyer trusts Amos, and who didn't, really, they might trust him in trying something a bit stronger. Just this once, mind you. This was Amos, the infamous, laid-back Edisto Beach hobo who was on first name basis with everyone from the mayor to the dishwasher at every restaurant.

"Kitty," Callie started again, in a slightly different direction. "Was he intending to sell either weed or coke through Edisto Calm?"

That popped Kitty upright, and a red flush washed up her neck and into her face. "I knew it. This is about Malorie!"

Callie kept her voice calm. "That's deflection, Kitty."

Kitty lowered her anger. Callie watched her emotions shift into something akin to that of a child caught cutting school. If only this were so innocent.

"He never said, but I suspected the weed." Then Kitty flashed up again, briefly. "But not the cocaine. Like I told you, he doesn't sell that."

"Where's his stash?"

"Of?"

"Anything. Pot or coke. He'd keep them in the same place, I imagine."

"He kept pot handy. On himself, mostly, but he also had a bag of it under the cash register."

"Did you ever handle it?"

"No!"

"Had you intended on handling it? Ever been curious enough to peer inside? To see how much was in there?" Callie would have in Kitty's shoes.

But Kitty gave little shakes of her head. "No. Didn't want to know."

Callie could see that. "Any chance you use People Finder on your phone and that you have Amos on it?"

Kitty shook her head. "Can you see him allowing that?"

No. Honestly, Callie couldn't see Amos wanting to be tracked by Kitty or anyone, with or without cocaine involved.

"So, you have zero idea where he is?"

"No," and tears filled her eyes again.

"One more question," Callie said, beginning to feel like she was almost beating up on the woman. Kitty wasn't far from being an innocent player in all this. "Did he mention anything about where he might be going? Tell me the truth this time."

"You mean more than just Charleston?"

Callie nodded.

"No. And he told me not to call, yet I did, Callie. I'm wondering if my calls messed something up." Her chin dripped now, and she used her arm to wipe it dry.

"You were worried where he was going."

Kitty sat straight and sniffed before clearing her throat. "What would you think if he didn't tell you where or with whom nor exactly when he'd be back? Only that he was handling the finances to keep my dream alive." The dam broke. "Does he love me this much that he'd risk . . . something, not sure what, just to make me happy?"

Callie reached around Kitty's shoulder and gave her a deep hug.

But she felt she had the answer to Kitty's heart-touching question. This was Amos. While he got along with anyone, with a personality even a stranger couldn't help but like, Amos took care of Amos first. Maybe he liked Kitty. Maybe he hadn't thought of using her at first, but Callie's instinct told her that he took full advantage of the opportunity to at least sell his weed. The coke was up in the air, but in her years of experience, someone didn't disappear over weed. Maybe he would come back soon. Maybe he would be home for dinner tonight. Callie hoped so, because she had a long list of questions for him.

She squeezed Kitty again and let loose, then stood. "Call me if you hear from him or when he comes home, okay?"

Kitty seemed hesitant.

"I'm going to talk to him sooner or later, Kitty. He's on my radar. He's got to talk to me."

Callie received a slight nod from the woman, which was good enough. Didn't matter. Callie would have enough feelers out. . . assuming he returned home.

She walked off, leaving Kitty in her misery. There was nothing Callie could say to make her feel better. Frankly, she could find it quite easy to make her feel worse, honestly, but there was no point since time would take care of that.

She entered her vehicle and headed west, having unconsciously chosen to deal with Kitty first and Attorney Dorothy Calloway second. One down, one to go.

It was mid-afternoon, so the counselor shouldn't be taking one of her five o'clock imbibing sessions yet. Residents, however, often walked the beach on days like this in the fall, so she hoped Calloway would be home.

A good sign was seeing a Lexus parked under the house on Mikell Street.

Callie pulled up, not surprised to see one of Calloway's friends from across the street poke her head out the door at the sign of a police car. Callie waved, getting a wave back then a hasty retreat.

Calloway answered the knock. "Chief. Come on in. Did you catch the thief? A Magnus Sims if I remember correctly, right?" Calloway had memorized the name from the driver's license picture Callie had shown her.

"Yes, that's correct. We're pretty sure this is our man, but he's gone to ground. There have been sightings of late, though, and I just sent one of my men to check one of them out."

"Good, good." Calloway left the entryway, leading them to the living room, the very place Magnus had been pilfering when Calloway caught him in the act.

"So, what's up?" Calloway asked, having poured herself a bourbon neat from the color of the liquid. She had poured her own drink so intuitively as to give the impression that was the rule upon entering this room. When she held up the bottle asking Callie if she wanted one, Callie motioned a no. The retired attorney topped the bottle then took her seat.

Callie let the stately woman assume her seat of choice before taking hers. "You haven't seen Magnus Sims around Edisto, have you?"

"Oh, no. I would have called you."

"I thought so," Callie said. "Listen, we believe he's started selling illicit drugs very recently, specifically cocaine. He has a partner we haven't identified yet. They are so lame in their dealings that I don't see a self-respecting dealer doing business with him . . . them. I think I know the answer to my question, but bear with me, I must ask."

Calloway held up her glass as permission to proceed.

"Do you keep cocaine in this house?" Callie asked.

There was no instant recoil and no adamant denial. Instead, Calloway sat back in her leather tufted chair, and Callie recognized a story to be told.

"You know," Calloway started, taking a hard look at her glass before resting it on the arm of her chair, collecting her thoughts. "I actually had a client who wanted to pay me with two kilos. Knowing my client, and knowing the value of his offering, for a split second I entertained the offer. But no, I don't do coke. I don't have cocaine in the house. Booze is my drug of choice, preferably expensive bourbon. Blanton's single barrel is my day-to-day go-to, but on special occasions, I take a sip out of a twenty-five-year-old bottle of Pappy Van Winkle, which my client ultimately gifted to me in lieu of a substantial amount of his fee."

"Nice," Callie said, meaning it. She could not imagine drinking from a bottle where each sip cost a thousand dollars.

"He probably stole it," Calloway said, laughing, "but I could not turn it down. I didn't even ask." She finished the Blanton's in her hand. "Be happy to share some with you," she offered again.

Callie held up a hand. "On duty," she said, realizing the Edisto resident wasn't aware like many that Callie fought to remain on the wagon. While expensive, the bourbon would be lost on her anyway with her drug of choice being French gin.

Calloway rose and returned to the bar, turned to the side and motioned, like Vanna White showing the next vowel on the board. She laughed, reaching out to touch the Pappy bottle. "That thieving idiot walked right by here, even rummaged around the shelves and drawers, and had no idea the value of what sat right in front of him." She tapped the Pappy bottle again then reached for her Blanton's and refilled her glass. "Told me right there the boy had no class."

She returned to her chair. "If I had coke, it would be for personal use, Chief. I know the law. I've tried it before and don't like it, so bourbon it is."

Callie believed the woman. She had no reason not to. She thanked Calloway who then walked her to the door. After another reminder to call if she saw Magnus or thought of anything that might assist them in their pursuit, she left the Calloway residence.

Assuming the attorney was telling the truth, Magnus was the likely suspect who invaded Edisto Calm. Callie's investigation kept taking her back to Kitty and the store being the source of cocaine. The fact that Amos had disappeared underscored that theory even more.

Then she wondered if Magnus and Amos had known each other all along.

Chapter 23

WITH THE SUN fading, Callie figured she could reach at least one more lady she wanted to address before calling it a day. It was late enough for Sophie to be at El Marko's but early enough that the restaurant would not be full. Callie drove straight there.

Sophie looked up from checking her phone. "Can I help you? Oh, what are you doing here?"

"Aren't you sweet?" Callie mocked. They were nothing alike, yet somehow they entertained each other, genuinely caring about each other's lives, families, and feelings. Didn't stop them from slicing and dicing each other at times, though.

"How about sitting with me a minute and answering a few questions?" she asked.

Sophie darted a glance toward the kitchen. "Mark might need me."

"Come on." Callie led the way to her private table in the back of the place, up near the kitchen door, and motioned for Sophie to sit at the tiny table for three. Callie reached over and opened the kitchen door. "I'm borrowing your hostess for a moment, Mark. She'll be right here at my table."

Mark walked to her, dishtowel wiping his hands from whatever he'd been creating for someone's meal. He leaned in for a kiss, and Callie honored his request. "Does she need to take off?" he asked. "It won't be horribly busy, but I will have to make allowances."

Callie shook her head before he finished. "No, give me a half hour maybe? Promise."

He studied her. "Are you working the Magnus case?"

"Yep."

"Making headway?"

"Maybe. Collecting pieces but haven't formed the whole. If you really need her, snag her, but I really could use her feedback on a couple things."

"Sure, go ahead. Love you," he said.

"Love you back." She returned to the table.

Sophie had already snagged them drinks, Sophie her lime water and Callie her Bleinheim's ginger ale. Mark kept a stash of their favorites in the refrigerator under the bar.

Callie took a quick swig out of her bottle. "I need your feedback, girl. Some of it is about your personal experiences, so don't get offended, okay?" Then before Sophie could turn on any drama, Callie asked, "Do you do coke?"

Sophie stiffened and looked at Callie like she'd grown another set of arms.

"It's not a hard question, Soph. I'm not looking to arrest you, for God's sake, and unless I caught you in the act, I couldn't anyway."

"I'm insulted," her friend replied.

"Do not get huffy on me, please."

Sophie leaned forward in secrecy. "I might do weed, but I draw the line right there. I do not do shit that kills people. You can't trust dealers. They cut that poison with all kinds of things. Weed at least has medicinal value."

Callie believed that. "Have you seen it around here?"

"Of course I have."

Callie hated hearing that. "Go on. Where?"

"I've been to affairs where it was out and about, but I'm not giving addresses. If it's a guest trying to sell or spread it around, I make them leave. If the hostess of the party offers the crap, I march out. My whole circle knows how I feel about that poison, so if it's going to be at a party, I don't get invited."

Yep, there was a reason they were friends. "Who's the main person trying to sell?"

"I'd rather not say. Besides, it's been almost a year since I saw him."

"Resident?"

"Nope."

"Repeat renter?"

"Maybe."

A case for another time. Callie had become aware of a cadre of women who acted as ladies of the evening during their summer trips, so apparently there was a thing about coming to Edisto and pretending to be something you weren't back home.

"What about Amos?" she asked. "I'm asking for Kitty's sake here. Nobody will know but you and me what you say. Off the record. I'm putting pieces together to catch who we think did the burglaries and maybe set the fire as well. Might be connected."

Sophie's mouth fell open. "It is arson! Oh, Kitty will be frantic, and Janet will crap a load of bricks."

"Sophie, we're talking Amos. Have you seen him deal? Where?"

Bringing her thoughts back around, Sophie leaned back in. "One time at a house party in Wyndham, he thought because they were wealthy that they were easy. Before the owner found out, I kicked his sorry self to the curb."

"Good for you. But I thought you two were buds from the way y'all act around each other."

She shrugged. "Most of the time he's fun. This beach is too small to hate anybody, Callie."

Callie had to commend her for that. "What about in Edisto Calm? See Amos do anything he shouldn't?"

Sophie scowled. "It was only open one day, Callie. How's anyone supposed to see anything? They were busy, and if I had a stash to sell, I'm not sure I'd do so right as she opened the doors, you know? Especially with the likes of Malorie strutting her wide ass around the place making trouble." Her mouth clinched like her friend ought to know better. "You were there most of the time, for God's sake. Selling anything illicit, even weed, would be plain stupid!"

"I know, Soph, but did Malorie have some basis in her complaint that the store was selling hard drugs out the back door?"

"Did she say she saw it happen?"

Callie shook her head.

"That bitch would tell you if she had, don't you think? I would've, to get some satisfaction after having had to pay Kitty five hundred dollars."

So much for Sophie's philosophy that you couldn't afford to hate anyone on Edisto Beach. But she'd flip on a dime, never holding a grudge long.

Sophie turned serious. "I don't believe Kitty knows anything. I hope not. I don't really know . . . but . . ."

"You wouldn't be surprised," Callie finished for her.

She got a sculpted eyebrow shrug. Then a light came on in Sophie's little mind. "You believe Amos is dealing the real deal, don't you? And that he had plans of using the store from the outset."

"Let's say it's open for consideration. Just call if you spot him. When's the last time you saw him?"

"The day after the fire, when a group of us was in there cleaning."

Callie started to ask another question, but Sophie spoke before she could. "We don't need that on Edisto, Callie. Even if it is Amos. I can talk to him for you if you like. Maybe make it all go away."

"No, let me, please. Just call me if he appears. Keep quiet about it, too. Very quiet. No confrontation, no winks, no squinty glances . . . Just nothing, okay?"

Sitting still, Sophie seemed to be cataloging what she could and couldn't do. "Squinty glances? What if I see you across the room." She showed her squinty glance. "Like this."

Funny. "No, sorry. Don't act like you know a thing. Play dumb, like you know nothing."

With nods of acknowledgment, Sophie got the point.

Then in one last effort, Callie raised her phone. "Seen this man?"

Sophie studied the photo. "Can't say I have. Call you if I see him, too?"

"Yes, ma'am," Callie said. "Go on back to work before Mark spanks me for taking up your time."

"Ooh." The old, reliable Sophie returned. "That sounds worth watching."

"Go to work, Soph."

Her friend gave a limp salute and exited the table. Callie checked her watch. It was almost shift change for the station. If she hurried, she could run down Marie before she left for home. She'd know Prince, Amos, and Calloway. She knew everybody.

Back the other direction Callie went, a grand total of two and a half miles. She appreciated every place being so easy to reach, appointments easy to make. En route, she radioed Marie and asked her to stick around a minute. Not an unusual request. Marie was ever willing and able.

Inside, Marie's fingers danced across her computer keyboard. The station's administrator lived back up on the island, similar to Thomas, having lived on Edisto her entire life. Born into a poor family and losing most of them to drugs, she'd been adopted by the police chief. An unofficial understanding required each police chief after to tend to Marie, seeing to her employment and happiness.

Marie could call and in a flash a uniform would respond. In return, she used her legacy of island knowledge to aid the police. She was rather proud of herself, and the town was rather smitten with her. She lived on the island, however, instead of the beach, because of the small house she inherited and the fact that cost of living ran high near the Atlantic.

"I'm working on that fire case, right?" Callie said as she walked in the door.

"Right."

"There's also some new cocaine being distributed on the island."

Marie got quiet, unable to connect the two thoughts.

"Sorry." Callie returned to the beginning, reminding Marie about Magnus Sims. Then she spliced the two thoughts by saying he'd possibly been seen dealing inland.

"Okay, I've got it," Marie said. "Now, what are you asking?" She never got flustered and acted like some wise old soul a decade her senior. Callie attributed that partly to being raised by a grandmother and partly being socialized and indoctrinated by the Edisto Beach Police Department. Callie respected the results.

"Have you heard anything about Magnus from your neighbors? Is there talk about a new man selling coke?"

Marie held up a finger. "First, I keep to myself."

Callie knew that, but Marie kept a keen ear open, too.

"Next, the residents of the island avoid talking much to me," Marie continued. "I may not wear a badge, but I'm considered the police. I've worked for every chief since I was eighteen years old, and people realize not only do I know a lot about this region, but I also answer to you." She smiled.

Callie loved that smile so genuine and sage.

"You may not realize how far your shadow reaches," Marie said. "For a little woman, you tote a big reputation."

Callie had heard that before. Didn't care. "So, nothing, huh? Not a soul out there near you asks for help or lets you know when they feel something is wrong . . . when they are afraid to do anything themselves? That kind of thing."

"I bring you what I hear. To be honest, I do have one thing. Not sure it's worth mentioning, but after hearing you just now, it might be."

There's the Marie she loved. "Shoot."

Marie continued. "My neighbor, the one I get chicken eggs from? About a half mile up the road? She says she has a nephew who tried drugs for the first time this week. At least she thinks it's his first time. He's a good student, never gotten in trouble, yet they caught him high, and he swears up and down he only did it once."

"Did she—"

"Ask where he got it from? Of course she did. From one of his friends who says someone just saw him walking home, stopped, and offered him the junk cheap. The friend happened to have enough money on him to buy enough for two, and he shared with this nephew."

This had to stop. "What's his name?"

"The seller? They didn't get his name."

"No, I mean the kid who did the original buying."

Marie took a light breath. "I don't know. I can try to get it for you."

"Get me the nephew's name, too. This seller is so harum-scarum he could hurt some good kids. This son-of-bitch is handing out cocaine like Girl Scout Cookies and needs to be stopped."

Marie gave a tight grin. "I'll talk to her tonight."

"Then call Thomas and tell him all this. He's scouting the island right now."

"On it, Chief."

Socially Marie called Callie by name, but when she called Callie *Chief,* Marie was on the job.

"As soon as you can, please," Callie reiterated.

"No other way," Marie promised, gathered her things, and left.

God help her, she almost wished whoever's cocaine this was found Magnus and solved all their problems.

With Marie gone, door locked, and phones redirected, Callie wandered to her office to check email . . . maybe do some research on Bruce. He was out there on this island. However, he was awfully sharp.

She had his name, Bruce Bardot, that he was ex-Ranger, and his approximate age was thirty-five. After the hurricane, she'd gone to Janet to hunt for whatever information she had on file for when the three Rangers rented a house. There was nothing on Bruce, and only sparse intel on Arlo Adkins, the spearhead of the trio in all their travels and adventures. In thinking after the fact, Callie surmised that Arlo put the only face out there for rentals for a reason, for control and limited exposure. Bruce, the medic, had protected the women, keeping them sedated, safe, healthy, and out of sight.

They hadn't hurt a soul, and each girl was returned safely without remembering what happened.

Bruce literally came out the hero, and even through the fog of her suspicion, Callie saw him in a positive light once he'd disbanded the team. She'd told him when they were alone that his team would have eventually screwed up and gotten caught. He neither confirmed nor denied, his action of walking away speaking for him.

She had doubts of finding much on the man when she began her online search, and it didn't take long to confirm those doubts. She found nothing other than an expired driver's license from Tennessee. She couldn't legitimize running a credit report, plus she had no social security number. Military records weren't easily accessed without proper authority which she did not have. She had no legal right to go after him. Funny how she was almost glad she didn't find anything more.

She sat back in her desk chair, staring at the dated picture on the far wall depicting the old Edisto shrimp boat, the Sarah Jane. She tried to put herself in Bruce Bardot's shoes.

How liberating was it to be so unattached to the rest of the world? Or was it work to remain so hidden?

What was it that made him want to bother with Edisto business?

And why did she care?

Sitting alone in her office, without those who knew her near enough to scrutinize, she made herself analyze the why of her attraction to Bruce Bardot.

Not an attraction in a Mark-like attraction, but she'd recognized a connection while in the hospital after the storm, back when Bruce had assisted her, stood by her, and dared to be seen by everyone when he preferred to remain hidden. Respect mixed with chivalry, amidst taking a chance. She suspected he'd risked being seen only in an attempt to get closer to her.

The depth to him appealed to her own sense of duty. That's as close as she could put into words what attracted them to each other. They lived on principles and shared a code with few people understanding the depth of what went through their heads thanks to a history of battles and the unfortunate need to take lives.

But why hadn't this man, so vagabond in nature, not left Edisto Island?

The thought that she might be the reason he hung around touched a nerve, a tender one. But if he admired her from afar, what was she supposed to do with that?

Or had she scrutinized him too deeply, taking the rabbit hole of guesswork into something romanticized too thin for good logic, all because she didn't have enough facts to go on.

She'd fallen so far into her thoughts that when her cell rang, she had to pull herself back to the present. Caller ID Thomas. He never called without strong reason.

"Got the make and model of the car, Chief."

"Good work." She was thrilled. If they acted fast, they might be able to shut down these dealers by close of business tomorrow. "Wait, you said car, not truck."

He laughed. "Prince took a picture of it. Said the guys didn't smell right. And you're right, it's a car, not Magnus's truck."

"Prince is protecting his regular dealer," she said. "He's ratting on these new infiltrators. This cannot end well. If we can run a tag, they can, too. I'd say the clock is ticking for these new boys. Who's the car's owner?"

"It's a 2009 blue Toyota Scion registered to Larue Rush," he said. "Address on the island. A small drive off Peters Point Road."

Rush was a common name in the region. She asked for the street number and pulled up the title of the house, wanting to know exactly where the address was and who she was dealing with. Eileen Rush owned the place.

"Meet me there," she said.

"Now?"

"Better now than later. Son of a gun, we might luck up and land Magnus tonight. I can arrest him on the spot. Once we take a statement from Prince and once we take one from someone Marie told me about, we can snatch up Larue as well. Thomas, there's a chance we can nip this mess in the bud tonight, tomorrow at the latest. I'm all over those odds."

"Ain't you the happy trooper," he said.

"Maybe," she said. "Find Amos in all this, and I'll give you a frickin' week off and your choice of duty assignments for a month."

"I already have those. I'm your favorite, remember?"

"I'll give you all the overtime you want for a month, for that boat of yours."

"Hot damn, you're on, Chief."

Chapter 24

Bruce

SEVERAL DAYS HAD passed since the fire. Bruce had given Magnus and Larue lukewarm interest in the novice drug venture to keep abreast of what they were up to. Not trusting where and when and with whom they'd do business, atop of not wanting to be seen, he'd defaulted to tending to Sere, doing the chores she'd expect Larue to do if he stayed under her roof, listening to them flaunt their ventures at night when they came home.

He had no idea what to do about them. To give them up meant they'd incriminate Sere, because there wasn't much loyalty in those genes. They'd try to blame him as well, but he wasn't overly concerned about that. It wouldn't hold water. He'd disappear, and the authorities would have nothing on him, so they'd forget he existed.

He wondered what Callie would think if he got swept up in this mess.

There was a sense of righteousness woven throughout all this he couldn't rationalize, when he preferred his world painted in black and white. It was why he steered clear of the general population. People were complicated. People were messy.

Yet here he remained without a plan, biding his time until he understood how to act. Closer to *react*, actually.

The first day after the fire the boys laid low at the house, scheming via the Internet, which Bruce found entertaining. How did someone search Google for *How to deal cocaine?*

The next day they went out, coming back that night, all a chatter with most of the drugs still in their possession. He could hope they'd been too scared to proceed, but they soon proved him wrong. Moving the three of them to the back porch away from Sere, Bruce settled in his regular chair. Magnus took the swing, and Larue, again, propped his butt cheek on the railing. This had come to be a hierarchy thing with them.

"Today we tested the water," Larue said.

"Scouting for open territory," Magnus explained, like he knew what the hell he was talking about.

In listening to the bragging and pontification, Bruce recognized them for what they were. . . clueless how to start and scared to start and get it wrong.

"Prince talked to us, though," Larue said.

Bruce waited for an explanation on who Prince was.

"He has a handle on the territories," Magnus said. "Don't want to step on toes, you know. He's the only one we sold to, and he bought enough. He said to come back tomorrow, and he'd have some more names for us. We might've sold little bitty amounts to guys we'd see walking the roads. You know, to spread the word."

Larue looked all proud of their accomplishment, the beginnings of a network. Bruce, however, wondered when Prince was going to take full advantage and come out the winner, with murder possibly a part of the equation.

Or whoever else Prince bought from regularly . . . or worked for.

The two studied the next day's navigation on their phones, a plan of where to start based on what Prince had told them.

Bruce had to ask. "Is this Prince to be trusted?" Bruce had a sound answer of his own, but this was the Magnus and Larue Show, and Bruce would get more out of them by playing dumb.

Larue lit up. "He's like the guru out here when it comes to needing . . . stuff."

"Did you know him from before?" Bruce asked.

"Before what?" Larue asked.

"Before you became dealers."

"No, but he said we were naturals, and whatever we provided, he could find a home for. He's only asking for product as payment."

Magnus wasn't as bubble-gum happy as his partner, but he was thrilled enough. "We're lucky he spoke with us. He was our first buyer. If the quality's up to his standards, he'll direct us to customers tomorrow."

"And he wanted product, not a cut of sales?" Bruce asked before he caught himself.

Larue was wide-eyed and shaking his head as Magnus said, "No, man. Said based on how we got the stuff, it was best we dispose of it quickly, and with this deal we'll get rid of it twice as fast. Beats us trying to find buyers. Considering we got nothing invested, we still come out ahead."

Bruce tried not to look at him like he couldn't be that dense. No place was virgin territory. Like anywhere, Edisto territory had to belong to someone else. The system in place didn't have to be sophisticated, but it would exist. Out here, the buyers would be a combination of the poor and unemployed who scraped pennies for their buy, and the more affluent who loved having a little something at their parties. Bruce couldn't see a big income from out here, but it was a good income to somebody. Magnus and Larue were trespassing, cutting into someone's profits.

Magnus foolishly assumed Prince looked out for their best interest while making a little bit on the side. Whoever had the region would hear about these interlopers soon enough. People like Prince played both ends against the middle.

"Prince is right," Bruce said. "Get rid of your stash fast. All of it. Tomorrow."

Larue scrunched his mouth up into his nose. "Dude, we got this. We were thinking a third tomorrow, a third the next day, then the last of it. That way word gets around, the need grows, and we can charge more. You snooze you lose, you know?"

Magnus chimed in. "We know who owns that stash we snatched up, you know. You do, too, right?"

"No," Bruce said. "I'm not from around here, remember?" The party had to be worried, pissed, or both about now. When they heard of these two new jokers catting about the island doing fresh business, especially since they were too moronic to be discreet, some nasty action could go down. These guys could never come back or be found in such a manner as to make a statement. No telling which.

"Well," Magnus continued. "We thought we'd get in touch with him, the guy we stole from, and form a union. We have the customers, and he can supply the goods, and we'll have a genuine business."

Jesus Christ. They didn't realize, first, there was nothing genuine about the drug business. Second, whoever they stole this coke from wouldn't be too damn willing to take on partners who had already proven they'd rob him blind. Third, he had his own circle established already. Whoever these idiots were selling to were already customers of the rightful owner. Actually, anyone in the zip code would be considered property.

"You don't think he'll be pissed at y'all stealing his product?" Bruce asked.

"Not if we give him part of what we sell," Larue said.

"He would've made more money if he hadn't had you guys to split it with," Bruce reminded. *And sold it for more than these ding-a-lings would.*

"We got this, man," Larue said.

Bruce said no more. No point. He'd remain around Sere and let the boys screw up on their own. He wanted to pull Sere aside and educate her, separate her from all of this somehow. He'd sleep on that. Sometimes ignorance was indeed bliss.

Day four. The guys left around ten in the morning, their conversation buzzing with hope for the day's enterprise.

Bruce helped Sere clean up then led her to the porch. A coolness swept in off the water, and despite the sun shining in extraordinary glory, a coat was needed. Sere, however, chose to bring out her favorite blanket, ease onto the swing where the sun shined on her back and made herself comfortable wrapped up with cup of coffee in hand.

Bruce watched her settle in her own perfect comfort, implanting that image on his mind for the days when he'd be gone.

"Sere," he started, and a brief smile creased her face before she lifted her cup for a sip. He noticed. "What?"

"You're worried about the boys," she said.

"I can't do anything about the boys. My concern is for you."

Her smile widened. "That's sweet. Why?"

"They don't know what they are doing. They could get hurt."

She swayed, her heels keeping the motion going. "They're grown. They'll figure it out."

He had to stop himself from sliding his chair closer, reaching out to touch her, doing something to make his point clearer.

"They are not your responsibility," she said. "Not really mine either."

"Neither are you my responsibility, but you're the one I have concern for."

"Again, that's nice, but not your issue. I'll be fine."

"You could go to jail," he said. "What they do could blow back on you. You've talked to them about selling. If they get caught, they'll give you up as a partner, if not the ringleader."

She gave him the slightest of a shrug. "We'll see. I can be quite disarming playing the old lady. They took advantage of me."

Was she really that naïve, or was she that shrewd? "What am I missing?"

She gave him that smile that said she was wiser. Sometimes she was right. "If they get caught doing something illegal, I didn't do it. I didn't steal anything. Even if I own up to saying they ought to get rid of it, what does that even mean to the police? An old lady who let these two boys hide in her house, heard them talk and mentioned something she saw on television. Maybe said it for fear they'd hurt her or take advantage." She raised both arms in a shrug, the cup still in her grasp. "How many times has Larue tapped my social security? Is some prosecutor coming after this?" She motioned with the free hand, sweeping from her head to her toes. "Besides, it doesn't change what they did, and they are adults."

Guess Sere wasn't so ignorant.

"You have to be worried about them," he said. "Today's the day they put their plan to the test."

She reached over, and he had to lean in for her to touch him. Her veined, knuckled hand patted him on his sleeve. "You just chop me enough wood in case they don't come back," she said, half in jest with words he suspected anchored in truth.

Sere was a hard-core realist.

"I won't be here much longer," he said. How many times had he said that?

"Didn't expect you to stay forever, baby." Her voice softened a little, taking him back to the days when it was just them. "My precious knight. You still haven't taken me up to the cave to do with me what you will," she said, reminding him of their first conversation, when they were strangers, and he needed a place to stay.

They watched the marsh slip into its lazy midday ritual, when the morning's feeding and socializing slowed to a crawl and creatures languished until the evening.

By midnight, after other marsh life had gone to bed, they remained awake, listening for a sound of Magnus's truck which never came.

Chapter 25

EARLY AFTERNOON and Callie had made her way to the Rush residence, not more than five miles outside of town, eager to connect the dots. She pulled up to a small clapboard style house in the typical square Charleston design, only painted sky blue.

From a distance the word quaint came to mind. Upon closer inspection, Callie noted a paint job a decade past due, sags in the roof whispering of problems to come, and no semblance of a yard whatsoever. The natural spread of live oaks with their draped moss and volunteer Palmettos reminded any visitor they were in the Lowcountry, but the property did little to imprint a positive impression. Everything had been left to its own devices.

Typical inheritance of a house they couldn't afford to maintain.

Callie pulled off in a worn, mashed area surrounded by overgrowth, finding an established footpath through it leading to the house's front door. No bell. No Ring cam. She lifted an old brass knocker that barely held onto the etched memory of an R and announced herself.

A woman answered of an age that might be in the right vicinity for Eileen Rush. Wrinkles on her neck and forearms said fifties or sixties, but one couldn't tell which end of the spectrum due to an apparent history of alcohol and cigarettes, the latter emphasized by the smoking cig held loosely between stained fingers, the former from the glaze in her eyes. The woman had a decent nail job, though.

"Can I help you?" she asked, the gravelly voice confirming lungs familiar with decades of a habit.

"Eileen Rush?" A waft of marijuana reached Callie. Big surprise.

Drawn-on brows rose high and peaked, someone having done well matching them to the dye in her hair. "I'd ask who wants to know, but all of that . . ." Eileen motioned with the cigarette in a top to bottom fashion. "That tells me who you are. What brings you to my lovely manor?" When Callie looked past her, to see if anyone else was in the house, Eileen noticed. "Sorry if I don't ask you in. The house is a mess."

"I'm here about your son, Larue Rush." Callie recognized the shift to a defensive posture. "Is he home?"

"Haven't seen him in going on a week," she said.

"You *are* Eileen Rush, and Larue Rush is your son?"

She took a puff of the cigarette, blowing it out long and slow. "Guess there's nothing wrong with admitting to that. If the little shit has done anything wrong, I'm not aware, and since he's an adult, I'm innocent."

Callie studied this Mother-of-the-Year material and had no problem envisioning Larue as a thief and owner of stolen cocaine. Callie held up the DL picture of Magnus. "Does he pal around with this guy?"

Eileen leaned in closer, having left her readers someplace. "Looks like his buddy. Haven't seen him as well. They're probably off together."

"When's the last time you've seen Magnus Sims?"

She studied Callie, likely pondering the direction where this was headed. Callie appreciated curiosity. Curiosity would keep Ms. Rush answering questions for a little while longer.

"They left at the same time. My son was in his Toyota. The other one in his pickup."

Okay, that rang true. "Where do they stay when they aren't here?"

She took another draw off the smoke. "First, I never let that Magnus fella stay here. Second, don't even know where he lives or where he holes up. But. . ." Another puff taken. "My son hangs with my sister-in-law when he isn't here. For some reason they get along. And since he's her only heir with my husband, her brother, dead and all, he nurses the relationship, if that makes sense to someone like you."

Callie didn't take the bait. It wasn't unusual for the islanders, especially the ones without a strong source of income, to take verbal shots at those who lived on the beach. With Callie being the chief of police, she'd be considered part beach nobility. She probably was compared to what some of these people made.

"What would your sister-in-law's name be? I need to find your son."

Eileen shifted her weight. "You haven't told me what about. Might make a difference whether I tell you anything."

If Callie told her, she'd phone a warning. She might be a crappy mother, but even buzzards loved their babies. "So you can call ahead?"

She literally winked. "Maybe."

"Honestly—"

"You mean you weren't up to now?" A tinge of an edge came through her words.

"Honestly," Callie repeated, voice firm, "we're looking more for

Magnus, and we were told he hung with your son. If your son cooperates, we might be able to come to an agreement." A chance, but Callie wasn't feeling those odds. Not the way things had gone thus far. Time would tell. The situation was still fluid.

The clincher would be how much of the cocaine could be recovered, and how little damage had been done to the citizens of Edisto Island. If anything reached her beach, however, all deals were off.

She'd prefer to grab Magnus first, but either would do. Larue wasn't here or dear old mom would've shot covert glances around, taking protective looks for signs of her son being half-witted enough to get himself seen. She hadn't, though, her focus on Callie. The only vehicle around was a low-end Kia easily a decade old. No sign of the Toyota.

"What's your sister-in-law's name? Rush, right?"

"Yep."

"First name?"

"Serenity. Call her Sere."

"How do you spell Sere?"

Eileen continued holding the doorframe up with her shoulder, one arm up against her, propping up the one with the cigarette.

"You've been good so far," Callie said. "Don't start interfering with an investigation."

"You work on the beach, not the island," Eileen said. "This isn't your jurisdiction."

Well, there was that.

"Then let's call Charleston County and get a deputy out here," Callie said, lifting out her phone. "I keep a few of them on speed dial, then there's always dispatch." Her thumb hovered over the screen.

Eileen came off of the door frame. She stepped onto the porch and defiantly threw the remainder of her drag onto a rubber rug on the porch, mashing it with a sneakered foot. "Serenity Rush Whaley." She spit off to the side, like she had a piece of tobacco on her tongue. . . or just wanted to spit in front of her irritating guest.

"Address?"

"Raccoon Island Road," she said. "First mailbox on the left, but you won't see it for a half mile or so. Mailbox still says Whaley on it if you look close."

Good enough. "Thanks for the help."

Eileen's lips puckered. "You might not see the vehicles from the road, so look close."

Extra information she hadn't asked for. Odd woman. Callie turned to leave.

"Who knows?" Eileen threw in, making Callie turn around. "You might find old Miss Serenity involved. All my boy does is scrape by and give part of it to the old woman, like he owes her. For what I'll never know."

Ah, there lay the reality. Mom was jealous of the boy's aunt, because for some reason, he loved the aunt more. Go figure why that would be.

Dear old mom slammed the door.

Families. But as badly as this one seemed to be mucked up, Callie was about to muck it up more.

PER GPS, CALLIE looked at a sixteen-mile drive to the address on Raccoon Island Road. She'd just passed the Old Post Office, an upscale restaurant with a history that, unfortunately, hadn't kept its doors open. She put in a call to Thomas. If he could make it, she'd appreciate the backup in case both men were hiding out at Serenity's. What was that nickname she used? Sere?

"Where are you?" she asked when he picked up. Hearing road noise, she could assume he was traveling the roads as promised, scouting for drug activity and reinterviewing those he'd spoken to before. By now, the island would be abuzz about the cocaine and the two men, at least in the right circles and the expected areas. With Thomas perusing roads, the buzz would quickly turn the story to one about cops being on the prowl.

"Just finished talking to Prince. Nobody's seen the two men since yesterday afternoon. They were driving Magnus's pickup," he said.

"In that case, meet me on Raccoon Island Road at the Whaley residence," she said. "You know Serenity Whaley?"

"I was about to ask you which Whaley, but out there that one makes sense. I haven't seen her since I was in high school, though, on a late-night gigging trip in my old boat with a couple of drunk buddies. She shot at us when we got too close to her place. Seems she watches from her back porch." He laughed to himself. "But that's been a decade, Chief. Haven't heard of her leaving, though."

"Well," she continued. "She appears to be Larue Rush's aunt. His mother hasn't seen him in a week. He has to be staying somewhere. In calling Magnus's home, and his neighbors, nobody has seen him, and they're none worried. Seems he and Larue are thick. Find one and we're liable to find the other."

"Meet you at the Whaley place then?"

"Please," she said. "I'm halfway there."

"I'm. . ." and he studied something, "maybe ten miles away?"

"Good. Meet me on the road. Don't go to the door until I get there. I'm not sure what we'll find."

Her phone rang with another caller. "Thomas, let me get this. It's Raysor. See you at the Whaley place."

She switched calls. "Callie here, Don. What's up?"

Don Raysor was her favorite Colleton County deputy, on loan to Edisto Beach PD through ten police chiefs. He was the extra that Councilwoman Donna had referenced a few days ago when they debated how many uniforms Edisto needed. The beach didn't pay for Deputy Raysor, but they still like to throw his presence in Callie's face when talking budget.

He was born and raised in the local town of Walterboro, across the big bridge and then a few miles. He'd fished every creek, walked every silt road, and eaten, visited, or gone to church suppers with most of the island people, whether in Charleston or Colleton County. Charleston wasn't interested much in the distant island, so Colleton SO and Callie's people took up the slack when things needed attention. People tended to remember the names of public servants who answered calls, and Raysor's name was spoken in every house on the island.

The fifty-plus-year-old was known far and wide, and multiple departments relied upon his knowledge. He filled in gaps nobody else could. Callie had a core of people that represented her go-to circle, and he was in it.

"Hey, doll," he said, using the tongue-in-cheek nickname he'd given to her as pure irritation when they first met and hated each other. "I need you to get to Russell Creek ASAP."

"Why aren't you calling the county?" she asked, puzzled.

"Aren't you hunting one Magnus Sims?" he asked.

Her thoughts hit a wall at Raysor being the one to call her about Magnus. "Working on running him down as we speak, Don." She hesitated again. "Why?"

"Might've found him for you."

"At Russell Creek?"

"Hold on." He shouted, "Don't you boys go in that water." Then he came back. "Sorry. Kids were fishing from the bank, and they happened to wave me down. You need to get here, doll."

"On my way. Don't touch anything until I get there."

"Already called the county. Just saying."

She pushed an additional twenty miles per hour out of her vehicle. "As you should, but I'll be there first."

"I heard that," he said. "Raysor out."

She called Thomas, told him to keep scouring the roads. She didn't want him at the Whaley place without her. No telling how this investigation would shift after learning what Raysor had found.

Chapter 26

CALLIE SPOTTED THE disturbed ground on the east side of Highway 174 and followed the mashed area down. Raysor stood with two boys in their early teens, the latter still holding onto their fishing poles with a green plastic tackle box a few feet behind them. Obviously, they were island boys born there and had probably fished since they could walk.

But then she saw the top of a vehicle poking up from the creek, maybe six inches above the water. The shape and size said small pickup truck, the color close enough to be Magnus's, about twenty feet out from shore. Momentum, slippery mud, and timing of the tide had placed it far enough out not to be immediately seen. The truck could've been under as much as five hours. Maybe more.

She prayed that none of this involved anyone seeking retribution for the foolhardiness of two unwitting young men. She could try to hope that Magnus put that truck there to buy him time to get out of town. Not wise, but he hadn't been exactly genius in his work, but that wasn't where Callie's gut was going. She just hoped there wasn't a body inside. Or two.

Parking next to the county cruiser, she found Raysor between the boys and the water, protecting the crime scene. He approached her as she came down the hill, so the boys couldn't hear.

"Could be the truck we've been hunting," she said, referencing the BOLO put out for Magnus and his wheels.

"Thought so," he said. "The Charleston SO will be here in twenty, maybe fifteen."

"Which means thirty."

He smirked in agreement. "What do you want to do in the meantime?"

Edisto was far enough out that nobody was ever nearby when it came to an emergency. She'd covered for both counties several times because they never had a unit near enough to be considered prompt. This truck in the water wasn't in her jurisdiction, but it was possibly connected to her investigation so her interest wouldn't be questioned. She would ask forgiveness and receive it. She only had moments to act. "Let's see whether anyone's inside," she said.

"Boys?" Raysor hollered, and the two came running. "You wanted to dive in and snoop around, right?"

The two boys, maybe fourteen, enthusiastically nodded. "We were going to before you even got here, Mr. Raysor, sir. You gonna let us?"

He looked down his nose at the two youths. "I cannot make you do this."

"We know. Don't care."

"Will your parents get upset?"

They laughed. "We seen shit before. Our mommas didn't raise no wimps."

"What about your daddies?"

One pointed to the other. "His is in jail. Mine died when I was five. Our mommas done raised us, and they tough."

If the situation wasn't so serious, Callie would laugh. She recognized one of the boys, the one whose father was incarcerated. His momma was made of iron and raised her three kids to be just as impervious. Kids raised on this island were cast of sterner substance than those in town.

However, the temperature was in the fifties. "Raysor, it's a little cool, isn't it?"

"Don't matter to them, doll," he said under his breath. "Look at them. Their pants legs are already wet. You don't see them shivering, do you?"

Yep, hard kids.

"Okay, boys. Now, if I was to look away . . ." Raysor said, dragging out his words and turning aside. "Don't touch anything," he hollered in an afterthought.

One pointed to the other, meaning he'd take one side, and his friend the other. Like two river otters, they dropped poles and dove into the creek, immediately underwater.

The water already had a small energy to it, like any water affiliated with a tide, but the boys' swimming movements made small eddies of their own on either side of the truck, showing where they were.

About the time Callie worried, their heads bobbed to the surface. "Only one person inside," said the one who seemed the leader of the two. "But you ain't gonna believe how he's in there."

"Lemme come over there and see," shouted the other kid.

"No, that's all right—" Callie tried to say, but the boy had already gone under and swam around, like a fish.

It didn't take long for him to pop up. "That's damn cool!"

"All right, you boys get out of there," Callie said, no longer happy with the exposure of these kids to the grotesque, regardless how hardy they appeared to be.

Chattering like magpies, they breast stroked themselves to shallow water and waded out. Side by side, they shook themselves, running hands over their hair. "Wanna hear what we saw?"

Raysor looked at them with a stern what-do-you-think expression and pointed to the one in charge. "Report."

"Grown man. Black hair. Dark long-sleeve shirt. Holding onto the steering wheel. His eyes are closed, and there definitely ain't no bubbles coming out of his mouth."

Callie could only imagine the families these kids lived around. One part might be admirable, but she was almost afraid to picture what else these boys had seen in their short teenage lives to be so grounded when it came to describing death.

She pulled out the picture of Magnus. "Look like him?"

Both peered in together. "Yeah," said the oldest. "That's him."

"Is he wanted?" the other asked.

Guess there was no harm in answering. "Yes," she said. "For questioning," she tacked on for good measure.

"Is he dealing?" asked the leader.

Callie frowned. "Why do you ask?" She hoped to God they hadn't been sold some of Magnus's product. Her blood pressure already climbed at the thought of such.

The boy shrugged. "I don't know. Maybe because his hands are zip tied to the steering wheel? Like someone was taking him out? It's what drug people do when you step on their toes, isn't it? In the city they just cap 'em and put 'em in a dumpster."

Jesus. The cavalier manner in which he explained drug turfs made her glad not to be raising little ones. They saw and heard too much way too early.

"What else can we do?" they asked, barefoot and dripping, unfazed by what they'd seen, and if Callie understood anything about human nature, they wanted to go forth and brag about it.

Time was of the essence now. "I need you to get gone before the deputies arrive," she said. "They might not take to y'all being in the water." Much less being so young.

They cackled. "City boys," one said, trying to act twice his age, elbowing the other.

"She said get gone," Raysor said, firmly enough to stop the laughter and make them scramble to fetch their tackle boxes and poles. "And don't go spouting off about what you saw, either."

"Thanks for letting us see that!" one said, skittering off.

"I mean it," Raysor ordered. "No spreading this around."

They quickly vanished into the woods, their giggling soon out of earshot.

"God, I hope some momma doesn't come rake me over the coals," Callie uttered, still watching the woods where they'd disappeared, knowing full well they'd tell the first person they saw.

"I'll talk to the mothers," Raysor said. "Trust me. These boys have seen worse."

Callie didn't want to ask the particulars of what that might be. Instead, she wanted to discuss the particulars of what was still in the water.

"Didn't get the tag," Raysor said. "It's under the mud."

They would confirm it was Magnus's truck when they raised it.

Deputies showed at the thirty-minute mark. They parked up on the road, however, to leave room for the coroner and the forthcoming towtruck. Callie and Raysor followed their leads and moved their vehicles, then wandered back down to the water's edge where the deputies scouted the bank, studying the water, trying to put two and two together.

Raysor explained how he came up on the scene, talked to the boys, then sent them on their way. "They seem to think there's a body in there," he said. "Which tells me they went swimming. I know 'em. They're harmless. And they damn sure didn't touch anything after that kind of a shocker."

Raysor and his ability to tell a tale, but everyone took him at face value because of his history out here.

"Explains the bank all muddied up," said one.

"Any idea who it might be?" asked another. Two had arrived. More were coming.

"Magnus Sims," Callie said. "I'm going by the truck, mind you. We've been hunting him for burglary, arson, and distributing cocaine. He's been on a tear for about a week."

A humorous *humph* came from the first. "Well, looks like he might've overdosed on his own product and underestimated the road."

Callie and Raysor said nothing. As soon as the tow truck arrived the deputies would change their tune. She and Raysor stayed the extra hour, long enough for the pickup to be lifted from the water, confirming what the boys had seen.

Magnus had indeed been zip-tied to the steering wheel, and he hadn't seemed to have given much of a struggle. That other deputy might be right about the OD part, but likely he was dosed, tied, and then pushed into Russell Creek. The killer knew full well that Magnus would be found once the tide went out.

Which made her wonder where the hell Larue was.

"Looks like a drowning, but the coroner has to say," said one of the deputies, while the coroner himself went through his checklist analysis.

Callie almost asked, *You think?* but the deputy was young, and she was there as a courtesy. He felt in charge, and she let him. She asked him about any other possessions or clues in the truck. There was nothing other than the wallet in Magnus's pocket.

She approached the coroner, stooping to his level. He knew who she was. "I have an open case with this man," she said. "Any chance you can let me know if he was full of drugs? Not sure it matters about the cause of death; the zip ties paint a pretty clear message, but I'd just like to hear from you, too, if you don't mind."

"No problem," he said. "But if he was full of drugs, it wasn't for long before they dumped him. It's looking like he drowned."

They wouldn't have wasted a lot of drugs on him. Just enough to make him easier to handle. "Thanks."

Callie took her own pictures, then approached the deputy again. "Want me to notify the next of kin?"

"It's my county," he said.

"I've already been to the house and met his family because of my case, so they might take it better from me." No cop alive liked making those calls. "I'd like to query them about my case while I'm there."

With her mission not being his, the deputy conceded. "Sure, go ahead. Give them this card if they want to inquire when they can collect the body, but I assume the county won't want to release him until they speak to you."

"Yeah, I'd appreciate that," she said, taking the card and excusing herself, making her way back to Raysor.

"I'm notifying the mother and girlfriend," she said. "Then I'm headed to Serenity Whaley's place. You familiar with her?"

"Yeah. Why?"

She hadn't kept him as up to speed on this case as she normally would, him being torn between his sheriff's department duties and those at the beach. Truth was, she'd kept details closer to home on this one, relying mostly on Thomas. Everyone was aware of the BOLO, and who wasn't aware of the fire, but all the little connections and suspicions hadn't been distributed very far or wide.

Maybe due to the loose connection to Bruce? Could she admit that?

Or maybe not so loose. Yes, Bruce had been directly affiliated with the burglaries, on the good guy side. But his appearance at the fire left her in a quandary, and until she understood more, she wasn't quick to share. To open the door to Bruce could open way more than she cared to.

She answered the waiting Raysor. "Magnus's partner is Larue Rush, who turns out to be Serenity Whaley's nephew," she said. "I spoke with Larue's mom who hasn't seen him, and yes, I believe her. But she led me to check Serenity's house because he stays there a lot. Mom confirms he hangs with Magnus and makes me feel he's hiding out with his aunt. I get the feeling mother and son aren't pals, and the aunt is more of a safe haven."

Raysor glowered, a regular response for the hefty deputy. "I can see that. Want me to take one of those chores off your hands? I can go to Serenity's place since I know her. Or if not, I can make the notification. Your call."

But she wanted to do both. The notification might give her insight into Magnus, but she held a greater sense of urgency to pursue Larue. With his best bud dead, with a ninety-nine percent chance of having been murdered, she fretted over Larue's health.

"You do the notification, if you don't mind. Ask when they last saw or heard from him. If it's been within the last week, call me ASAP. If not, we'll chat later. I'm sensing a clock on all this, Raysor. With one idiot dead, the other might be a walking target."

"Assuming he's not dead already," Raysor tacked on.

Just what she was thinking.

She radioed Marie where she would be and that she'd redirected Raysor to the notification in Ravenel. Then as Raysor pulled away from the scene and headed across the big bridge, she turned the other way. Per GPS, she was five miles from the Whaley residence.

She'd have to turn off onto Pine Landing, go a bit, then take a left onto Laurel Hill. Before she made that last turn, however, she pulled over. She needed to call Mark.

"Hey, what's up?" he answered.

Theirs was usually a texting conversation throughout the day. For her to call meant she wanted feedback. Nine times out of ten it involved a case, and with a case came a degree of danger he wanted to be aware of. He'd made her swear to keep him apprised. She thought hard each time before doing so, because he'd want to come running to her rescue since he had the skills.

He was aware of the burglaries, the fire, and the hunt for Magnus and Larue. Reluctantly, she'd told him about Bruce and him thwarting two burglaries and observing the fire. She wanted Mark fully informed. She had an edgy, creepy crawly feel about today thanks to Magnus's death. All of this had escalated to a different level, and she felt the realities of it hanging just outside her reach. The only way to understand was to proceed into the unknown.

"I don't like Bruce," was Mark's first reaction.

"He saved Stan. Frankly, he came close to having to save me after that hurricane."

"Yeah," he said. "You keep telling me that. I wasn't there."

That little zinger didn't sit well with her. "You were incapacitated. We had an emergency. He was the best person to help me lift trees and get Stan to medical help. What about that isn't believable?"

He got quiet. He understood the undisputed facts and that him being only two days out of surgery made him worthless moving downed trees and debris. He'd hated Bruce from the outset. They hadn't had a dozen words of conversation, but he'd expressed his wariness well enough to Callie, right in front of Bruce.

"Besides, I'm going to an old lady's house to hunt for her nephew. Bruce has been seen driving that nephew's car."

"Seriously, Callie?"

"Stop, Mark. This is my job, and I'll be careful. With Magnus dead, I wanted you to know where I was before you heard anything from someone else."

He didn't really have a choice. "Got backup?"

"No. I will, however, be informing Thomas, because he's out here on the island hunting information on the drug dealing. I can tell him to meet up with me at some point, but right now, I'm right around the corner from Serenity's place and the day is waning. I don't want to wait until tomorrow. I need to know what Larue knows, and I need to be the one to inform him about Magnus."

She was on a roll, pissed yet trying to lessen Mark's concern at the same time. She hated even making these types of calls to him, but she'd promised. All it did was make him worry. His worry had roots in helplessness, but he could save that emotional bit for when they got home, not when she was about to go somewhere that required her full attention.

"I love you, and I've got to go," she said, her tone daring him to make this worse. He had enough cop sense in him not to. Oh, the games they played.

"Love you," he replied, hard, like he had to say it harsh enough for it to stick and make her remember.

She hung up, telling herself to force the love of her life to the back recesses of her mind. She expected to run into Larue and had to prepare herself for doing so. There was no telling what frame of mind he'd be in, assuming he was alive.

Then a small piece of her hinted a thought she hoped was nothing. What if whoever dealt with Magnus had already found Larue. And what if they were at Serenity's house on Raccoon Island Road?

She hadn't told Mark that.

Chapter 27

Bruce

NEITHER LARUE NOR Magnus had come home last night. Bruce and Sere had waited up until midnight. Finally, he helped her to bed with assurance the boys had likely stayed at Larue's mother's place, not wanting to come in late.

But he stayed up, just in case.

The two men said they had ground to cover that day, to supply all the promises made the day before. They'd developed a list, mapped the territory, and set out awfully proud of themselves late morning. They'd even invited Bruce, thinking his presence gave them . . . something. Maybe a degree of strength? Maybe they could use the unfamiliar face to pretend they had connections? Who knew what played through the minds of those pea heads.

Not coming home wasn't good. Not answering their phones was worse.

By midday, Sere received a call. Bruce tried to appear disinterested from his place in the yard where he did chores. She was already on the morose side today.

"No, they're not here," she said, then listened. Listened for a while. "Yes, I'll let you know." More silence. "Shut the hell up, all right?" This time she hung up. Unable to slam the phone, she threw it into the sink. The rattle told him it wasn't full of water, thank goodness.

He put down the ax and wandered inside to the kitchen. All he had to do was stand in the doorway. He'd never been one to mince words, and she'd been pretty good about reciprocating same.

She exhaled a deep, penetrating sigh.

He just waited.

"That was my sister-in-law, Larue's momma. Said the police came by hunting for the boys. They didn't stay there last night, either."

Before he had the chance to ask a question, she added, "The lady chief from the beach is the one asking questions."

Which was what he'd wanted to know. Which jurisdiction. Which cop.

Chief Callie Morgan was making headway. He had no doubt she'd already checked at Magnus's house. Only made sense to come to Larue's.

"She'll be here next," Sere said before he could. She looked to him for answers.

"Talk to her when she gets here," he said. "That's all I can say."

Sere did a slanty-eyed stare at him. "You ever met this woman?"

He hadn't told Sere much about himself, and it was like she was afraid to ask him much. "Met her in passing," he said. "She probably doesn't even remember me. You know her?"

Sere watched him harder. "Same here."

The silence substituted for words neither wanted to say. Sere had probably aided and abetted Larue a time or two, when it came to advice and a place to store his pilfered wares. Bruce had a history with the chief nobody needed to know about.

Silently they agreed not to push each other. They only wanted to share the pieces of each other that worked.

The day dragged on. Larue didn't answer his phone. Neither man showed. Bruce could see Sere's worry. He could go hunting for the two men, but something told him to stay close.

In the afternoon, halfway between lunch and supper time, they stoked the fire inside as the temperature dropped to the low-fifties. Just a light one. He'd chopped enough wood to fuel it up more when night fell.

They heard a car pull up outside.

Sere stood from her recliner, and Bruce rose from his knees before the fireplace.

"Finally," she said, expecting the men to be back, anxious to hear if they'd succeeded, failed, or returned with the fear of God in them from something gone wrong. Being gone through the night was not cool.

Bruce didn't expect the car to be theirs.

One couldn't identify a car from the front door through the trees to the road. From behind the screen, Sere hollered, "Larue?"

"Sorry, not Larue, ma'am," came a voice that Sere didn't immediately recognize from the puzzlement in her eyes.

Bruce did, though, and Sere soon put it together. She remained on the stoop at his suggestion, and he slipped just out of view yet close enough to hear the conversation.

"Ms. Whaley?" asked the lady officer. "Serenity Whaley?"

"That's me," Sere said, hands playing the folds of her dress. "And I assume you're that lady police chief from the beach."

"Yes, ma'am." She gave her full name and title. "I have questions about your nephew."

Bruce peered through the crack of the wooden door, past the back of Sere to Chief Callie Morgan standing below the steps. She attempted congeniality, but she wasn't there to be nice. It was written all over her that she had news to deliver, and Bruce prayed it was about Magnus and not Larue.

"Larue ain't here," Sere said.

Callie turned toward the road, pointing off to the side where the parking area was. "Isn't that his car parked over there?"

"Yes it is, but he isn't here. They left in the truck."

Bruce winced at Sere volunteering information without being asked, but it was what it was.

"They," Callie repeated. "Who is his friend?"

Sere's posture shifted, and she cleared her throat. She recognized she'd released info she hadn't meant to. "Do I have to tell you?"

"What does it hurt for me to know who your nephew's friend is? I could ask the other guy's family. I could ask Larue's mom."

"You've already been there. She would've told you if she knew."

Callie sighed. "Just say his name, Ms. Whaley."

"Magnus Sims," she said, like she'd given up the combination of a bank safe.

"When did you last see them?" Callie asked.

"Yesterday."

"About when yesterday?"

"Mid-morning." At each question, Sere's body language stiffened, and she fought to keep her answers brief.

Bruce may not have been around Sere but a couple of months, but he was a fast read of people. Sere had clammed up some, not trusting Callie, halfway expecting bad news and subconsciously thinking not co-operating might stop the news from being delivered.

Callie held up the driver's license picture of Magnus for the ump-teenth time. "Is this the friend?"

Sere looked, hesitated, then nodded.

It was then that Callie paused, and Bruce recognized her preparation in delivering bad news. She took to her phone again and pulled up another picture. "Ms. Whaley, this is how we found Magnus a couple hours ago."

Just as Callie showed the picture, Bruce came out of hiding. He reached Sere's side as she realized what she was seeing.

Callie didn't react to his presence. Instead, she remained focused on Sere, who covered her mouth with a hand. "Oh. No. Oh . . . is he dead?"

Bruce put a hand under Sere's elbow, letting her know he was there.

"Yes, ma'am, he is," Callie said, her gaze on Bruce.

"What . . . about Larue?"

But Callie quickly dispelled that concern. "He was not there, Ms. Whaley. I'm here to see if you know where he is. I'd really love to find him before whoever did this to Magnus tries to do the same to Larue."

Bruce felt the shiver in Sere's whole body, and he moved his grip from her elbow to around her shoulder. Sere wasn't talking at all now. Anyone could see that she was imagining all style of danger pursuing her nephew.

Callie came closer, unhappy with having scared the woman. "I'm so sorry having to put you through this, but we must find Larue. Where would he be, and is he trying to sell drugs?"

Sere shook her head, not wanting to answer.

"Tell her, Sere," Bruce said.

But now it seemed like the woman couldn't make herself do so, so he did. "They had cocaine they stole from that store that caught on fire in town. They broke in to rob it but tried to light some of those candles spread around the shop and wound up catching things on fire. They grabbed a bag from under the register, only to learn later that they'd taken somebody's stash. Enough for dealing. They couldn't be deterred from trying to sell it themselves."

Callie pierced him with a gaze. "You could not stop them?"

He was fit, he was young enough, he was smart, and he was trained. Bruce fully understood the point she made. He could have maneuvered both men into restraints before they knew what hit them, and he could've returned the cocaine.

What she wasn't thinking, though, was how he lived. He didn't get involved. He avoided the public. He'd followed Magnus and Larue, trying in his own way to keep them out of trouble, off book and under the radar.

He was only at the house because he'd befriended Sere, and she'd befriended him, that friendship prompting him to quasi-compromise himself in trying to protect the men. That had morphed into sticking around in case she needed him just like this. In case whatever the boys did blew back on her.

He had never wanted to be anyone's keeper.

And if Callie would only think straight, she'd realize that he couldn't draw too much attention to himself or become connected to a case. That would mean putting him on record, giving an interview, and someone looking at who he was and where he was from, which he preferred to keep off anyone's record.

"You don't want me on this case," he finally said. "And you know why."

Her expression said she did know. She'd let him escape his partners during the recent storm. She'd let him evade suspicion for kidnapping. There was no going back and explaining the why of any of that.

"I remain here for Sere," he said. "And I remain hidden for you."

·

Chapter 28

CALLIE'S RECOLLECTION of Bruce contained minimal conversation. He let others speak, preferring to read people than talk to them. So this time, when he told the story of Sere, Magnus, and Larue, she let him go uninterrupted.

It's what any smart cop did when interviewing someone. When they wanted to talk, you let them.

He confirmed Magnus's and Larue's activities. He confirmed the burglaries, and he had explained why Edisto Calm caught fire. He saw the bag that contained the cocaine that had been mistakenly stolen when the two men thought it was full of cash.

Sere, on the other hand, was not talking. In Callie's opinion, she was worried about anyone getting caught and so she acted the ignorant old lady. But whether she was aware or not wouldn't factor in unless she was involved. That remained to be seen. This moment was more about Larue.

"Were you aware of their plans?" Callie asked.

"I was, vaguely, but I trusted them to know what they were doing," she said.

Bruce added to that. "She was not involved. How was she to stop them?"

Callie again wanted to remind Bruce he could have stopped them, maybe even for Sere's sake.

"I told them not to," Bruce said, "and I told them to turn it in." He motioned for her to show him her phone pic again.

She didn't even ask which photo of Magnus. He was familiar with the guy alive, so she showed him the one of him dead. Bruce studied the image.

Then, with Sere unable to see, Callie flipped to another picture.

"Hmm," he said at the zip tied hands.

"We need to find Larue," Callie said, and he understood.

"I'll come with you," he said, then to Sere added, "Lock the doors and don't let anyone inside while I'm gone. We'll find him."

Callie put away her phone. "How well do you know the area?"

"Well enough," he replied. "I've been here since . . . well, you know."

Which meant he had been on the island since September. She was surprised she hadn't noticed him until last week, but this was Bruce, accustomed to blending in or hiding out.

"I'll take Larue's car," he said.

"I already have an officer scouting the area," she explained, "but you take the roads to the right of the highway between here and the beach, and I'll take the ones to the left. Keep me apprised of where you are, especially once you've covered a road and marked it off."

"Marked?"

"Yeah, I have a map in the car. I'll give it to you."

He turned Sere around, giving her undertones of assurance as he escorted her inside. Not a minute passed before he returned with car keys in hand. He locked and shut the front door behind him, pausing, hoping Sere did as he told her. He didn't want her part of this mess.

Callie saw no bulge of a handgun tucked in the small of his back or under his shirt. He was going out with his physical skills and wits. That didn't make her feel any better.

Chapter 29

Bruce

HE WATCHED THE chief take off, to scout her side of the highway for Larue. Bruce followed her to Highway 174 and waited. She turned right, but he circled around, returning from whence he came.

Logic and a sixth sense had told him to start here, where he was, close to home . . . to Larue's home. It was what he would've done in grabbing the boy. Keep him near his residence, where most law enforcement would not expect a kidnapper to go, they would menace the boy with fears of hurting his aunt.

Is that your aunt's place? We can kill you then take her out on the way.

Larue wasn't that stable. He'd give up where Sere lived early in the game. He wasn't bright enough to weave very complicated thoughts to outsmart captors.

Yes, Bruce thought he was already taken and held nearby. Maybe already dead.

From the highway back meant Bruce taking Laurel Hill Road, but instead of turning west toward Sere's, he continued to the road's end, on a little extension called Crooked Creek Lane. Driving all the way down, he hunted for silt roads, less traveled paths, and trails that might give tire tracks of recent activity or signs of someone being where they shouldn't. He took each one of them to their dead end, usually in a marsh, then he'd turn around once he found nothing and start again a little further.

He reached Herbert Smalls Road, short with a dead end into a piece of St. Pierre Creek.

Bruce had learned in his two months of being an Edistonian that regardless of how long, rural, and deserted a road seemed, when it approached water, someone found a way to stake a decent house on it, turning a nothing piece of land into a one- or two-million-dollar home. He'd have hit these houses for valuables if he'd been Magnus and Larue, instead of wasting time at the beach. The seclusion alone made them simpler, more lucrative targets. It would be easy to learn when someone was gone, simple to clock, and you'd be in and out, nobody able to see you, and nobody having a friggin' clue who might've done it. There were ways around cams.

Back up again to Laurel Hill, he turned left and headed out on Raccoon Island Lane, only taking it down past Sere's house, speeding up a bit to avoid the slightest chance she'd be outside and see Larue's vehicle. He slowed at the fork. Both sides, he learned, ambled through heavy woods that rose and fell in and out of boggy areas, with respectable houses on the higher grounds.

Along the second road, though, sometimes he'd have water on both sides, and other times land, with the thoroughfare taking him across tiny islands that wouldn't accommodate construction.

It was on one of those islands that Bruce almost passed the reflection of a car's tail end, near the water, half hidden in the trees.

One could go hours out there without seeing a vehicle, and with the autumn evening approaching, shadows growing dark in the dense vegetation, nobody would see you. This was a tiny island. Unless someone was fishing, or some horny dude had brought his lady friend out here for a booty call away from his wife, nobody should be there. Anyone there didn't expect to be found.

He didn't pull in. Instead, he drove past, coming to the edge of the water where the road crossed to land along a larger part of St. Pierre Creek. There he parked.

It wasn't dark enough for a flashlight, but dark enough to take the colors of day to more muted ones that would be grayscale within the hour, so he'd wedged a small light in his pocket, just in case. Woods could rob you of details as the sun set old and low in the sky.

He hoped his gut still worked like it used to. He hadn't been forced to go clandestine for a long, long time, but the second he entered the clusters of pines, myrtles, oaks, and spiked ferns, his training kicked in.

He felt naked in normal civilian clothes, nothing to surveil a jungle setting. Jeans, beige tee, and a brown windbreaker, though when a chill came in off the creek with daylight waning, he appreciated the jacket. Sound died underfoot with the moist leaves and needles, but still he paid attention, ensuring he remained stealthy in choosing his footing and barriers to hide behind.

After ten to fifteen minutes of covering such a little stretch of the island, covertly picking and choosing his movements, he came within ten feet of the silt path he'd seen earlier, only closer to the water. The car, a dark sedan, as cliché as one could get when it came to criminal types, was covert enough almost to blend into the darkness of lush undergrowth and hundred-year-old tree trunks of grays and black.

He couldn't be so lucky.

But he wasn't a winner yet. He saw no people. More importantly, he saw no Larue.

He looked to see if the car showed movement, indicative of lust in the backseat, but it stood still. He was unable to see anyone inside from where he stood.

He reached inside deeper to hear, pushing past the sounds of birds and wildlife that took on twice the life this time of the evening, as he'd learned from Sere's back porch. A man's low mumble reached his ears, and he tried to filter for the sound of Larue's voice. Nothing.

Too far to tell much more, he closed his eyes, placing the approximate location of the unintelligible voice, and then slinked in the opposite direction. He made a wide swing and moved in closer, keeping the car between him and whomever continued to talk.

Then slipping around to the front of the vehicle, still wedged into the woods' darkness, he took a quick glance beneath again for a better angle. They stood closer to the trunk. Two men, like he thought.

One looked like someone a few steps past middle-aged. Retirement era but still agile. A man who loved leisure more than physical labor.

What were they standing there for? What was worth the wait?

Backtracking into the woods, he dared for different angles, taking maybe ten minutes or more to gain intel and determine if this was no more than two men furtively meeting to make plans they wished nobody to hear. They made phones for that, though.

Then he heard the third voice, moaning, further away from these two. A young man's sporadic, unconscious moan.

Bruce moved for better vantage, to put some piece of image together with the sound. He had to stand to see, though, and with that would come the danger of being seen.

He stood. What the hell?

Larue lay spread eagle, anchored in the pluff mud of the creek, water having stolen its way up to his chest, the tide climbing his body. From the looks of the vegetation and the moisture of the ground around him, Larue was staked to be slowly swallowed up by an early night tide, these two men overseeing that the deed got done.

With the image of Larue's body vivid in his mind and the realization he only had a little bit of time, Bruce debated whether to confront the captors or call Callie. He didn't do tide tables, but the water looked high enough to be threatening.

He chose to walk back over his tracks, fighting not to run, then at the road he raced to his car, easing inside.

She answered but didn't get two words out before Bruce said barely above a whisper, "I found Larue. The first marsh island down the left fork past Sere's house. Know it?"

"Yes," she said, equally as quiet.

He heard tire noises over the phone. She was turning around mid-highway. "Larue is staked out in the marsh," he said. "If you cannot get here fast enough, I'll take them."

"Do not do a thing until I get there," she said. "I'm ten minutes away, tops."

"Larue . . ."

"How high is the water?"

"Chest high."

She hesitated. "He has ten minutes."

"You aren't sure. I hear it in your voice."

"I'll be there in five, then. Wait. Better they deal with me than you," she said and hung up.

She thought she could protect him and save Larue. This was why he debated whether to call her.

He wasn't waiting on the road to wave her down. He retraced his path through the woods, pausing to see Larue before approaching the car again.

The boy appeared unconscious, his body floating up a bit, to the limits of the tethers on his legs. Bruce had no idea how fast a tide came in, but it had made a difference since he'd been there. Not a good sign.

And he couldn't locate the bigger man.

A beam pierced through to his brain. He threw up an arm and bent down, seeking darkness, but he was blinded for the moment by a tactical flashlight.

"Who the hell are you?" said a man. Bruce blinked, peering at the ground, struggling to find his vision.

Regardless, he remained calm, per his training. He slowed time and weighed the situation. They wanted to know who he was. They didn't know how much he'd seen. They had no idea he had called Callie.

In a speedy move, the bigger man, the one not speaking much, snatched him around, putting Bruce's back to the water as he was shoved over against the jungle side of the car.

"Down on the ground," the man ordered, in a voice twice deeper than the other. From the feel of how he handled Bruce, the man was bigger. He carried some weight on him but not so much as to compromise any fighting skills he might choose to wield. He moved too easily to be clumsy.

If he wasn't an enforcer of some kind, he'd missed his calling.

Bruce sat as he was told.

"On your belly," came the order.

But when Bruce didn't comply, the man surprisingly let the order go unfollowed. "Who are you?"

Bruce's presence had thrown them. He stared straight ahead, past the man, blinking hard for effect but still measuring from the shadows what he could see. Measuring height, muscle, the way his captor placed his two-hundred and fifty pounds in those expensive Italian loafers began coming into focus. Also, how he held his hands.

Dress slacks were muddied around the cuff. Bet he didn't like that. His loafers would need a heavy cleaning then a polish like never before. He hadn't dressed for this environment, the quality of his trousers being a tight weave, cotton wool blend, the crease sharp as a butcher knife. At least that's what Bruce could tell from his seated position, though he acted like he still couldn't see.

He'd been in way worse moments than this.

The nonchalance didn't sit well with the captor. Studying Bruce, as if he contemplated what he had to deal with, he leaned over a smidge, analyzing. Then he looked up and across the vehicle at the other, lesser man. "You know him?"

"Nope," came the clipped response, like he was trying not to talk and not to be noticed.

Bruce kept trying to place the other man; the older, smaller, less put-together man. He hadn't met him, but he had seen him. Yes, the night of the fire.

Bruce would continue acting like he was ignorant, but logic told him no way would they take the chance of letting him go. Bruce expected to be tied next to Larue in the marsh. He didn't get the why of that method of death, though. Maybe they needed information out of Larue . . . or the location of the drugs. This dragging out killing someone only improved the odds of something going wrong.

"Look at this guy," the big man said. "You're from around here. You should know everybody. You claim that all the time."

"I said I never seen him," said the other.

That exchange, that little delay was when the mistake was made.

The big man fully straightened with attention on his compadre as he spoke, taking his attention off Bruce for those few seconds.

Seconds that mattered.

Bruce leaped up.

Quicker than expected, the bigger guy flipped his attention back, reaching for what had to be a gun.

But Bruce expected that.

There was too much weight to the man to spin him and get behind, so going light on his feet, Bruce stepped into the man, their bellies in contact. The tightness between them wouldn't allow his opponent to reach into his belt for his weapon.

Pressing closer, Bruce pushed such that even in the shadows and grays the man saw him smile. Then right hand under the man's chin, left gripping around the back of the head, Bruce wrapped his own body tight to hold the man in place.

Then snapped his neck.

The pop satisfied him.

"Shit!" said the other man, forgetting his effort to stay silent.

Bruce didn't smile at him.

But he didn't expect the guy to draw his own weapon, either. Suddenly he was staring down the barrel of a nine mil.

He glanced over at Larue, now neck deep in the water.

The tussle had taken them toward the front of the car, leaving Bruce more in the open.

"Stay right there," the last man hollered. "Shit," he said more to himself.

He had no idea what to do, like he had options other than to take out Bruce. But from the way he held the gun, Bruce guessed he'd never shot a man before.

Larue gurgled from the marsh. Coughing, sputtering, he struggled. The water at his chin, sweeping into his mouth and nose, had awoken him. The writhing, however, only served to move the water more, slapping his face, compounding his inability to breathe. Not being able to move exacerbated panic, creating a cycle that he wouldn't comprehend and think his way out of in time. A cycle that wouldn't last long.

"Save the boy," Bruce said. "I take it your partner here was on your ass about the drugs."

"He wasn't my partner."

"He was related to your drugs."

The abductor stiffened. "Who the hell are you?"

"A friend of Larue," he said, taking a step forward.

"Quit walking," the man yelled.

Yelling was good. Callie might be close enough to hear. Those five minutes were ticking awfully fast.

Bruce took a sidestep, coming around the car's front.

The man slowly pivoted in kind, not realizing it. "What the hell are you doing?"

"Trying to see Larue," Bruce yelled back.

"You know this kid?"

"I do."

The gun toter repositioned the piece in his hand, like he had to think harder about this situation. Bruce would need to be killed just as much as the kid, and this man was having to come to terms with that.

Bruce moved to his left, again.

The gun man did in kind.

The gun man also started wondering harder about this dance. "What the hell are you doing?"

"Making for a cleaner shot," Bruce said, taking yet another step.

"Stop!" the man cried.

"Amos!"

Amos swung around, handgun and all.

Bruce leaped in his direction, but Callie shot first.

She'd called him so he'd take his aim off Bruce and position himself such that Callie could put a bullet in him.

She hit dead center.

Chapter 30

BRUCE LEFT IT TO Callie to confirm Amos's demise. Instead, he bolted toward the marsh.

Larue had arched as high and hard as he could for as long as he could, his head now underwater, strength gone from his body.

Pulling a knife from his pocket, Bruce freed the tethers on his wrists, lifting the boy up to air. He wasn't breathing.

Bruce cut the ankle tethers then dragged Larue to shore.

Callie rushed over. "How is he?"

"Not breathing," Bruce said, beginning CPR, his medic training kicking in.

Evening had begun to fall, and Callie held her mini-Maglite to aid Bruce . . . hoping Larue wasn't really as pale as he looked coming out of the water.

"They coked him up," Bruce said, between breaths.

Callie phoned dispatch for an ambulance and a crime scene unit. She reported the two bodies. She made no mention of Bruce.

Larue coughed up water, and Bruce rolled him over.

"Thank God," Callie said, sitting back on her haunches.

But Larue wasn't much conscious.

"Told you," Bruce said, dragging the kid further back from the water, sitting him up against the car's front tire. "He's doped up. I can't treat that. They'll need to. Don't know how much is in his system."

Callie didn't ask why they'd poison the boy in addition to laying him out in the marsh. She guessed they did it as punishment for stealing their stash, and to quiet him so nobody would see him drown. A gunshot would have echoed far and wide.

"Good shot," Bruce said, seating himself beside Larue. "Thanks."

Callie peered back over to Amos's body. "Son of a bitch, I didn't want to do that," she uttered. She tried not to tell herself that Bruce might've handled Amos alone. Maybe she could've leaped out of Amos's fire point while Bruce took him alive.

Had she saved Bruce's life? Could he have saved himself? Those were thoughts for one of those nights when she rehashed taking someone's life. This wasn't her first.

No doubt it would be deemed a righteous shoot. That didn't make taking a life any easier, though.

Larue was awake but couldn't speak, couldn't focus, and had no idea where he was. They worked to keep him awake until he was earnestly trying to keep his eyes open.

"You need to leave," she said under her breath to Bruce, her hand on Larue's shoulder, halfway holding him up.

"Maybe it's time I quit being smoke," Bruce said. "I can stay."

But she shook her head. "In my searching for Larue, I started near his aunt's place."

Bruce nodded and listed to the story she began to weave.

"I saw the tail end of this car, just a piece of it, while it was still light," she said.

He let her go on.

"I came up to see Larue drowning and that man on the ground, apparently his neck broken. Amos stood nearby, watching Larue's life inch away. I called his name, and he swung around, his handgun drawn. I took him down."

Bruce watched her with zero expression.

"Close enough?" she asked.

"Don't like it," he said.

"It's harder to explain what really happened." She changed the subject. "Where's the coke?"

Bruce stood and peered inside the car. "On the seat."

"Which they took from Larue."

"What about his car I drove here?" he asked.

"Drive it back to Sere's," she said. "Don't tell her about Larue. Just tell her someone will be in touch soon and that she can breathe easy."

"Then I leave," he said.

"Don't see any way around it." She stopped herself from saying his name around Larue who struggled to come back to life.

She was doing her level best to be terse, solid, and professional about this. Ordinarily, she'd be eating herself up over what she'd had to do to Amos, but he'd no doubt helped kill Magnus, and he was in the process of killing Larue. Maybe he was being forced to participate . . . maybe not. But he had. And he'd drawn a weapon. And he'd paid the price for doing so.

She pondered the man standing opposite her, looking down at the boy. She rose. Larue was trying to collect his wits, so she motioned for Bruce to follow her to the edge of the woods.

Keeping Larue in view, she dared to peer into Bruce's eyes, his pants dripping, his stare something that made her hold her breath and ponder just what this man was made of.

"I wish you could stick around," she said, holding back from touching his sleeve, for a moment aching for a hug.

There was a depth to him she really admired. A strength that delved to a level she'd never seen before. An instinct that penetrated to his DNA.

He was meant to be a soldier, yet here he was, unable to be such. He wasn't exactly flapping in the wind, because he never seemed to be without some degree of anchor. He didn't allow the unpredictable nor did he invite loneliness, yet she felt sorry for him. He needed someone to counterbalance who he was. Someone to save. Someone to protect. Someone to use his talents for whether a country, a cause, or an old woman who lived alone in the marsh.

Bruce had experienced too much, done too many questionable things to be invited back into the military. So where did that leave him?

For some unexplainable reason, she wished he could find a way to remain on Edisto.

He smiled, like he was reading her mind. "I like you, too, Chief Callie Morgan."

How could she not smile to that?

Then she softly scoffed. "How did your compass get so screwed up? You're a good man, Bruce Bardot."

"You're pretty nice yourself."

And there they stood.

She spoke up first. "You'll be missed." It went unsaid that he had to keep moving, or at least he couldn't stay here. He could try, but something would trip him up. Someone would get curious about him and dig. Callie wasn't so sure she wanted him in the shadows, either, waiting for that to happen, sensing that he hovered here or there, searching for another soul to save. He seemed to enjoy saving people.

Her whole focus should be on Mark, the love of her life. Having this ghost of a being in Bruce, someone she mentally could relate to, wasn't healthy for anyone.

Bruce held his arms wide.

She fell into them, wrapping arms around him. In spite of it being November, in spite of the dampness in his clothes, he was warm, and she sucked that in for a moment before making sure she was the first to let go.

"You take care of yourself," she said.

"Ditto, Chief."

He slid into the woods, but not without looking back once before the pines and wax myrtle swallowed him into their darkness.

Despite the two bodies, despite the kid high on coke, Callie stood alone, thinking how sad she'd feel about Bruce not being *maybe* gone, but really gone.

To some, he was a criminal. To others a savior. To her, he was just a solid, principled man. Such beings were few and far between.

She heard the car turn on the silt road and head back to Sere's. On her way out, she'd make sure it was there when she relayed the news to the aunt.

She really hoped he was gone by then.

Chapter 31

THE SUN HAD completely set, night blanketing the island when Callie stopped at Sere's house. Larue's car was there. A limbo feeling wrapped around her as Callie sat in the front seat of the patrol car, convincing herself to walk through those trees to the front door.

Sere answered when Callie finally knocked. No sign of Bruce. Of course not. Even if he were there he would remain hidden. He'd crossed a line for her, and she had to either honor it or . . . no, there was no *or*.

"What happened?" Sere asked, seeming older in the dark.

"Larue is alive, ma'am, and on his way to St. Francis in West Ashley," Callie said, referencing the nearest hospital forty-five minutes away. "Do you want me to drive you there? He's going to need someone."

"Will he live?" she asked, telling Callie she probably hadn't seen Bruce. He would've at least assured her before leaving.

"I honestly can't say. The good thing is we found him alive and kept him that way until help could arrive."

"That's good." The woman gaze rested past Callie, off into the trees.

"Ma'am, let me take you to the hospital."

Sere refocused. "No, no, that's okay." Her shoulders hung limp from the day's burden, spent at the relief. "I'll grab a few things since I imagine I'll be staying there."

Callie hesitated. "Are you driving yourself?" Then she added, "Or is someone taking you?" *Like Bruce?* He'd come to the hospital after the storm for Callie. It would be like him to do the same here.

Sere shrugged. "Got nobody to take me. I'll drive myself. Larue's momma will have her boyfriend take her. They don't want much to do with me. Hell, she'll probably blame me."

The woman was borderline rambling. Callie waited for more. Surely there was more.

Like where Bruce was.

Instead, Sere questioned the police chief. "He's gone, isn't he?"

When Callie didn't immediately answer, not sure how to, tears welled in Sere's eyes. "I'll miss him." She peered down at her hands, not knowing what to do with her emotions.

Though the woman was taller, wider, and heavier, Callie swooped in with an embrace.

The old woman fell into her, sobbing. "He was my knight," she whispered. Callie didn't bother asking what that meant, respecting whatever the meaning.

They released each other in an unspoken, shared understanding of a feeling that couldn't be formed by words.

Callie cleared her throat and spoke of the formalities, using more general terms to repeat the same story she told the Charleston County authorities when they had arrived. The record would show she found two nameless captors, one man having killed the other, and Callie saved Larue. She didn't like making that claim, but it was a claim that had to be made.

"Thank you," Sere said, under her breath. "That half-witted boy is all I have left, and this dumbass attempt for a few dollars almost cost him . . . and me."

The two stood on the stoop in seriousness and silence.

Callie was about to just take Sere to Larue herself, but Sere came back to life first with a sudden thought. "Hold on." She ran inside and returned with a cotton twill bag. "This needs to go back to whoever it belongs to."

Inside was the gold coin, a small jade statue, and the missing jewelry items belonging to Attorney Calloway. With a melancholy grin, she thanked Sere. "The owner will appreciate this. One piece belonged to her deceased husband."

"Don't feel right keeping it. Put all that blame on Magnus, if you don't mind," the woman said.

Callie got it. Nobody had seen Larue driving the getaway car anyway. Magnus, however, had become the familiar face of the Edisto burglaries. Easy enough.

"I'll do my best," she said.

Callie waited while Sere gathered her things, giving her a warning to put something on the seat since the previous driver might have gotten the front seat wet. Then she escorted her to Larue's sedan.

Callie would've given the old lady a blue light escort all the way to St. Francis if Sere had wanted, but she knew better. Still, in an odd respect, maybe in honor of their shared relationship with a man who showed up out of nowhere and left an indelible mark regardless his ability to stay invisible, Callie followed Sere all the way to the McKinley Washington Bridge.

She pulled over the cruiser and watched Sere's taillights cross the bridge and leave the island.

Callie tried to imagine if Bruce had already crossed ahead of them, or if he lay in wait in the woods, spending one last night on the island before he made his way elsewhere. Maybe he'd thumbed a ride and was already on the Interstate an hour away, heading west.

He could be watching her right now. That would be his way, making sure that some of the ends were tied up before he vanished.

An ache in her chest made little sense. He was like he was by choice. While she could feel sorry for him and his veiled means of living, she shouldn't. A piece of her wished he'd stick around, live in her jungle, be the vigilante here and there. He needed purpose. Of that she was certain. Now he had to begin anew finding a world he could exist in.

Twenty minutes passed before she caught the loss of time. Things were made right here, weren't they? Messy, but more on the side of justice than the side of crime. That's what drove her gyroscope. . . justice. She was sure that drove Bruce's as well.

She took a deep breath and with no traffic coming or going, she u-turned on Highway 174 and headed back to the beach. Kitty needed to be notified.

After that, she needed Mark.

Anyone else could wait until tomorrow.

KITTY LEFT EDISTO two days later after being notified about Amos and queried about her potential involvement in the drugs and fire. Edisto Calm was shuttered.

She appeared to have no idea of Amos's motives, and while Callie avoided saying Amos might've used her, Kitty spoke about how naïve she was to believe all his dreams, notions, and plans for the future. She'd lost everything personally and financially. Nothing connected her to the crimes, and Callie told the Charleston SO detective so, from both a professional and a personal perspective.

Janet returned the For Rent sign to the fire-scarred building, waiting for the insurance to do its thing so she could put the place back to a state it could be rented again.

As expected, at the shock of Amos's death everyone craved to know the how and why. When they heard he was wrapped up in dealing drugs and died amidst a deal gone wrong, they accepted the karma of it all despite his jovial personality. Words were used like *sad, unfortunate,* and *heartbreaking,* but after the initial shock, everyone admitted they really weren't. Even Malorie felt a certain level of remorse but was frequently heard saying, "I'm not surprised."

Callie was, though. Amos had been a staple of the town. Whether he danced the line of criminal or not, he left a bit of a hole in some circles. He'd be missed at parades, at the Pavilion, and during happy hour in certain establishments. It was difficult to explain how he'd only sold marijuana and a little coke. After all, he could've distributed fentanyl, heroin, meth, ketamine, MDMA, and so much more. He could've seriously had a hand in marring the landscape of Edisto Island with drugs. . . but he hadn't.

The Charleston County SO spoke of quickly closing the case, relying heavily on Callie's personal accounting. Only Mark and Stan, those closest to Callie who would understand, were trusted with the official story about the man dying at her hand. And again, only Mark and Stan heard the story about Bruce.

That was twice she'd assisted Bruce in dodging charges. Not her finest moment, but far from her worst. She'd lost too many people she cared about in her life by trying so hard to do the right thing. Sometimes the right thing for the moment was the wrong thing in other's eyes.

The coincidences here were worth noting as well. Amos had been a small-time dealer by choice, for years, but it took Kitty's arrival as opportunity to take his criminal career to another level. Then those two simpletons, Larue and Magnus, had stumbled in the way . . . and what were the odds that Bruce had been on Edisto to intercede?

Sophie would call that some heavy-handed karma. . . if she was allowed to know.

Callie returned the stolen goods to Callaway and closed the burglary cases. When the subject came up, Magnus was the name used for every misdeed. She was good for her promise to Sere.

Larue spent a week in the hospital, then came home to his aunt, not his mother. Callie visited the day after. Sere had put the fear of God in him since he'd regained consciousness, and Callie underlined the fact he'd dodged a bullet, almost literally, thanks to her and the transient guy long gone from the island. Larue seemed changed, the wind gone from his sails. Time would tell for how long.

He didn't recall Bruce being there at the marsh's edge. He didn't see anyone die.

He cried talking about Magnus.

"You came awful close to dying," Callie told him, the three seated on that back porch overlooking the marsh, hot apple juice in hand to chase the small chill in the air. They let the boy have the swing. "The odds won't be on your side next time," she said. "Find yourself a regular job, Larue."

The kid carried a haggard look, and he'd aged at the loss of a friend and his own whisper miss from death. "They said you killed Amos," he said.

Callie just sat, not comfortable in confirming that evening's events.

Larue didn't seem bothered at her not answering. "Bruce. . ." he started, and Callie held up her hand.

"He led me to you. Now he's gone. Be happy he helped."

He gave a tired squint, very tired. "He was a different sort of dude."

"He was."

"Where'd he go?"

"No idea," she said, in full honesty.

"Where do you think he'd go?" he said, hoping for a clue.

She exhaled, long and slow. "He wasn't one to tell you his business, Larue."

"Yeah," he said, seeing his question worthless.

Callie stood to leave before Larue could throw her more questions. "Just stay straight, okay? People have died over you. Take some responsibility in using that for good from here on out."

He nodded, his gaze darting to the edge of the marsh.

Sere walked her to the car. Once away from Larue's hearing, she spoke. "Hope he's all right."

Callie knew she didn't mean her nephew.

All Callie could do was nod in response. She hoped so, too.

There were shades of good and shades of bad. The naïve wrongly saw them divided by a cemented, fat line. Bruce's character held so many shades of gray that nothing ever seemed totally wrong, nor totally right. At least to those looking in. From his mind, he had his act together. Callie almost envied that.

She left Sere's and drove back to the beach, to her world, to an evening at El Marko's, and shared dinner with Stan. Donna said she had things to do, which showed just how good a person she was giving Callie alone time with her old boss who'd shared her every trauma. Sometimes they only wanted law enforcement around the table and tonight felt like one of those times.

During a lull in customers, Mark joined them, the three talking about anything but Edisto Calm and all that ensued because of it. They knew her well enough not to discuss the topic of how it had all concluded. She'd killed someone, and that wasn't something you shared over dessert.

That night at home, Mark avoided their usual small talk, and the two of them crawled into bed, cradling.

Callie drew him tighter, so grateful for him and how he read her moods. She wasn't wanting to share her thoughts yet, and she wasn't sure she could share them all. Mark knew better than to ask what occupied her mind. He would assume it would be Amos, which admittedly weighed heavy. She wouldn't tell him there was more.

Nestled in the crook of Mark's arm, Callie compared her man and Bruce, something Mark would not understand. But she couldn't help but do so. Mark had weathered his own nightmare in law enforcement and come out the other side intact, strong, both physically and emotionally. . . admirably. He survived with ample scars, but nothing he couldn't handle. She loved him.

Bruce had his own scars as well, only his owned him, leaving no room for other people. That bothered her. He had no one to share his darkness with. Alone in the night like this, secretly she wished he had room for her. Not in lieu of Mark, but in addition to Mark . . . or was that even a possible thing?

The best Callie could do was wish him well and wonder what he would be like if he hadn't been so damaged. Still, a piece of her would instinctively scout for a man walking Jungle Road, with no real place to go . . . except for maybe to have a conversation with her.

After all, he had no place else to go . . . not really. Or so she liked to think.

The End

Acknowledgements

This was not the most difficult to write of the Edisto Island books, but it was by far the most difficult to publish. Thanks to Debra Dixon at Bell Bridge for shouldering the huge burden of helping me get from Point A to Point B for reasons only she and I know.

Love to Cowboy/Lawdawg/Sweetie and all the other names Gary W. Clark, Sr. answers to throughout the long journey of a book, but especially this one. The trek had a few more obstacles than normal, but he was right there for each page, chapter, and word.

Appreciation to Tara Jerdan for the incredible logo for Edisto Bridge Books. Your creative talents proved to me the advantages of a human artist over the atrocities of AI.

Thanks to a sea of beta readers who opened my eyes.

Thanks to Joan Dempsey for a week in Maine when she gave me her ear and shoulder as I trudged through ending this book and starting another, through a tsunami of change in my life.

Blessings to my readers, who have adopted these characters and come to adore this island as deeply as I have.

About the Author

C. HOPE CLARK has a fascination with the mystery genre and is author of the *Carolina Slade Mystery Series* , the *Craven County Mystery Series*, as well as the *Edisto Island Series*, all set in her home state of South Carolina. In her previous federal life, she performed administrative investigations and married the agent she met on a bribery investigation. She enjoys nothing more than editing her books on the back porch with him, overlooking the lake, with bourbons in hand. She can be found either on the banks of Lake Murray or Edisto Beach with one or two dachshunds in her lap. Hope is also editor of the award-winning FundsforWriters.com

C. Hope Clark

Facebook: facebook.com/chopeclark
Instagram: instagram.com/chopeclark
Author website: chopeclark.com

www.ingramcontent.com/pod-product-compliance
Lightning Source LLC
Chambersburg PA
CBHW031613220925
32966CB00012B/690